"You're scared, aren't you?"

Nora nodded. "Sometimes it swamps me."

Jake held her, as if his arms were a defense against the terrifying world beyond them. If only.

"I wish I could promise that he'll be caught. That you'll be safe forever."

But he couldn't. She was still trapped in the web, and she could still feel it vibrating with threat. She knew her attacker was getting closer.

Jake touched his lips to hers.

Instantly all concern flew from her head. That a kiss could have the power to fill her with heat, to expand the need deep inside her into an aching pool of fire, amazed her.

"You're not alone," he said. "And as long as I breathe you won't be until this is over for good."

She wasn't sure how he could keep that vow, but for one moment she almost believed it.

Conard County: The Next Generation

D0448429

Dear Reader,

Writing *Killer's Prey* proved a very difficult emotional journey for me. While I'm grateful to say I've never been stalked by a killer, I have experienced many of the abusive kinds of experiences Nora endured. I reached into some painful places to bring her to life. It was, in many ways, a cathartic journey for me and a great reminder of how wonderful my life has grown as the years have passed.

But her fears, her tendency to revert, are what I knew from my own experience. Watching her grow and blossom in this book was like watching a birthing. She took the reins from me early in the story and told it in her own way. It may have started with things I've known, but this is definitely Nora's story.

It's also Jake's. Young people often act in ways they can't explain and have trouble understanding even in hindsight. Those are the things that often keep us from sleeping at night as we recall them and wish we had never done them. Jake's own struggle to figure himself out held me transfixed.

But with time comes understanding. If we're lucky, with time also comes self-forgiveness.

And if we're really lucky, we find the perfect love.

I hope all of you are as lucky as Jake and Nora become.

Hugs,

Rachel

KILLER'S
PREY

—

Rachel Lee

(H) **HARLEQUIN**®ROMANTIC SUSPENSE

Recycling programs
for this product may
not exist in your area.

ISBN-13: 978-0-373-27841-1

KILLER'S PREY

Copyright © 2013 by Susan Civil-Brown

Printed in U.S.A.

Books by Rachel Lee

Romantic Suspense

**The Final Mission* #1655
Just a Cowboy #1663
**The Rescue Pilot* #1671
**Guardian in Disguise* #1701
**The Widow's Protector* #1707
**Rancher's Deadly Risk* #1727
**What She Saw* #1743
**Rocky Mountain Lawman* #1756
**Killer's Prey* #1771

Silhouette Romantic Suspense

Exile's End #449
Cherokee Thunder #463
Miss Emmaline and the Archangel #482
Ironheart #494
Lost Warriors #535
Point of No Return #566
A Question of Justice #613
Nighthawk #781
Cowboy Comes Home #865
Involuntary Daddy #955
Holiday Heroes #1487
    "A Soldier for All Seasons"
**A Soldier's Homecoming* #1519
**Protector of One* #1555
**The Unexpected Hero* #1567
**The Man from Nowhere* #1595
**Her Hero in Hiding* #1611
**A Soldier's Redemption* #1635
**No Ordinary Hero* #1643

Harlequin Nocturne

***Claim the Night* #127
***Claimed by a Vampire* #129
***Forever Claimed* #131
***Claimed by the Immortal* #166

Harlequin Special Edition

The Widow of Conard County #2270

*Conard County
**Conard County: The Next Generation
***The Claiming

Other titles by this author available in ebook format.

RACHEL LEE

was hooked on writing by the age of twelve and practiced her craft as she moved from place to place all over the United States. This *New York Times* bestselling author now resides in Florida and has the joy of writing full-time.

To all the Ugly Ducklings: I know there is a swan inside you.

Prologue

Cranston Langdon sat in the chair in his den, pant leg pulled up so he could study the tracking bracelet that had been attached to him when he'd been released on bail. Just the sight of it made him furious. He was an upstanding member of this community, a business owner. They should have released him without this damn bracelet.

Hell, he wasn't even being charged with murder. Rape, yes. Aggravated assault, yes. But guys who'd done a lot more than take a knife to a woman had been allowed to walk out of court on bail alone.

But not him. He blamed his soon-to-be ex-wife for that. She'd gone into that hearing and claimed he was a violent man, that the whole reason their child was receiving counseling from Nora Loftis was because of *his* violence. She had even said she was afraid of him.

He would never forgive her for that. Just as he would never forgive Nora Loftis for surviving. He'd dragged her to a ditch in the woods and she should have rotted away before anyone found her body.

Instead, she had managed to climb out of that ditch hours later and flag down help. So now here he was.

He knew he could cut that bracelet. He'd read about it online. It could be done. He could set himself free. He just had to be sure he did it right, because he wouldn't have much time.

Ten or fifteen seconds before the alarm sounded at the police station. Five to ten minutes before the cops managed to respond.

So he had to plan it carefully. Very carefully.

Then, one way or another, he was going to take care of that cheating wife of his and finish off the Loftis woman. Two birds. Then off to Canada and parts unknown. He'd already moved his money. He'd taken care of that a long time ago, stocking away most of it in the Caymans.

So he'd be fine. He just had to make sure that he cleared out fast enough. That he dealt with his wife swiftly. Hunting Nora Loftis might take more time, but no one would expect that. No one would even begin to guess how badly he wanted to see her die, not when he'd insisted in the face of the evidence that he'd never hurt her, that they'd been lovers.

No, they'd think his wife was the end of it, because he'd never told them the truth. He'd let them think he was having an affair with Nora. Little did they know that he still wanted that woman's blood and her essence.

But he knew.

Chapter 1

When Nora Loftis had emerged from a roadside ditch, bloody and beaten, raped and tortured, dazed and half-crazed, she'd at least thought she had survived.

Little did she realize that her battle for survival was hardly over.

Three months later, still healing in so many ways, she arrived at the baggage carousel in the Denver airport to be greeted by one of the last people she ever wanted to see again.

Jake Madison, larger than life, towering over six feet, built like a cheesecake dream, wearing jeans and a loden-green chamois shirt under a light jacket. His hair was still intensely dark, and his eyes were still that peculiar green, a color that seemed to be lit from within. If anything, the years had made him more attractive.... Stronger, broader, more like an oak than a sapling.

And he was still one of the reasons she had avoided her

hometown of Conard City. He was a big reason, but not the only reason.

He saw her and nodded, but something about his eyes seemed to narrow.

Well, she looked like hell, and he hated her anyway, and they had a history she would have preferred to utterly forget. Why wouldn't his eyes narrow? And why had her dad sent *him* of all people?

She fought down an almost overwhelming urge to turn and run. But while she might need a place to lick her wounds, she had also developed some backbone, and she was damned if she would give him the satisfaction.

"Nora," he said when she approached. His voice had deepened, too. Everything about him had reached the fullness of manhood while she'd been gone.

"Jake." She hoped she sounded cool. Inside she felt as if nerves already stretched too tight had just stretched tighter still.

"Your dad asked me to get you," he said, explaining. "His car is acting up."

"Thanks." Short and ungracious. Well, he didn't deserve any better from her, not after what he had done to her. She'd avoided *him* for twelve years and Conard City for ten. Now her choices had become limited to one.

She turned to watch the carousel, where the first bags had begun to appear. Maybe she could pretend he wasn't even there.

"You won't find the town much changed," he remarked.

"I didn't think I would. It never changes."

"Oh, things change," he replied calmly. "Lots of things."

She let that lie. Bad enough that she had to come home without hearing cheery stories about how things had changed for the better. She wouldn't believe them anyway.

He picked up her luggage for her, leaving her with only

her rolling carry-on to tag along behind him out to the parking garage, where he stowed her bags in the back of his tan Jeep. Then she climbed into the passenger seat, looking straight ahead, thinking that if there was *one* thing she didn't need now, it was a couple of hours in the car with Jake Madison.

He seemed to feel the same, surprisingly enough, and didn't offer any kind of casual conversation. Good, she thought. Good. Because she just plain wasn't up to it.

The doctors had told her she would tire easily for weeks to come, and that she needed to conserve her energy for what was most important. Already she could feel her nerves letting go, simply because she couldn't maintain the tension. Not now, not for a while.

After Jake paid the parking fee and pulled out onto the exit road, he spoke again. "I heard what happened."

"I don't want to talk about it."

A mile passed, then another, before he spoke again. "I'm just letting you know that people are talking.

"Surprise, surprise. Apparently *that* hasn't changed."

He glanced at her. "Bitter now, too?"

"Maybe I have cause."

"Maybe so." But he let it drop.

Pointedly, she closed her eyes, not wanting to talk to him at all. Then, without warning, fatigue crashed down on her between one instant and the next. She fell soundly asleep before they'd made it all the way out of the suburbs of Denver, and she didn't wake until they were drawing near her home.

The familiar state highway into Conard City carried Nora Loftis back too many years. Way too many years. It also carried her to a home she had vowed never to visit again.

The wide expanses of ranch land—brown now as winter drew closer, tumbleweed snared in fences—still looked desolate. Had she ever seen the beauty out here? But the purpling mountains ahead were still beautiful, still drew her as mountains always had. She had missed them during her years working in Minneapolis. Gentler hills were just not the same.

But the rest of it, she assured herself, she had *not* missed at all. Not the endless roads that seemed to go nowhere, not the outlying ranches or the few small subdivisions. And certainly not the main street, captured in an early twentieth century kind of amber, a mixture of archaeological finds left over from the 1880s to a few newer World War II era buildings. The town had enjoyed a number of booms and a few busts, and the last bust still lingered, a kind of genteel poverty for all but a handful, who managed to prosper anyway.

Outside town, before she faced the sorrow of the main street, she saw a sign announcing the construction of a new ski resort. Another boom in the making, maybe, one that would change the character of the town yet again.

It needed some changing.

She hated coming back, but she had nowhere else to go. Not now.

The speed limit lowered, taking them along a flat stretch of road that boasted little but an occasional roadhouse. Closer to town, she saw the modernity of some new fast-food joints that didn't appear to be doing well. That much modernity had arrived here, too. Even with so few people and despite the closing of the semiconductor plant that had been this town's last boom. The ranchers hereabouts were barely enough to keep the place going.

"I saw it in the papers," her father had said when he phoned, the first words he'd spoken to her in a decade.

"Come home, girl." An offer made too late, but one she had been unable to refuse with her life in ashes all around her.

What else could you do when the big bad world had treated you so horribly you were almost afraid to stick your nose out the door? What else could you do when you'd become famous—or infamous, depending—and the world wouldn't leave you alone to lick your wounds?

He'd seen it in the papers. Even here. That meant Jake knew, too. All those sordid details.

Her hands tightened into fists until her knuckles turned white and her fingers ached. She couldn't bring herself to look at Jake as he managed the town streets with the ease of familiarity.

A sharp right turn, then a left, and they were on the main street, a veritable visual essay of the town's past, most of which seemed to have been a matter of aging as gracefully as possible.

They drove past the hulks of Freitag's Mercantile on one side and the Lakota Hotel on the other. One busy and surviving, the other barely holding together as a sort of rooming house. Past her dad's pharmacy, and then past the courthouse square and the sheriff's office.

Past Mahoney's saloon, with a history stretching back to the brief boom of the 1880s. No matter how good or bad the times, people always wanted drink. Even more so when times were bad.

Then a sharp left turn onto her dad's street. Victorian houses, built on long narrow lots, lined the street, along with trees as old as the houses. People who had never lived here found it charming. It made Nora feel claustrophobic.

And finally, Jake pulled into the driveway behind her dad's car, an old white Caddy he'd been nursing for so many years it was probably now an expensive collectible.

"Here we are," he said, as if she wouldn't know.

Only then did Nora realize that she was shaking, physically and emotionally. *Stop it,* she told herself. *Stop it.*

On joints that felt far older than her thirty years, she climbed out of the car, stiff and aching from the long drive.

If her dad had seen it in the papers, so had everyone else in town.

No escape.

Jake pulled all three of her bags out of the back of his car and dragged them up onto the porch ahead of her.

She climbed the front porch steps like a stranger instead of using the side door. Wood creaked beneath her weight, which was much less than even a few months ago. Like a stranger, she knocked, then put her fisted hands at her sides, waiting. She could almost feel eyes boring into her from the surrounding houses.

"See you around," Jake said. She turned her head, watching as he climbed into his Jeep and drove off. Leaving her alone with the rest of her past.

Then the door opened and her dad faced her. The past ten years had taken a toll on him, too. Every one of them seemed to have etched itself deeply into his face, and his rotund figure had become lean. He regarded her steadily from blue eyes just like hers, shook his head a little.

"Come in, girl. It's getting chilly. I'm making breakfast."

Breakfast for dinner. His favorite meal. He turned and walked toward the kitchen, so she followed. A kind of numbness filled her as she moved through familiar rooms, the typical "gunshot" design, from front room through bedrooms to kitchen and bath. Only one addition gave any privacy, and it had always been her bedroom. Probably would be again.

"Have a seat," he said, motioning to the small table

with its cracked plastic top and four chairs that were older than she was.

She sat and let him pour her a steaming mug of coffee. He placed it in front of her and she reached for it, realizing she needed some kind of warmth and fortification for whatever was coming.

At last her body began to react to her environment rather than her fear and anger. She smelled the sizzling bacon, the coffee, the bread browning in the toaster. Good smells. Not everything about home was bad.

But very little of it was good.

Her dad kept his back to her as he worked at the gas stove. Rude? Unwelcoming? Or just her dad at his oblivious best? What had she expected? A hug?

Of course not. Too much lay between them, both time and events. Even though she had accepted his invitation with huge reluctance, she suspected he had offered it with even more. Angry words, fights, accusations. Too much history.

And maybe not enough.

She still couldn't understand why he had called her to come home. The only reason she could imagine was that everyone knew what had happened. God forbid he should look uncharitable to the church that was the center of his life.

"How's everyone?" she asked finally.

"About the same." He didn't even glance her way. Then the first prick. "'Course, you been away awhile."

"Yes."

He made up the plates with eggs, toast and bacon and brought them to the table, placing one in front of her. She realized she still wore her coat, so she slipped it off and hung it over the back of her chair while her dad grabbed some flatware.

He sat across from her and bowed his head, saying grace. He didn't ask her to join him, though once he would have insisted. These days she didn't feel like giving thanks for much of anything.

Her dad spoke as he spooned marmalade onto a slice of toast. "Jody said you should stop by."

Jody, her best friend during all the growing-up years until Nora had finally left town for good. Once they had dreamed together of escaping to the larger world. Only Nora had escaped. "How's she doing?"

"Pretty busy with four kids."

"Four?"

Her dad let his gaze skim her way. "Two boys, two girls. Married Dave Anson."

"I remember Dave. That's a lot of kids in ten years."

No reply from her father. Fred Loftis had pretty much let his attitude about women's roles solidify in the Stone Age.

"Why did you send Jake?" she asked. Jake, the guy she had so brazenly offered herself to right after high school graduation only to be scorned in a way that had left a permanent scar.

"He could get away." A simple response. She wondered if it was really that simple. Fred Loftis wasn't tone-deaf, he just didn't listen.

Great. "And Beth?" The girl Jake had scorned her for.

"They divorced. No kids."

"Oh." Could she be excused for feeling a twinge of vengeful satisfaction? Of course not. She didn't have to become an ugly person just because the world was full of ugly people. But that probably explained what Jake had meant about things changing.

Her dad finished his first slice of toast, then used the other to dip in his egg. Nora forced herself to eat a few bites, even though her stomach was so tight there didn't seem to be room for even a mouthful of toast.

"Not much has changed," her father said after a bit. "Folks are hoping a new ski resort will liven things up. I'm not sure about that."

Of course he wasn't sure about that. Owning the only pharmacy in a hundred miles had made him a secure man, if not a wealthy one. Why should he care that others needed more and better jobs? Besides, growth could bring in one of those chains to compete with him.

She knew all the arguments. She'd grown up with them, and a whole lot of others besides. Arguments about her, mostly, but some about her mom, too. Maybe the ugliest ones about her mom.

She watched her dad wipe his plate clean with a final piece of toast. Only then did he look at her again.

"You need to eat," he said flatly. "You're all skin and bones."

"I just got out of the hospital. It'll take time." She didn't mention having been in jail, falsely accused. She still couldn't bring herself to say that out loud.

Eventually she managed to choke down the two pieces of toast. The sight of the eggs and bacon sickened her.

And for once he didn't expect her to do the dishes. He picked them up himself, rinsed them and put them in a dishwasher.

"You have a dishwasher!" She couldn't believe it. Her mom had wanted one for years, and he'd always refused.

"Don't have time to wash up myself."

The bile of anger filled her mouth. Didn't have time to wash up after himself? Just one person?

Jumping up from the table, she decided to get her bags from the porch. It would have been nice to stomp out and never come back, the way she had ten years ago after her mother's funeral, but there wasn't a place she could go. She was stuck. Stuck.

"Your room's ready," he called after her.

"Big deal," she said under her breath, between her teeth. One by one she grabbed her bags and wrestled them to her bedroom off the kitchen. He didn't offer to help.

Of course not. He never had. Instead he plopped himself down in front of the television and turned on a football game.

No, nothing had changed. Except a dishwasher.

And her entire life.

A few hours later she woke from a nap feeling a bit better. The trip had evidently taken a lot out of her, but now it was nearly 10:00 p.m. and she felt wide-awake. Her dad would be in bed already, so that meant she could get up, find something to eat that she could manage to swallow and maybe take a short walk. The doctors had insisted on walks to rebuild her muscle strength.

It would be cold out there; it always was at night this time of year, and as winter crept closer the chill would begin to really bite.

She found a bag of pretzels and ate a few. Then she grabbed the spare house key off the peg by the side door and slipped out, wrapped in her coat and scarf, to walk streets that would be quiet now. Utterly quiet, as long as she stayed away from the saloon.

How many nights as a teen had she walked these very streets, troubled by a sense of alienation that had arisen from a lot more than her age?

She tucked her hands into her pockets, and as she strolled under a streetlight realized she could see her breath. Some of the houses she passed had gone totally dark. Others displayed life in the form of flickering light from TV screens. That hadn't changed.

But she *had* changed, in ways she had barely begun to understand.

The purr of an engine crept up behind her, and the back of her neck prickled. She turned and saw a police car pulling up beside her. She waited until it stopped, and the passenger window rolled down.

"Cold night for a walk," said the now-familiar voice of the older Jake. "Want a lift?"

With *him?* "No. Thanks."

"Coffee," he said. "I'm going for coffee, and maybe a roll. Look, Nora, I'm not exactly the same ass I used to be."

"You're a new kind of ass?"

Silence issued from the car, then a laugh. "Aren't we all? Come on. Get in. I don't bite, and I hate to imagine how alone you're feeling right now."

As if he would care. And then there was the whole police-car thing. Her fists clenched as her heart began to pound. "I...can't," she said finally.

Silence, then the sound of the motor changed as he put the car in Park. He climbed out of the driver's side and looked at her across a short distance, but a chasm of years. "I heard about it, Nora. You can sit in the front seat. I swear, we'll just go to the diner and then I'll bring you home."

Why was he pressing her this way? But as much as she wanted to turn her back on him, she realized something else: he was going to keep after her until he got whatever it was he wanted. And he must want something or he wouldn't be after her like this.

Almost closing her eyes so she could pretend this wasn't a police car, she walked around the vehicle, reaching for the door handle then sliding in by feel.

At once she wished she hadn't. Scents had always triggered impressions in her, and in this car she could smell fear, anger, anguish and alcohol, each scent bringing to mind imaginings of earlier passengers in this car. She clenched her teeth, battling down the torrent of feelings.

She kept her eyes closed, seeking the quiet mental sanctuary she had created for herself, a place she visualized as utterly empty and still. A place where the hyperawareness of odors usually couldn't reach her. Where nothing could reach her.

Jake said nothing as he drove the three blocks to the diner. She couldn't get out of that damn car fast enough, and she was walking through the door of Maude's before Jake had finished locking up.

Maude stayed open until midnight, the only place in town that did other than one convenience store and the truck stop. She was by herself, behind the counter, taking care of paperwork. All day long this place was full, but Nora couldn't help wondering why Maude bothered to stay open this late in a place where the sidewalks rolled up by 9:00 p.m.

Maude straightened on the chair she had pushed behind the lunch counter, blinked as she saw her, then actually smiled. For Maude that was as unusual as Mount Rushmore moving to another state.

"Well, ain't you a sight for sore eyes, Nora."

She managed a smile. "Hi, Maude. Keeping busy?"

"Enough to get by, which is more than some can say." His eyes shifted as Jake entered behind her. "Evening, Chief."

Chief? In spite of herself, Nora turned to look at Jake. "Chief?" she repeated.

"The town took a wild hair recently. Before you know it, we have a city police force," Maude answered, her voice souring to her usual grumpy mood. She sniffed her disapproval.

"Really." Nora slid into a booth, absorbing this information, wondering if she had lost what was left of her mind. Having midnight coffee with a man who had crushed her ego and was now a police chief to boot? Yes, she must have lost the dregs of her sanity.

"It's no big deal," Jake said. "The city council decided they needed a little more authority or something. I don't know. I have six officers, is all, and we spend a lot of time cooperating with the sheriff." He shrugged.

"I thought you were a rancher."

"I still am. At the rate things are going, I may be back at it full-time soon."

"Why?"

Jake smiled faintly. "It was a power grab by the city council. They didn't like feeling that the sheriff was running everything, the town included. I sometimes think we're a sort of auxiliary."

"Useful as teats on a bull," Maude grumbled.

Nora figured he was minimizing it but didn't know why. "It must be expensive to have a police force."

"Not with federal grants. It helped swell the city budget. Maintaining it may prove to be different."

"So why did you do it?"

"I was already a part-time deputy. This pays a little more. Ranching isn't what it used to be."

Little was what it used to be. "Are the politics of it hard?"

"Nah. Gage Dalton is a good man. He doesn't mind that we help him patrol the streets in town. His budget is tight, too. And I give him someone else for the city council to holler at."

Maude brought them both coffee and thick slices of

apple pie heavily laced with cinnamon. Nora looked around
the diner, mostly to avoid looking at Jake, and felt the in-
tervening years slip away. If it hadn't been for some wear
and tear around the edges, she could have believed she was
still in high school. Red vinyl booths, a couple of battered
wood tables, stools at the counter, some of which had been
patched with duct tape.

But finally she couldn't avoid looking at Jake any longer. God, he was handsome, more handsome by far than in
their youth when she had often been content to just stare
at him. The years had favored him, and experience, good
or bad, had etched a few faint lines.

By contrast, she knew how she must look to him: ema-
ciated, too pale, her once-thick blond hair now thin and
lifeless. Stress and mistreatment could do that to a person.
Her blue eyes, unfortunately like her dad's, were three
sizes too big for her shrunken face.

"You've been through hell," he said bluntly.

"I don't want to talk about it."

"I can understand why," he answered. He picked up
his mug and sipped his coffee. Apparently he still liked
it black.

She reached for a little container of half-and-half and
poured it into hers. Then she added a second for safety's
sake. No telling how her stomach would react to the assault of Maude's strong coffee at this time of night, especially when she was feeling wound as tight as a spring.

Her hand was shaking, and Jake took the second
creamer from her hand and poured it for her.

"Look," he said as he dropped the container on the sau-
cer, "I know you have plenty of reasons to hate me. Hate
this whole town, I guess, but most especially those of us
you grew up with. We were merciless. But we're not kids

any longer, Nora. And most folks think you got a hell of a raw deal."

"Thanks," she said shortly.

From the corner of her eye, she saw him tilt his head. She didn't want to look at him, didn't want to feel again the impact of his good looks.

He sighed audibly. "All I'm trying to say is that you may find folks here are easier to get along with than it must have seemed to you back in our school days."

"Really." She tried to keep the tone noncommittal, even though she wanted to ask him what made him think she wanted to get along with *anyone* in this town. Funny how painful even the oldest scars could become when faced directly with their source again. In just this short period of time, her distant past had reared up to claw at her nearly as strongly as her recent past.

But then, it all came down to the same source, didn't it? Everything bad that had happened to her, far past and near past, had happened because she was different. Cursed, as her dad had said more than once.

Jake sighed. Apparently the tone hadn't been as noncommittal as she had hoped.

"You've been hurt," he said finally. "Badly. And I get as much blame as anyone. I'm sorry."

She glanced at him then and wished she hadn't, because with that one look she remembered something she hadn't allowed herself to think about in more than a decade: Jake had been one of the few kids she had grown up with who *hadn't* picked on her throughout her childhood. In the end he had proved to be no better. But for many years he had refrained from the name-calling, the nasty pranks, the ugliness that had framed her days. Not until the very end had she realized that he'd thought the same hideous things about her.

She said nothing, because she wasn't going to ease his conscience and accept his apology. After what she had been through, apologies seemed like empty words.

"Nora."

Her gazed skipped back to him, then away.

"Nora," he said again. "What would you think of me if we didn't have a past? If we were meeting for the first time?"

"I'd hate you," she said flatly. "I'd hate you just because you're a cop."

Jake supposed he deserved that. Even without all that had happened to her in the past months, he would have deserved that. But leaving the past out of it, given what she had endured from the police in Minneapolis, he could well understand her reaction.

He left her alone and began to eat his pie, trying to think his way through this, something he should have done before impulsively picking her up and bringing her here.

He'd been a bastard twelve years ago. He knew that. He could still cringe inwardly in shame at the way he had thrown all those epithets she'd been hearing for years in her face when she'd been utterly vulnerable, counting on him, at least, to be a friend. He still didn't know exactly what had possessed him to be so cruel, but who could understand the mind of a twenty-year-old male anyway? Not even the male involved, evidently. There was more than one stupid act in his youth, although his treatment of Nora probably topped the list.

He ate another mouthful of pie, hardly tasting it, wondering what he could say to start building a bridge he never should have destroyed in the first place. It was clear she didn't even want to hear an apology.

Finally he said the only thing he could think of. "I wouldn't have suspected you."

Her face lifted and she looked straight at him. He felt a pang as he once again saw how thin and pale she had become, how worn she looked. Even her beautiful blond hair seemed to be on the brink of death. He didn't know, might never know, all that had been done to her.

"Really?" she asked, her voice brittle. "Even my defense attorney wouldn't agree with you."

His head jerked a bit, as if she had slapped him. "What do you mean?"

"He agreed with the cops. I'd worked with the guy's kid, so I must have known him. Must have had an affair with him. Must have tried to conceal his identity to hide the affair. Must have obstructed justice. Never mind that I never met him, only his wife."

"I'm sorry."

"Sure. Everyone was sorry afterward. But that didn't get my job back. It didn't protect me from the endless hounding of the press. It didn't spare me from people who believed that simply because I was arrested I must be involved somehow. Do you have any idea how that felt?"

"I can't begin to imagine." And he honestly couldn't, although he was trying.

"So they finally let me out, and the D.A. said something to the press about how they had proved unequivocally I was in no way involved with the man before the attack. People avoided me like the plague for all of a week, and then the media were all over me all over again, demanding to know my relationship with the man, what I'd done to make him so mad at me and then…and then…" She stopped, breathing hard, her voice breaking.

"And then he threatened you."

She looked down, her long hair veiling her face. "Don't go there," she whispered. "Don't go there."

"You should have had protection."

"Well, I didn't. He was an upstanding member of the community, no flight risk… Yeah, I heard it all. Even *I* didn't think he'd be stupid enough to make those threats."

He wanted to reach across the table and take her trembling hands, wanted to promise her a safety no one could promise her.

But before he could say or do anything, she pushed herself out of the booth. "I'm going home. Now."

Home. The place that had been part of her misery when she had been growing up her. To a dad who had been less than a dad. A dad who had treated her as harshly as her schoolmates.

Maude caught his eye and he saw a frown there as Nora hurried toward the door. Okay, he'd been stupid again, and Maude had heard it all.

Jake hurriedly tossed bills on the table, then followed Nora into the night.

"Wait," he called after her. "Wait. I said I'd take you home."

"I don't want anything from you. Nothing!"

From the looks of her, he doubted she had the energy to keep up that pace, and certainly not for three blocks. Hopping into his cruiser, he did the only thing he could: he followed her.

She didn't even glance over at him as he drove beside her. She made it to the next street and started up the gentle slope toward her father's house. Just a couple more blocks.

But she didn't make it. The small hill defeated her. Her steps slowed, and then she stumbled. He threw the car into Park and climbed out, rushing to her side.

It wasn't just weakness that was giving her problems,

he realized, but the anger, as well. She was gasping as if she'd just run a marathon.

She had enough strength to glare at him, though. He didn't care. *This* time he was going to do something right.

Without even asking, he scooped her off her feet and carried her to his car. Ignoring the way her fists pounded weakly at him, he managed to free a hand and open the door, thinking that she couldn't weigh a hundred pounds soaking wet.

Bending, he put her gently on the seat, and even though she refused to look at him, he touched the side of her face gently.

"Nora," he said softly. "Nora, honey, you've got to take it easy. You've been so ill...."

"I'm not your honey!"

Then she coughed, and started panting again.

"Easy," he said as he would have said to a restless mare. "Easy. I'll get you home."

He climbed into the driver's seat, but before he put the car in Drive, he turned to look at her. "It'll take time to get your strength back. Give yourself time."

She gave a short nod, but still wouldn't look at him.

Okay, he thought. This was it for tonight. He'd just get her home, see her safely to her door, then leave her alone for now.

Everything else would just have to wait.

Chapter 2

Nora awoke with a start in the morning. Confusion filled her momentarily as it often did now that her nights were plagued with nightmares about the attack and the threats to repeat it. Then she recognized the drab, faded curtains on the window, saw the thin slices of a gray morning slipping by them, and knew.

She was at home, at her father's house. Once the worst place in the world to be, and now only the second-worst place. That didn't say much for it.

She didn't want to get up, but she rarely did any longer. She felt tired, lacked energy, lacked the desire to do anything anymore. Depression. Pills for it stood on her nightstand, and she took them only because the alternative was worse. But she had a *reason* to feel depressed, and she wondered if pills could really help that.

The sheets on her old bed smelled musty enough that she suspected her father hadn't washed them. They probably hadn't been washed since the last time she'd been here, for her mother's funeral. It wouldn't surprise her.

She listened, hoping it was late enough that her dad would have gone to work. She had nothing to say to him, and he had nothing to say to her. Not anymore.

Unfortunately, the late-night coffee, little as she had drunk of it, insisted she get up anyway. Pulling on her robe and slippers, she left her room and padded to the ancient bathroom off the kitchen. It hadn't changed. Not one bit. Except maybe the tile had been regrouted. She couldn't be sure.

A glance at the clock when she emerged told her she was safe, at least for now. It was ten after nine, and her father was surely behind the pharmacy counter now.

It was at once a relief and a disappointment. Being alone with her own thoughts was a bad place for her these days. Too much pain, too much despair, too much anger and no answers in sight.

She reheated some of the coffee that was left in the pot on the stove and sat at the ancient table, cradling the mug, annoyed that her dad hadn't even remembered that she liked half-and-half.

But that was him. Fred Loftis, penny-pincher extraordinaire. From the way they had always lived, no one would guess he was as successful as any businessman in town. Hand-me-down clothes for Nora, all of them chosen from church rummage sales where he'd allowed the purchase of only the ugliest of them. How much fun it had been to always be the girl in school who looked like a ragamuffin from the Great Depression—or an old lady oddly cased in a young girl's body.

A twisted young girl's body. The years of wearing that damn hideous brace for scoliosis hadn't helped, nor had it helped that when she'd needed eyeglasses he'd always

insisted on the cheapest frames. Not one bit of fashion
in her life. He'd carped about the cost of them, too, and
about the cost of the scoliosis brace and the doctors, but
he hadn't been able to get out of that without gaining the
disapproval of the town.

If there was one thing her dad really cared about it, it
was his public reputation. He was a God-fearing, righteous
nineteenth-century man, whose frequent discourses on
sin and vanity in the small church where he was a deacon
had managed to convince everyone in town that dressing
his wife and daughter in modest, ugly clothes had made
sense—given his beliefs.

But that was the thing about small towns. They made
room for every kind of eccentric short of the criminal.
Their kids, however, were far less tolerant.

Nora squeezed her eyes shut. She had enough to deal
with in the here and now, she didn't need to be wandering
to the distant past. Of course, being with her father wasn't
helping that part one bit. She wondered if she had enough
left in her savings to find a small place to rent.

But then the fear clamped her so hard she could barely
breathe. After that man had attacked her, after his hideous
whispered threats on the phone, she couldn't stand being
alone. Even here, in this house that echoed with the past
and seemed so far removed from the life she had been
building in Minneapolis.

They'd put one of those electronic bracelets on him
after the threatening calls. He could only leave his yard
to go to work. That should keep him confined, shouldn't
it? Although even her own lawyer couldn't explain why
they hadn't just jailed him pending trial. Not to her satisfaction, at any rate.

But she was a thousand or more miles away right now,
and if he strayed so much as a hundred feet the cops would

be all over him. So said that lawyer. But after his threats, it was hard to believe. The guy was crazy. Clearly. He'd had no good reason to attack her in the first place. How could she believe he wouldn't do something crazy again?

She realized her fingers ached from gripping the coffee mug, and as she crashed back into the present she had to face the fact that her day was empty. Empty hours scared her because they gave her too much time to think.

But how could it possibly have been any better locked up in her old apartment in Minneapolis with that man in the same town?

No, that would have been worse. She needed to find a job, that's what she needed. If only she felt stronger, and looked stronger. Right now she doubted anyone would want to hire the scarecrow she had become.

Even though her appetite had never come back, she forced herself to look in the refrigerator for something to eat. She was supposed to eat six times a day. Small meals, but six a day until she started to feel hungry again.

Nothing looked good. Nothing. She finally grabbed a package of cinnamon rolls, her father's one weakness, and cut one roll in half, leaving the other half in the package. If she could get this down, she'd be doing good.

Then maybe she would have the energy to take a walk, something else she was supposed to do every day to recover her strength. Hemmed in by orders, all for her own good, she had to force herself to obey them. She'd have preferred to find a dark corner and curl up.

Except… Well, that wouldn't be good, either. In a dark corner she'd be even more alone with her thoughts and memories.

Trapped. As surely as a lab rat in a cage, she felt trapped, and she didn't know how to break out.

She felt a weak sense of triumph when she swallowed

the last of the roll. Thank goodness the coffee washed it down or it might have stuck. Going to her bedroom, she found some jeans, a flannel shirt and her walking shoes. She had just pulled her jacket off the peg by the door when the phone rang.

She hesitated. She knew who it had to be. But with a sigh, she answered it.

"Get down here, girl. I could use someone on the register for a few hours."

Wasn't that just like her father. Get down there and get to work, just as he had demanded of her in high school. And somehow those words released a surprising and unexpected burst of resistance.

"No. I have to go for my walk. The doctor said."

Then she hung up and experienced a sense of satisfaction, something she hadn't felt in a long time.

The phone rang again, but she ignored it. She slipped her jacket on, grabbed the spare key and left the house.

Winter tinged the air. Although there was no snow, nor any sign of it, she could almost smell it coming. Some aroma in the air had changed, something she had never been able to pinpoint, but she could always tell. Conard County was slipping quickly into winter.

And then what? she wondered dismally. Living with her father was apt to drive her even more nuts than it had before after so many years of ordering her own life. He wouldn't allow her that independence. He'd feel that since he was supporting her she owed it to him to follow his rules in every respect, from how she dressed to working for him and doing chores for him. He wouldn't give her an ounce of independence. He never had.

He'd claim she owed everything to him. One of the biggest and most momentous decisions of her life had been to go to college on her own. Paying every penny for it herself. Building a life as far away from here as she could get.

Getting contact lenses. Learning to wear more attractive clothing. Finding confidence first through her school achievements and then through her job performance. Then one sicko had come along for reasons known only to him and had stripped all of it away, including her job. Because notoriety had made the school system ask her to quit, with the excuse that parents had questions about her.

Well, why wouldn't they have when the police had had so many? She wasn't sure who had wounded her more, her attacker or the damn cops and their doubts.

Or the school administration that had refused to stand by her after her years of excellent work for them. They *had* promised her a stellar recommendation.

Although she could understand the school, she thought as she walked slowly down the hill toward the more level part of town. Parents were talking, afraid of what their children might hear. The guy might be crazy enough to come after her again. What if he came after her at the school? And besides, she was honestly in no condition to counsel anyone. She couldn't even counsel herself right now.

In fact, she was in no condition to work at much. Still, it had hurt, but how many months of disability would the school be looking at? How many months before she was capable of providing adequate counseling? How many months before the parents stopped worrying?

And how many months before the trial, while it would never quite fall from the news or people's minds? Followed by the resumption of her notoriety.

Hell, she couldn't really blame the school for all of this. Her severance pay sat in the bank, not enough for anything long-term, her disability checks would continue just a few more weeks, but now that she had resigned, they would dry up. Bills continued to roll in, like her credit card and her student loans. It might be months yet before her victim compensation was approved.

She heard the growl of an engine behind her again and didn't even need to look to guess who it was. Jake. Why the hell couldn't he just leave her alone? Seeing him was like picking the scab on a wound that refused to heal.

It was Jake, all right. She didn't even turn to look as he drew up alongside her and slowed down to pace her.

"Wanna go horseback riding?"

That stopped her in her tracks. Slowly she turned and saw that today he was in his tan Jeep. "Riding?" she repeated. Her mind couldn't quite make the leap.

"Riding," he said. "I know you used to love horses. Well, I've got a couple that could use a walk today. Why don't you join me? We'll go out to the ranch and ride."

"Are you out of your mind?" The words came out sharply.

He cocked his head, still motoring beside her. "Actually, no. Wandering the streets here in town will bore you pretty fast. Being all alone is probably even worse. I'd like the company."

She really did love horses. Surprised that he even remembered that about her held her rooted. Not that she'd had a whole lot of opportunity to ride in the past, but a couple of times...

The decision was made almost before she knew it. "I'm not dressed right."

"Jeans are fine. My mom's boots will probably fit you, well enough to ride anyway. Come on. Let's blow this town before we grow cobwebs."

She doubted he could grow a cobweb if he tried, but she well might. Without another word, wondering if her mind had taken a final break from reality, signaling her total descent into madness, she climbed into the car beside him.

This car was okay. It smelled like leather, like hay and like Jake. And he no longer smelled like the guy who'd hurt her so long ago. His scents had grown more subtle, and they weren't swimming in cologne these days.

"I used to hate that cologne you wore," she announced. God, had she forgotten the last of her civility?

"Beth gave me a bottle every birthday and Christmas. I should have taken the hint."

"Hint?"

"That I wasn't okay just the way I was."

That jarred her out of her self-preoccupation. "I'm sorry," she said because she didn't know what else to say.

"I was, too, for a while. Then it struck me I'd been a fool in more ways than one. At least we didn't have kids."

There seemed to be no answer to that, either. But he didn't seem to expect one.

"I'm still wondering," he continued, "why she married me. She sure as hell didn't like ranch life. In the end she didn't much like me, either."

Nora, older and more educated now, knew something about that. Jake had been the best looking and one of the most popular guys in school. Dating him was a feather in the cap. Marrying him, maybe not so much. But she didn't say that. She'd been one of the drooling girls herself. Back then.

Jake at least left her recent past alone. He didn't ask any questions or offer any useless sympathy. He talked occasionally about the ranch, about the new police department, giving her a sense of what he was about these days. Casual, safe conversation for the most part.

At least she wasn't thinking about herself. She tried to think of something to say and finally offered, "I really don't get why they wanted a police department. Wasn't the sheriff doing okay?"

"Of course he was. But he's an elected official and doesn't answer to anyone except the voters. Me, I answer to the city council."

"That must be a lot of fun."

"Oh, yeah." He sounded sarcastic.

"So why did you agree?"

"Like I said, better pay. And by agreeing, we were able to open up five new jobs. We may even add a few more come spring. If so, that's good."

"Are you very busy?"

"Busy enough. Drunk and disorderly, speeding, domestics. Mostly small-town stuff, which is fine. If I wanted to deal with the big-city stuff, I'd move."

"But the ranch isn't doing well?"

He seemed to shrug. "It's getting by, but a little extra cash is welcome. The money isn't in cattle anymore, so I'm thinking about raising something else. I've been cutting back my herd size steadily. Something is going to have to replace it. We've been talking about it at the Grange, trying to figure out how to adapt. Feed prices are skyrocketing, so we don't get what we used to when we take the steers to market."

"Biofuels?" she asked.

"Partly. And commodity traders. Single-family operations are heading the way of the dodo. So we're thinking about forming some kind of co-op and getting into something else."

"That's sad, about family operations."

"Things change. Times change. The key is to keep up."

She supposed it was. Right now, though, she wasn't ready to apply that theory to her own life. She had to find some kind of acceptance before she could move on. Some way to absorb all the blows and knit them into a whole person, not the remnants of one.

She thought about his comment about the police force being a kind of power grab by the city council and realized it almost managed to amuse her to think that he was right. As she recalled, the council had been nearly a non-entity when she grew up here. Basically they had taxed and licensed businesses and put up some cheesy Christmas decorations on the light posts. Had they ever done anything else? Not that she was aware of. So, yes, they'd probably feel a whole lot more important running a police force, however indirectly.

But thinking about that reminded her that she was riding in a car with a chief of police. She wanted to yank her thoughts away from that as a wave of darkness threatened to descend over her once again. Instead, she forced herself to reach for a semblance of normalcy.

"So people in town call you now instead of the sheriff?"

He chuckled quietly. "It doesn't make much difference to them. We share a switchboard. Whoever happens to have the closest car responds. Mostly that's the sheriff. I've only got six of us, me included. That's nowhere near enough for round-the-clock coverage, assuming the officers get time to sleep, eat and see their families."

He swung the car onto a narrow road that led to his ranch. "You could say we cooperate fully. The difference is I have no jurisdiction outside the city limits. The sheriff continues to have jurisdiction in town. Like I said, I feel we're more of an auxiliary."

"Would have made more sense to hire more deputies with that money."

"I won't disagree."

Yet he was doing this anyway. More money, he'd said.

It troubled her to think of that when she remembered the days when that hadn't been a huge concern for his ranch.

All of a sudden, panic struck her. No matter where she looked, she saw nothing but fences. Like when she'd staggered out of that ditch in the dead of night far outside Minneapolis. Nothing. There was nothing out here, and she was alone in a car with a man....

"Take me home!"

The panic in her voice must have been unmistakable. He jammed on the brakes, pulling to the grassy shoulder, and rammed the car into Park. "Nora?"

Her heart hammered so hard that she could hardly hear him. She was panting like a runner at the end of a long sprint. Her mouth turned as dry as cotton, her palms gripped the armrest, slippery with sudden dampness.

"Nora?"

She tried to grab on to his voice as the world seemed to shift dizzyingly from then to now and back again. "Don't touch me. Don't touch me!"

"I won't. I swear I won't."

She wanted to get out of that car, but a vast wasteland was all that lay out there, offering no safety, no help.

"Nora, can you look at me? Please?"

She knew that voice. Jake. Somehow she managed to turn her head one jerk at a time toward him. He had turned in his seat, one arm on the steering wheel, one on the back of his seat. He had moved as far away as he could get in the confines of the car. Giving her room. His posture un-threatening.

"Jake," she croaked.

"Yes, Jake," he said quietly. "I'm Jake. You're safe with me. I won't touch you. If you want to go home, I'll take you right now."

Home. The image of her father's house, the emptiness

inside it, made her shudder. Being alone wasn't good. It was never good. "No," she said finally, a mere whisper. "I don't want to go back there."

"Will you be all right? It's only another mile or so to my place."

She looked down at her lap. "I'm sorry."

"For what?"

"Sometimes...I remember."

"I'd be surprised if you didn't." He turned and put the car into Drive, resuming the trip. With each turn of the tires on pavement, her heart slowed down. Her mouth moistened again, and the tension seeped out of her.

She forced herself to think about riding a horse, something she hadn't done since she'd left here. One of those promises she had made herself, that she'd find a Saturday and some money and go to a stable for a few hours, but had somehow never gotten around to.

As the panic slipped away, a sense of anticipation tried to replace it. Closing her eyes, she recalled the marvelous scents of stables and horses and leather. After all these years, they remained as vivid as just a few minutes ago.

The car turned and she opened her eyes to see the ranch house ahead of her. It looked like a haven—gleaming white clapboard in the bright autumn sunlight, a well-kept barn not far beyond and a paddock where a half dozen horses grazed.

"It hasn't changed much," he remarked.

No, it hadn't. She'd been out here once before, for a hayride with a youth group. Once had been enough for her, but surprisingly she suddenly remembered how Jake had silenced the few who wanted to know why Nora had been invited. At least after that they'd left her alone.

For the first time in many, many years, she felt some warmth toward him.

He came around to open her door for her but didn't offer a hand, as if he guessed that was too soon. She felt better with her feet on solid ground and looked around, taking in details—from the flowerpots that lined the wide porch, filled now with dying plants that struggled to hang on to just a little green, to the wooden porch swing.

The door opened and a matronly women with pitch-black hair streaked with gray stepped out, wiping her hands on a bib apron. A wide, warm smile creased her face.

"Nora, this is Rosa Gonzales. She and her husband, Al, work for me."

Rosa came down the steps, her smile fading slightly. She offered her hand, then changed her mind and touched Nora's shoulder. "You come inside. I have lots of food for lunch, and we can eat a little early."

Nora didn't argue, even though the horses drew her gaze again. Six meals a day was a pain, but an order not to be ignored. Right then she'd be more comfortable with a woman around anyway.

The inside of the house hadn't changed much, either, from what she remembered, but it had been well maintained.

Rosa insisted they use the dining room, over Jake's good-natured objections that the kitchen table would be fine.

"Not the first time you bring a lady here," Rosa said firmly.

Sitting at the big polished table, with Jake at its head and her to his right, felt strange to Nora. As far as it would be possible to get from her past experience.

More, Rosa insisted on serving them plates loaded with saffron-flavored rice and pulled pork.

"She's really putting on the dog for you," Jake remarked.

"She usually doesn't object to Al and me standing in the kitchen in our work gear eating from the counter."

For the first time in what seemed like forever, Nora felt herself smile. It was hard not to, since Jake looked uncomfortable with this development. "Just tell me she doesn't call you *patrón*."

At that, a laugh sparkled in his green eyes. "Hell, no. She calls me Jake. Or other things, depending on my latest transgression."

The rice was perfectly spiced, the best thing she had tasted in forever. The pork was so tender it practically melted in her mouth. "What transgressions?"

"Forgetting to take my boots off when I've been in the yard. I have a tendency to think floors are for walking on, but she seems to think we should be able to eat off them."

"She sounds like a gem."

"She and Al both are. I'd be lost without them."

"Where do they live?"

"I don't know if you ever saw the bunkhouse out back? Well, we fixed it up for them. Their bad luck turned into my good luck."

"Really?"

"They were homeless and out of work. I needed help. They didn't even want to be paid, but I won that battle. I think it's the last battle I won with Rosa."

And that probably explained his need to make extra cash as chief of police. She stared at her plate, surprised by how much she was eating, reevaluating Jake. At least a bit. And wondering if she should eat any more than she had. She didn't trust her stomach to hold it down, not when she'd been eating so little for so long.

What the heck, she thought, feeling suddenly reckless. It tasted good. If she got sick... Well, she'd already freaked on Jake. If he could handle that, he could handle her getting sick.

She ate slowly, though, taking only tiny bits onto her fork, awaiting any warning sign that she was making a mistake.

Finally she had to put her fork down and look sorrowfully at the plate, which was nearly three-quarters full. Jake had cleaned his plate and sat back.

"Want to go meet the horses now?"

At least he didn't try to encourage her to eat more. Her friends back in Minneapolis had driven her nearly crazy by urging her to eat just one more mouthful.

"Yes," she said promptly and rose. When she reached for her plate, Jake stopped her. "Don't offend Rosa."

Offend her by clearing the table? Nora found it hard to imagine, but Jake would know.

Jake grabbed a pair of leather cowboy boots from the hall closet. "Put these on."

So she eased out of her running shoes and shoved her feet into the boots. They were an almost perfect fit, finely tooled leather. "Your mom didn't wear these out in the yard," she protested.

"Actually, she did. She reserved Wellingtons for mucking out the stalls."

So many things she didn't know about ranch life. At the moment, though, that didn't seem terribly important. As they passed through the kitchen, she thanked Rosa for a wonderful meal. The woman beamed at her. "There's more. You eat some later, okay?"

"Okay," Nora agreed, not sure whether she'd be around later or back at home with her father. As soon as they stepped outside, she was grateful for the jacket she'd worn through so many Minnesota winters. It seemed to have grown a lot colder in just the short time they'd been eating.

She half expected to meet Al when they went out to the paddock, especially when she saw that a horse had been saddled. He was nowhere to be seen, however.

"I want you to try riding on a lead at first," Jake said. "I don't know how strong you are."

"Not very," she admitted. And the closer she got, the bigger the horses looked. How could she have forgotten that part? "Maybe I shouldn't do this."

"You can try it. Daisy over here is as gentle as they come. She won't give you any trouble, and if you start to feel tired, just say the word."

"Daisy? Really?"

"Mom liked to name the mares after flowers. Dad drew the line at Begonia."

An unexpected laugh escaped Nora and she felt her spirits beginning to rise. The nightmare seemed so far away right now; it was a beautiful day, and the scents of the horses called to her as they always had.

"Where are your parents now?"

"Can you believe they turned into traitors and moved to Florida? To a condo?"

That drew another small laugh from her. "Less work," she suggested.

"And warmer. Plus, according to my dad, he gets to play golf all year. Mom swears she can't get him out of the house in the summer to play, but he denies it."

Jake climbed the paddock fence, pulling a long leather lead from where it was wound around a fence pole. He clucked quietly, and called, "Daisy... Here, girl."

To Nora's surprise, the saddled horse, a spotted gray with huge, soft brown eyes, responded promptly. The mare stood patiently while Jake clipped the lead to her halter.

Then he turned back to her. "Now comes the hard part. I doubt you're strong enough to mount by yourself."

She eyed the distance between the ground and stirrup and shook her head slowly. "I could try."

"Or you can just sit on the top of the fence and I can help you. But I'll have to touch you to do that, Nora. Will that be okay?"

He probably hadn't imagined that difficulty when he invited her out here. But then neither had she. She closed her eyes a moment, waging an internal struggle. This was Jake, not *him*.

When she opened her eyes, Jake still waited patiently. "I want to try." It was important in ways she felt deep inside but couldn't have named. She knew a lot about psychology, but it didn't seem to be applying to her own mess.

Determined, she climbed the fence rails and managed to reach the top one, legs inside the paddock, steadying herself. The effort left her feeling weak, and she hated it. Hated the weakness, the slowness of her recovery. She was breathing a little hard, too, and her heart was racing, although she wasn't sure it was just from exertion.

"Give yourself a minute," Jake said. He led Daisy closer and began to rub her neck. "Have you ever seen horses nuzzle each other, the way they wrap necks and rub?"

"In pictures or on TV, maybe."

"They're very social animals. But they have this spot right here where they nuzzle each other." He patted and rubbed. "Someone finally got around to studying it. It's like petting a dog or a cat. It calms them down, lowers their blood pressure, eases their stress. Wanna try?"

Daisy didn't look stressed to Nora's untutored eyes, but she wanted to touch the mare anyway. Jake eased her even closer so that Nora could reach out and pat the horse's neck right where he'd showed her to. Daisy quivered slightly under her touch, then relaxed. The horsehair wasn't soft like a dog's or a cat's; it was much tougher and more bristly. But it still felt good, and at the moment she suspected that petting Daisy was calming her at least as much as the horse.

She began to relax, felt her fears disappearing. "I could do this forever."

"She'd almost let you, believe me. Unfortunately, like most of her kind, she needs to graze and move, so she doesn't stand perfectly still for long. Ready?"

"I think so." Although she still couldn't imagine how they were going to do this.

But Daisy was now close enough that her side nearly brushed Nora's knees.

"I'm going to guide your foot into the stirrup," Jake said. Apparently to try to avoid surprising her by reaching out. The man figured out things quickly.

He told her each thing he was going to do before he did it. As soon as her foot was settled safely in the stirrup, he told her to grab the pommel and try to rise. "Let me know if you need a boost."

She summoned every bit of strength and determination she had, and not only managed to stand in the stirrup but also to swing her leg over Daisy's wide back. She had forgotten how wide a horse could be.

"Good job!" Jake said approvingly. Moving around to the other side, he guided her right foot into the stirrup.

"I'm going to shorten them up just a bit."

She hardly noticed. She was astride a horse for the first time in so many years, and it felt wonderful. Daisy, bless her, didn't even twitch. Well, her ear twitched, and Nora leaned forward to pat her neck in that important spot.

"All set?" Jake asked when he'd finished adjusting the stirrups.

"Oh, yes!"

"I'm going to take it very slow here," he advised her.

"Just relax and let your body move with her. You'll find your balance quickly. Keep your weight in the stirrups as much as you can."

It was the kind of horse ride a child would have gotten at a fair, but Nora didn't mind at all. Jake kept Daisy on a very short lead, and they ambled their way around the outer edge of the paddock. Every now and then one of the other horses would look up from the scattered hay they were dining on, give it all a disinterested look then lower their heads again.

"If you get tired, let me know."

"I will." But what she felt like doing for the first time since the attack was throwing her arms up and shouting for sheer joy. The world looked different up here, and the power of the mare beneath her gave her an unexpected sense of her own power and strength.

"This is wonderful!" She spoke with an exuberance she had doubted she would ever feel again.

"It is, isn't it?" Jake agreed. "I love riding. As you get stronger, we'll take longer ones."

"This must be boring for you."

"Not at all." He looked over his shoulder, smiling. "Just seeing you look like you do right now would make me do a whole lot of things a lot more boring than walking around the paddock."

The statement startled her. What did he mean by that? Probably exactly what he said. She'd certainly been a drag since he'd picked her up at the airport. It must be a relief to see her smiling. Having dealt with many depressed people in her career, she knew how hard it was when nothing you did could make someone feel better.

She resolved to try to at least put a better face on things. And why not? She was away from that man—whose name she could never bring herself to think, let alone say—in a safe place in a town that looked after its own. She was mending, however slowly, and with time even the emotional and psychological damage would heal. Some things left permanent scars, but it was possible to deal with those scars and not let them rule your life. She, of all people, should know that.

It was time, she thought as Daisy carried her around the paddock for the second time, to live in the now, not yesterday, not last month.

Easier said than done, of course, but most things were. She tipped her head back, letting the sun wash her face with its tingly warmth, feeling the chilly air whisper over her skin, listening to the steady clop of Daisy's hooves and the quiet sound of Jake's boots.

It was a magical moment, and that man's madness had no right to deprive her of enjoying whatever good came her way.

Jake spoke, drawing her out of her almost defiant reverie. "Try clamping your thighs against Daisy's sides. To build up muscle for longer rides."

God, he was acting like a physical therapist, something she'd had to give up when she lost her job. She obeyed, though, pressing until the muscles began to tremble, then letting go until they settled down. Over and over again.

Then, as if someone had just let the air out of a balloon, weakness and fatigue hit her. She began to shake, and even pressing into the stirrups became too much.

"Jake…"

They stopped instantly. He took one look at her. "I'm going to help you down. Can you handle that? I'm going to reach for your waist as soon as I get your feet free of the stirrups."

She nodded. Either she let him help, or she was going to slide off.

Daisy stood stock-still, thank goodness. He freed her right foot, then hurried around to release her left foot. Then, something she would have been sure she could never tolerate again happened—he reached up, clamped her waist with strong hands and pulled her out of the saddle.

When her feet hit the ground, she could barely stand. He didn't release her, he released Daisy. Wrapping a powerful arm snugly around her waist, he nearly carried her to the gate. No climbing the railing this time.

"Al?"

She saw a man emerge from the barn. Tall and almost painfully lean with dark hair that looked as if it had been dusted with powdered sugar, he answered, "Yeah?"

"Take care of Daisy, will you?"

Then Jake focused all his attention on Nora. "Let's get you inside, get you a warm drink."

It embarrassed her to be so weak. To be so completely lacking in stamina. She wanted to hide in a hole. And sometimes she wished she had just died.

Chapter 3

Rosa had evidently sized up the situation. After Jake settled Nora in the living room, he went to the kitchen and found Rosa already making her own brand of hot chocolate: very chocolaty, not very sweet and sometimes with a bit of chili pepper.

"No pepper today," Rosa said.

"I think that would be wise."

"She's very sick."

"Yes, I'm afraid so."

"Not dying?"

"No, recovering."

Rosa nodded and began to fill a plate with cookies from the cookie jar she never allowed to run empty. "Maybe I should add some extra milk to her chocolate."

"I honestly don't know." Jake leaned back against the counter. "I like the way you make it."

Rosa smiled. "My family recipe. I only put in a little sugar for you."

Jake laughed quietly. He suspected Rosa's preferred brew would be more like drinking black coffee than anything he had once thought of as hot chocolate. As it was, the way she made it for him it was nearly a bitter brew, saved only by the little sugar and small amount of milk she added for him. And he especially liked it when she spiced it up with a dash of chili powder.

Her version, he often thought, was probably closer to the way the pre-Colombians had used chocolate.

He wound up carrying a tray to the living room, and Nora's mug had some extra milk and sugar in it. Breaking her in easily, he thought with mild amusement.

He set the tray on the coffee table, then turned to look at Nora. She had curled around herself in the armchair and closed her eyes. Maybe she was sleeping?

He retreated to his own favorite chair and sat, just studying her. He'd felt sorry for her most of the time they were growing up. The way she had to dress, that father of hers, the horrible scoliosis brace that must have been awful to wear...but mostly because there was enough about her that was different that she was an obvious target for the other kids.

He knew he'd damn well been her only protector a lot of the time, except for that other girl, Jody, who was now the mother of four and looking matronly at thirty. But Jody had been a bit of an outcast, too, for some reason or other.

He'd never really understood some of that stuff. At least not until the night Nora had asked him to take her to the senior prom and offered to sleep with him afterward. His own words still had the power to make him cringe, never mind how they had made her cringe. He'd been wanting to apologize for years, but that would have to wait. She clearly had more important issues right now.

Unlike most of the folks who had to depend on news coverage, as a cop he'd gotten a damn good look at the more detailed reports of what had been done to her, including the initial suspicion that she was covering an affair with a student's parent to protect her job as a school psychologist. Obstruction of justice? A pretty thin thing to hold a woman on when she'd been nearly killed by a brutal rapist.

He couldn't imagine what those cops had been thinking. But he knew enough of the details not to be at all surprised that she was finding recovery slow. There was just so much a human body could take, and she should have died in that ditch. The psychological trauma had to be beyond imagining. And now here she was, back in her hometown and living with that caveman the town called Deacon Loftis.

It was a good thing Jake had been raised in a different church because if he'd grown up listening to that man, he'd have believed God had abandoned the world to Satan. Or maybe that there was no God at all.

How was she supposed to deal with Fred Loftis on top of everything else?

But he could understand why she had come back here. No job. And worse, that man was out on bail. He couldn't figure that one, either. How any judge would think Nora's attacker shouldn't be in a cell until the trial...

Well, not for him to reason why, but if he were Nora, he'd have wanted to get as far away from Minneapolis as possible, and without a job her options had clearly been limited.

She stirred a little and opened her eyes.

He found a smile to offer. "Rosa made her special hot chocolate for you. I warn you, though, it's not very sweet."

She astonished him with her non sequitur. "This chair smells good. Rosa deodorizes it, doesn't she?"

"Yep. That commercial spray, once a week."

"I like that smell. I used it all the time…before."

He didn't miss the slight hesitation, and wondered if her entire life had become a series of "before" and "after." Then she stretched a bit, sat up and reached for the mug nearest to her. "Bitter?"

"Not as bitter as what she makes for me, but I'm sure it's more so than what you're used to."

"Thanks for the warning."

He saw that her hands shook a bit, just a bit, as she brought the cup to her lips. She took a cautious sip, then smiled. "That's really good. I like dark chocolate."

"Sometimes she puts chili pepper in it. That's great, too, but we decided not to hit you with the full treatment your first time."

"Probably wise. My stomach can react oddly at times."

As could she, he thought. He was astonished, when he thought about it, that she had allowed him to touch her at all after that incident in the car. He'd even had his arm around her waist. The memory of that darkened his thoughts. He could feel the bones, could feel that she was way too slender for good health.

Her hair, once among her best features, didn't look very good, either. He supposed that would come back as she recovered, but looking at her right now was enough to make him ache, thinking of the hell she had been through and the hell she still had to deal with.

Thinking about that left him with little to say. He didn't want to talk about anything that distressed her, and right now that seemed to be about the only thing worth discussing.

"Daisy likes you," he remarked finally, looking for neutral ground.

"Did she? How can you tell? I liked her for sure."

"She tosses her head a bit when she doesn't like her rider. Not that she gets rough or anything. She's too gentle for that. But you can tell."

"It was so much fun I didn't want to stop."

"Then we'll do it again. Soon. Maybe even a little later today."

"I'd love that," she admitted. Then, more shyly, added, "I get my energy in spurts right now. I'm not wiped out for the day just because I get tired every now and then."

"That's good to know. Do you have any directions from the doctor you have to follow?"

"Take a couple of walks every day, as far as I can, and eat six times a day, small meals. I felt so bad leaving all that food on the plate."

He could imagine where that came from, knowing her father. "Don't. Rosa can't imagine serving anything less, and I'm sure she saved the leftovers. You'll probably go home with them."

She surprised him with a little giggle. "How do you and Al manage not to gain weight?"

"Hard work." He smiled back at her.

"So is being chief of police much different from being a deputy?"

"More work and a hell of a lot more politics." He leaned forward, reaching for his own mug of hot chocolate, then sat with his elbows on his knees. "I think the city council invented new paperwork just for me. Then these guys don't always get along well, and they try to put me in the middle. I'm not sure what I'm supposed to do from there, but they try. The six of them are a private soap opera, but a lot less interesting."

She nodded. "It seems silly having a separate police department."

"It is. But Gage likes it. Even though he's elected and doesn't report to them, they used to give him a hard time. Now they reserve it for me."

"Is it worth it?"

"Right now. I could change my mind at any moment." He winked and was glad to see another smile. "Gage would take me back."

"It's good to know that." She sighed and rested her mug on her thigh. "I'm trying to decide if I should look for someplace to live."

"Your dad giving you trouble?"

"Not yet. But he hasn't changed a bit. It's like…" She bit her lip, clearly uncertain if she should speak, but finally the words burst out. "It's like exchanging one nightmare for another. It's like being a child all over again."

And that hadn't been a happy time for her at all. He didn't need her to say it. "That's not good."

"But I guess I need to find a job, too. He wants me to work at the pharmacy but I…" She trailed off and shook her head. "I'll figure out something, but it's not going to be that."

He was glad to see the spark in her. "Your father is a handful, all right."

"He should have been born in the nineteenth century," she said vehemently.

"I never thought of it that way, but you're probably right."

"I know I am. I got away, and amazingly enough there's a whole world out there where women don't have to bow and scrape, where people can actually have a good time without feeling like sinners. Of course, I'm just waiting for him to tell me none of this would have happened to me if I'd just stayed home like a good girl. That sin brought this all down on me."

Rage began to seethe in Jake, and he could feel every muscle of his body tense. "If he ever, *ever,* says that to you, let me know. I'll have more than a few words for him."

Her look grew forlorn. "What if he's right? What if I hadn't gone to Minneapolis?"

He cussed then, words he was sure her father wouldn't like. Maybe words she still wasn't used to hearing. He didn't give a damn. "Bad things happen to good people. They just happen because life is random. Blaming yourself for being in the wrong place makes as much sense as blaming yourself for being born. Trust me on this, Nora. It could have happened to anyone, including a nun. So don't even edge near those thoughts."

"It's hard to avoid them."

He figured it would be. He had ten years of experience in law enforcement, and he'd heard that kind of self-blame before. In Nora's case it was augmented by the blood-and-thunder pulpit pounding she had grown up with. God rewarded the good and punished the bad.

"I've seen a lot of good people get hurt," he said evenly. "Kids. Kids who never had a chance to do anything wrong. What does a six-year-old do to deserve leukemia?"

She didn't answer, but sat staring down into the mug on her lap. Finally she asked in a small voice, "Then how do you figure it?"

"Bad things just happen. If there's ever any fault, it's with the person who does the bad thing. It certainly isn't with the people they hurt."

"But I don't even know why that man attacked me!"

"You may never know. He may never explain it. His lawyer is sure going to tell him to be quiet about it."

"So how do you explain people like him?"

"I have to believe there's something wrong with them. Most of us stop ourselves from doing bad things even if we happen to think of them. A few of us don't. The whole difference is whether we act on those things. This guy acted. And he's going to prison for a long time."

"I hope so."

He fell silent, realizing that she had to work through this in her own way. Hammering it for her wasn't going to help.

But it made him furious to think he might take her home today to a man who could blame her for this. Her own father, for the love of Pete. The one person who should be on her side more than anyone else.

The phone on the table beside him rang. "Excuse me." He answered it and immediately shifted into another gear.

"Nora, I'm sorry, but I'm going to have to take you home. Something's come up at work."

Something he sure as hell didn't want to tell her about.

Nora arrived home with enough rice and pulled pork to feed both her father and herself a large dinner. Rosa had insisted, and Nora hadn't wanted to argue. It was a generous offer, and might take some of the sting out of her dad when he got home, probably still angry that she had refused to come to work for him today. As if she could have stood at a register for much more than ten or fifteen minutes.

She guessed he thought life was going to carry on as if she had never left. Of course, it couldn't. Any chance of that had died when he'd blamed her for her mother's death, claiming she had died because Nora had gone away to college and hadn't been able to take care of her.

Nora knew better than that, but the ensuing fight after the funeral had been ugly enough for an entire lifetime.

What the hell had she been thinking, coming back here? Surely she hadn't hoped the man had changed. As a psychologist she knew how unlikely that was. Could she have even for one foolish moment have thought he had? All she knew was that she had become desperate, and maybe she hadn't been thinking clearly at all.

But she couldn't stay in Minneapolis, not while that man was still there. Not when he'd whispered more threats on the phone to her. Panic had driven her more than anything. And where else could she have gone? When she got well enough, she was going to find another job, far away from here, but in the meantime... In the meantime, her resources were too limited.

She sagged in a chair at the kitchen table and put her head in her hands. For a little while today, with Jake, she had tasted a normal life once again. She had enjoyed herself riding Daisy. She'd had a normal conversation with someone, although she was still a little surprised it had been with Jake.

Just yesterday she'd been appalled at seeing him, wishing as she had wished so long ago that she never had to see him again. Then today... Well, today had certainly been a surprise.

Although perhaps no surprise that he had offered to defend her against her father. He'd done that kind of thing so often when they were in school. In that regard he evidently hadn't changed: defender of the weak and picked on.

But she absolutely couldn't imagine how he could stop Fred Loftis from being Fred Loftis. The man was as set in his ways and his beliefs as if they'd been poured in concrete at his moment of birth.

And she wished something hadn't come up, that she could have ridden Daisy once more today. Somehow it had carried her out of herself to a place she had almost forgotten, a place where she was glad to be alive.

But Jake had promised they would do it again soon. She was counting on that.

Jake walked into the sheriff's office, still in mufti because he hadn't wanted to upset Nora by putting on a uniform. He was immediately waved back to Gage Dalton's office.

Gage sat behind his desk, one side overloaded with a stack of papers, the other side burdened by a computer. In between there was a battered nameplate that identified him as sheriff and looked as if it had fallen to the floor countless times.

"You've taken an interest in Nora Loftis," Gage said without preamble.

Well, of course, the whole damn town probably knew by now. If he hadn't been seen picking her up, if folks didn't know he'd gone to Denver to get her, Maude still would have mentioned to someone that they'd been in the diner together last night. Life was like that here.

"I've known her all my life," Jake answered, settling in one of the two wooden chairs in front of Gage's desk.

"I'm not questioning you, Jake. Fact is, I have only a vague memory of her as a child. She seemed to blend into the woodwork and say very little. But I do know Fred Loftis. Nora gets my sympathy for that alone."

"He's a harsh man."

"To put it mildly. Now to the point. After you expressed interest in the case, I very nicely asked the Minneapolis P.D. to keep us informed. They told me that they discovered this morning that Cranston Langdon slipped his bracelet."

Jake tensed. He'd feared that when Gage had called him in, mentioning that he had a concern about Nora. The concern had been itching along his nerve endings since the call. "I was afraid that's what you wanted to tell me."

"He cut it off last night. Then before they could start checking, he was gone. Apart from what he did to Nora, this is one scary guy. He went after his wife last night, presumably because she was able to state unequivocally that Nora had never met the man. Anyway, the wife is unconscious, probably comatose, and our rapist and would-be killer is on the loose."

"What's the likelihood he could find her here?"

"Damned if I know. I've got the guys in Minneapolis scouring everything they've got to find out if it was ever mentioned anywhere in public that she came from this town. They don't think it's likely. Are you willing to bet on that?"

"Hell, no. She probably had friends who would know, if nothing else." Jake's voice became a low, almost savage growl.

"Me, neither. But I don't want to scare Nora out of her skin unless it becomes necessary."

Jake leaned back, squashing his fury, trying to sort through more logical thoughts. Getting angry wouldn't fix a damn thing, and might lead him to foolish action.

"They're sending us the guy's description and mug shots. We can get them out. You know strangers stick out around here."

"Except at the truck stop." Plenty of strangers passed through there. "I guess we should give Hasty the mug shot." Hasty owned the truck stop.

"I guess so." Gage drummed his fingers on the desk. "I hate shadow boxing."

"I'd have thought you'd done a lot of it in the DEA."

"That's why I hate it." Gage smiled crookedly, the burned side of his face barely moving. Long ago, as a

DEA agent, he'd been targeted by a bomb. "There's no guarantee this perp will have any idea where to look for Nora. There's also no guarantee that he won't. And if he could slip his bracelet, he's no dummy."

"My main concern is protecting Nora," Jake said flatly. "To hell with the rest. Living in that house with her father is hell enough, and he'd be no damn good in a crunch."

"Stashing her could be good, but stashing her would mean telling her why we want to hide her somewhere. Do you think she could handle that?"

"I think she's a lot stronger than even she realizes. She should be dead. She survived being accused of obstructing justice to protect herself and her rapist. She's a mess right now, but she's a survivor." Jake shook his head. "You're right, though. I don't want to scare her needlessly."

"Then we got us a problem." Gage sighed and shifted in his chair, a grimace of pain crossing his face. Jake had gathered that the bomb had done more than burn him. It had also injured his back and left him with a permanent limp.

"I think she's as tough as you are," Jake said.

The remark surprised Gage. For a moment he froze. Then he shook his head. "I spent a long time getting to sleep at night by tossing down a couple of whiskeys. I doubt that young woman is drinking anything stronger than lemonade."

"Not in that house."

"I don't know how to figure Loftis in this. Does he care for his daughter? If so, how much?"

"Nora seemed to think that he's going to blame her for the attack, claiming she sinned by finding a normal life for herself."

Gage swore quietly. "Somebody tell me why men like that never meet an untimely end."

That almost surprised a laugh from Jake. He wasn't used to hearing Gage talk that way.

Suddenly Gage leaned forward. "Okay. I'm going to talk to my wife, Emma. I bet she can offer Nora a job at the library, doing something that won't wear her out too much. Give her a little income. Maybe she can get out of that house then and she won't be alone, at least at work. In the meantime, we get everyone to put eyes and ears on for strangers. Quietly. And hope to God we're wasting our time."

Jake was far from a happy camper when he left a few minutes later, but he *was* glad that Gage was taking this so seriously. He sat outside in his car for a few minutes, trying to decide just how much of a threat there really was to Nora. This was damn near the back of beyond, hardly a blip on the map. Truckers came through here only because the state highway provided a shortcut to the interstate.

But it was not totally off the radar. Who could guess how many people Nora might have mentioned her hometown to? Or what sort of information about her Cranston Langdon might be able to access?

Nobody. The guy was clearly crazy. He had to have known that attacking his own wife was only going to deepen his troubles. Apparently he either didn't care, or wasn't capable of caring. Hell, if people feared consequences, there'd never be a murder.

Sorely troubled, he sat a while longer, watching pedestrians stride along the sidewalks, everything looking so damn normal he couldn't believe how much had changed by the insertion of one wounded woman into his life.

Nothing looked the same anymore. Nothing. All because of Nora.

And dammit, he had to do something more to keep an eye on her than rely on the loose cordon Gage was instituting. A whole lot more. But just what? How could he insert himself further into her life? She'd warmed to him a bit over the past twenty-four hours, but he doubted she wanted him camped on her doorstep.

And then there was Fred Loftis. He'd have to find a way around that man or be forbidden to set foot on his property.

He paused in midthought, as it struck him that he seemed like an odd choice for Fred to have sent after Nora. They weren't friends. Far from it. Fred could have asked anyone from his church.

So why the hell send the chief of police? The more Jake thought about it, the more disturbed he was by what had initially seemed to be nothing but a neighbor's request.

What the hell was Fred Loftis up to? Did he know something about that long-ago night and what Nora had done? What *he* had done? Had asking Jake been intended to cause more pain?

Or was it Fred's way of reminding his daughter that she was a sinner?

Damn! He wanted to pound the steering wheel. He wished like hell he could read minds.

But he couldn't. And he was beginning to have a horrifying feeling that Nora might be tangled in more than one spider's web.

He had to figure out something. Anything. And soon.

Nora sent a few text messages to friends back in Minneapolis, assuring them she was okay but was careful to avoid telling them where she had gone. Denver was the closest she had come to telling them her plans when she left, but she imagined none of them suspected she was here. After all, she'd made no secret of where she had come from, and no secret of her problems with her father. She doubted any of them would think she had come home.

She could hardly believe it herself. What was she doing here in this house, a house that still echoed with angry words spoken so long ago, when her father had insisted her mother had killed herself because Nora had gone away to college to live a sinful life? Him shouting those damning words, and her shouting back that if anything had made her mother suicidal, it had been life with a harsh, judgmental man who wouldn't even allow her a single thought or act of her own.

A man, she thought bitterly now, who had gotten a dishwasher when he no longer had a woman to clean up after him. A dishwasher! Her mother had asked for one once, when she often had tons of dishes to do after contributing to a church supper, when her hands had become arthritic and the job had begun to pain her, and the answer had been, "Idle hands..."

Yeah, idle hands. Her mother's hands had never been idle, even when they got so bad she could no longer do her crewelwork or her knitting. Nora had stepped in as much as possible with the chores, but the desire to escape that house had overwhelmed her, too. College had been her way out. There had been none for her mother.

Maybe her father was right. Maybe her leaving had taken away her mother's last support. Maybe she had left Gretchen Loftis feeling hopeless. Certainly, her mom had been left without anyone to buffer her against her dad.

Nora, at least, had often provided him another object for his endless sermons and criticisms. With Nora gone, Gretchen must have born the full brunt.

God! She couldn't afford to think that way. She had to remind herself that when she announced she was leaving, her mother hadn't offered a word of protest. Not one sound, unlike Fred, who had told her she was on the path to hell.

No, Gretchen had helped her daughter pack. Had taken

her to the bus station. What wrath that must have brought down on her head.

Nora felt tears seeping out of her eyes but she didn't wipe them away. Gretchen had wanted her daughter to escape. Of that she was certain. But whether that had anything to do with her mother's final act of despair, there was no way to know.

So maybe she was responsible, at least in part. But not fully. Never fully. Not with Fred Loftis in the picture.

God, what was she doing here? Had she sunk so low she had to come back here? Couldn't she find enough strength to stand on her own two feet?

Escaping Minneapolis made sense, at least until that man was in prison. And yes, she was still very weak from her injuries and needed time yet to regain her strength. But surely she could have gone somewhere else.

Agitated, she rose and walked through the house. No pictures of her or her mother remained. They had been erased as if they had never been. Even the wedding photo showing a young Gretchen and Fred had vanished.

Why the hell had her father told her to come back here? Some vestige of genuine caring? Or just the sense that he had to do something that would look good to the people whose opinions he really cared about?

She would never understand that man. Never understand how he could care so much about some things and so little about others. How he had become so hard and implacable.

How had he become so righteous and wrathful and so lacking in compassion? Had he been raised that way? She would never know, as she knew nothing about him except what he showed her in any passing moment. If he had a past he never mentioned it. He might have sprung out of the ground as a fully formed adult for all she knew.

She had to get out of here. A glance at the clock told her he would probably be coming home soon. He generally took an afternoon break then returned to the pharmacy as the evening business picked up and remained until closing.

But where would she go?

Anywhere. Anywhere at all.

Once again grabbing her jacket and the key, she left the house. Walk slowly, she reminded herself. One easy step at a time or she wouldn't get anywhere at all. There was the library, if she wanted relative quiet, or Maude's if she wanted coffee.

But there'd be too many people at Maude's, even at this time of day.

So, walking as slowly as an elderly lady, she set out for the library. She could hole up there at least until her dad went back for his evening shift. It was a much longer walk, but if she managed it, she'd have something to feel good about.

And she desperately needed something to feel good about.

Chapter 4

Emmaline Dalton, known to everyone in the county as Miss Emma for reasons long since forgotten, was a beautiful woman in her early fifties. Nora had a soft spot for the town's librarian mainly because Miss Emma had allowed her to hide out there for hours and read whatever she liked, while insisting to Fred Loftis that, of course, the girl was always doing her homework.

Homework had been Nora's excuse for coming to the library every single day until her father insisted she started working. And Miss Emma had given her a home away from home.

Emma recognized her immediately and came out from behind the desk to hug her warmly. "It's so good to see you again, Nora. I just wish the circumstances were better."

"I never intended to come back here," Nora told her frankly, returning the hug. "Never."

"I can't say I blame you. We're quiet right now, so why

don't we share a cup of tea back in my office? There may be something I need to tell you."

That ratcheted up Nora's anxiety, but only a bit. She didn't fear Miss Emma the way she feared her father.

Emma had an electric teakettle on her desk in the tiny office that seemed to be overflowing with both books and papers. "My aerie," Emma said wryly. "Or, my pending work. We're starting to collect a lot of letters and diaries from the families that have been around here for a long, long time, putting together a really detailed history of the county."

"That's a super idea."

Emma smiled. "It will be when it's done. For now it's hanging over my head."

"I could help. In fact, I'd love to."

"There's a lot to be done. We need to microfiche everything, and then I want as much of the database as possible on the computer so it's searchable. Sometimes I think I could use a tech geek."

"I don't know about the geek part, but I could help with the cataloging. As long as I don't get lost in the stories."

Emma settled her in a padded chair then turned on the kettle. "Getting lost is easy. I wouldn't have believed it possible, but I got lost in one woman's diary. She was a ranch wife, and dutifully recorded something every day for five years. Guess what she mostly recorded?"

"Family stuff?"

Emma laughed. "The weather. Day in and out. Once in a while she'd mention her grown daughter had come to visit, or her grandson, but most of it was a careful record of the weather. I guess that tells you what was important in daily life."

"I guess so." Nora paused. "Imagine it. I can't actually. To record the weather every day and leave almost everything else out. Not the price of beef, not the number of cattle, or how many calves or…"

"Exactly. That's what surprised me. I assume that information was probably recorded in ledgers of some kind, but if so I haven't found them yet. For her personal diary, though, it was all weather and an occasional visit. And she didn't even detail the visits, just mentioned them."

"And she probably thought that everything else about her days was too mundane. How many loaves of bread she baked, how many loads of laundry, whatever. It was probably invisible to her."

"I hadn't thought of that." The kettle whistled and Emma poured steaming water into two cups, where tea bags already waited. "I hope you like Earl Grey."

"Love it."

"I don't have any milk, but I do have sugar if you want."

"Black is fine."

Emma brought out a small package of tiny doughnuts. "My sin. Don't tell anyone. My boys would have fits if they knew I was eating them."

"Why?"

Emma laughed again. "Because I make them eat healthy foods."

Nora giggled and felt her spirits lifting. The tea tasted especially good after the chilly walk, too.

Emma leaned back, sipping from her teacup. "What I alluded to earlier. You need to know something about me, because I want you to know you can turn to me if you need to."

Nora tensed again. "Yes?"

"The story had pretty much quieted down when you were very young, so you probably don't know. I never finished college."

Nora was startled. "Really?"

"Really. I couldn't. I was attacked, much as you were, and left for dead in a Dumpster."

Nora clapped her hand to her mouth, closing her eyes, feeling black waves of horror pour through her, as Emma's words reawakened her own memories. "Oh, my God," she whispered.

She felt a hand on her shoulder and realized that Emma had come around the desk. "Breathe," Emma said gently. "Breathe, Nora."

It took a few minutes, but gradually the world swam back into focus. "Okay?" Emma asked.

Nora managed a nod, and Emma returned around her desk. "The guy who came after me tried it a second time. Thank God for Gage."

Nora barely managed a whisper. "Again?"

"Again," Emma said. "In my case, it was apparently ritualistic. Regardless, I'm sure that won't happen to you. I just want you know that if you need to turn to someone, I understand. Fully."

Nora supposed she would. Her hands were shaking, so she put down her tea. "I'm so sorry."

"I'm sorry, too. I didn't want to upset you, but sometimes we need someone to talk to who really understands what it's like. I'm here, any hour of the day or night."

Nora felt a wave of warmth wash through her horror. "I'm afraid," she admitted. "I'm afraid that he might come after me. He can't, they've got him on one of those electronic bracelets, but I'm not going to feel safe until he's in jail. That's why I came home."

"I can certainly understand that," Emma said gently. "It's going to be a while before you start to feel safe again. I know that for a fact. But you will, eventually. I can promise you that."

Some of Nora's tension eased, but she was looking at

Miss Emma in an entirely different way than she had during all her years growing up. The woman who had always seemed so strong and kind had had her own demons and scars to deal with. Maybe she was still dealing with some of them.

Nora spoke impulsively. "I want to grow up to be like you."

Emma smiled. "I think you've already grown up far more than that. So, you want to help with the cataloging? Are you sure?"

"Absolutely." It would keep her out of that house, away from her father, at least during the library hours. It would give her something to focus on outside herself. "I need to be busy."

"Then I'm hiring you. I have a small budget for another assistant, but I haven't had one in a while. Libraries aren't as busy these days." She rolled her eyes. "I can't imagine why. Regardless, I'll pay you for as much as you can work."

"I'd better warn you that I run out of steam quite a bit. It doesn't last, but I'm still...recovering."

"That's not a problem. At the rate this job is going, it may not get done for another generation. But it's making me feel guilty to have folks donating so much stuff and not being able to keep up. You can have my office to work in, except for when I want tea." Emma winked.

Emma quickly explained where the already cataloged items were being placed, the spreadsheet on which the description of each item was being recorded and how the items were being numbered. Nora felt confident enough with this part of the task and was soon busy at it.

She felt useful again, and what's more, she felt safe here. Her mind didn't wander down frightening paths, but instead took a trip into the pasts of others, most long gone, who had left their marks, big and small, on this county.

All too soon, though, the afternoon waned, the early twilight arrived and Emma suggested she call it quits for the night. Nora glanced at the big clock on the wall and realized it was nearly six. Her dad wouldn't be home again until nine, so it was safe.

"I'll drive you," Emma said. "Candy is taking over for the evening."

Nora had never met Candy, or at least couldn't remember meeting her. She appeared to be about twenty or so, with an ear-to-ear grin and a smattering of freckles across her cheekbones and nose.

"So you're the new archivist," Candy said. "I wouldn't take on that job for anything."

Nora managed a smile. "I'm enjoying it." And she was. It took her out of herself, and far away, a welcome change.

But now it was time to go home. To a blessedly empty house. Empty enough that she'd probably start thinking again. She didn't want to think about it yet, though. She'd deal with it in the silent house. Somehow, some way, she had to come to terms with what had happened, and she knew she couldn't do that by avoiding it. She was enough of a counselor to know that.

Still, those long hours loomed in front of her, and the tension she had managed to forget while she'd been going through papers in the library began to build anew as Emma drove her through the darkening streets.

"Will you be okay?" Emma asked as they pulled up in front of the Loftis house.

"I have to be."

Emma sighed and nodded. "I remember. Damn, I remember. Let me give you my cell number. Don't hesitate to call me."

With Emma's phone number tucked in her pocket, Nora

walked up to the dark house. She should have left a light on, but she hadn't expected to be out so long.

Her hands shook a little as she inserted the key in the lock and her stomach began to flip-flop uncomfortably. At this point she didn't know if it was the attack that was unnerving her, or being home again. It was all a mess. All of it.

Once inside, she locked the door and switched on lights as fast as she could, checking each room as she went. Her fear inside was not as bad as it could get outside, because she hadn't been taken from her home, but from her evening walk. Still…

No one in the house. Maybe she could arrange to be in bed before her dad got home. Then she got mad at herself for wanting to avoid him. Darn it, she was a grown woman now. She had nothing to fear from that man that couldn't be settled by packing her bags and living somewhere else.

And now with a job at the library, she could probably afford to rent a room somewhere. Real freedom.

But freedom had lost some of its appeal following the attack.

The phone rang, almost as if someone had seen her come home. It had to be her dad, she thought, and unfortunately she was proved right.

"Where you been, girl? I been looking for you all day! I needed you here."

"I'm not well enough to work there. I visited a friend, and then I got a job at the library."

"How can you work at the library if you can't work here? Don't make no sense."

"I can work there sitting down, and at my own pace." Nora felt her spine stiffening. "Dad, I'm still sick. So I took a job I can handle. Live with it."

He started demanding to know who she had visited, but she hung up before he finished the question.

She had to get out of this house. *Had* to. It was like being sixteen again, dependent, questioned about every little thing, criticized if she didn't do exactly the right thing…or at least the thing that Fred Loftis wanted.

No independent thinking or action had ever been tolerated in this house.

Sitting at the table, she ignored the phone when it started ringing again, sure her father wanted to holler at her for being rude, and tried to decide what to do.

She couldn't go back to living under her father's thumb again. It had seemed better than staying in Minneapolis until the trial, but now that she was here, she wondered if she shouldn't have stuck it out.

Fear was driving her entirely too much. Somehow she had to get a handle on it. Yes, it would take time to get her strength back, but that didn't mean she had to be browbeaten by Fred Loftis.

No, she had to find another way. Once again the phone rang, and once again she ignored it.

Jake was going nuts. Nora wasn't answering the phone. He knew Loftis was still at the pharmacy until he closed up around nine. So where the hell was Nora?

Sleeping, he told himself. He'd seen how weak she still was, so she was probably sleeping. Or maybe she'd gone out for a walk. He drove up and down the streets in his cruiser, hoping for a sight of her, but the length and chill of the approaching winter's nights had cut down on pedestrian traffic except right on Main Street.

He waited another twenty minutes, then called again. Still no answer. Enough was enough. Three unanswered calls when she was home alone. At least he thought she was. She could have gone to visit someone.

But he couldn't let it go. He drove over to the Loftis house, determined to settle his mind, paramount after what Gage had told him today. There was surely no real reason to think the Langdon creep would or could follow her here, but as long as there was even a remote possibility, it seemed he wasn't going to rest easy.

With the streets so quiet with the deepening chill at night, it would be a perfect time for someone to slip unnoticed into town. Few enough folks were out without purpose right now, unlike summer, when everyone seemed to be out and about on the long evenings.

He parked in front of her house and called her again. Still no answer, but he could see that a lot of lights were on. Concern crawled along his nerve endings, propelling him out of the car and up to her door. He was in uniform, and he had already gathered she had a problem with that, but too bad. All she had to do was open the door and then he could rest easy.

It seemed to take forever after he knocked before at last a curtain twitched. Then the door opened and Nora stood before him. She almost looked as if she had been crying.

"Why don't you just leave me alone?" she asked.

That smarted after the progress he had thought they'd made that day. "I was worried when you didn't answer the phone."

"That was you? I thought it was my dad again." She hesitated, biting her lip. "Jake, you don't owe me a damn thing. I feel bad about the position I put you in about the prom. I get that you probably feel bad, too. So…" She trailed off. "I can't ask you in."

"Why?"

"Dad."

She spoke the word with enough bitterness that he didn't need much explanation. "House rules?"

"Plenty."

"Dammit, Nora, you're grown up."

"Tell me about it. First of all, I'm not feeling very grown up at the moment, and second, I'm living under his roof. At least for now."

He paused, seeking a way around old impasses and new ones. He wasn't quite sure why it was so important to him, except possibly that he still felt guilty. But then he remembered something else.

"Get your jacket. If you can stand five minutes in my patrol car, we're going to go somewhere and talk."

"Talk about what?"

"Anything. Everything. Twelve years ago or earlier this afternoon."

She bit her lip. "Jake, what's going on?"

"Maybe I give a damn. Someone should. Will you get your jacket?"

Her hesitation was so palpable he almost turned away, but then she stunned him by saying, "All right."

Why that relieved him so much he couldn't have said. Yes, the incident all those years ago still had the power to keep him awake with shame some nights, but it was something else. Something about remembering Nora at eighteen, prettier than she had probably ever imagined, so vulnerable and so innocent and reaching for something so ordinary and normal that her entire life had denied her.

Maybe it was that image, overlaid by the shrunken, frightened woman some lunatic had turned her into, that was getting to him.

Something sure as hell was, and it wasn't only today's unpleasant news.

When he'd gone to pick her up in Denver, he'd done so

out of a sense of old debt. A small way to make up for the hurt he'd inflicted so long ago. But now...now he wasn't so sure. He'd felt protective of her during their youth, but he'd been raised that way. Now he was feeling protective again, and the reason behind it was totally different. Even he was self-aware enough to realize that.

This wasn't just something he was doing because it was right. At that moment, he wondered if it really had ever been that simple.

She took only a moment to get her jacket, then stepped out into the chilling night and locked the door. As she turned, he saw her breath like a puff of steam on the night air. That cold already?

She hesitated again as she looked at the police car.

"Is it about being arrested?"

"Partly. I was stunned. Completely stunned by that."

"Well, that's not going to happen here, I promise you. I'm astonished it happened in the first place. Some idiot wasn't doing his job right."

He opened the door for her, careful not to touch her, and was relieved when she made it inside.

Maude's, he decided. There'd be enough people around to make her feel like she wasn't alone with him, but not so many at this hour to cause her other problems, like the feeling she was being stared at or whispered about. In fact, after her unusual reception by Maude yesterday, he suspected that Maude herself would step in if anyone was rude.

He switched on the ignition and turned up the heat a bit. She didn't have enough meat on her to keep warm, he figured. He'd save her some energy.

"What did you mean about it only being part of your problem that you were arrested?"

He waited, and finally she said quietly, "I don't talk

about it, but I'm extremely sensitive to odors. They're evocative to me. I can smell sweat, fear, anger and alcohol in this car."

"Ouch. I guess I need to get it thoroughly cleaned." Then he said, "So that's why you mentioned that cologne I used to wear."

"Yes." She paused. "You smelled better when you forgot it."

"I forgot it as often as I could."

A tiny laugh escaped her. "I noticed. I probably wouldn't have, except I'm so sensitive to that stuff."

"How do you stand crowds?"

"I got used to it, the constant swirling of all kinds of smells. You have to get used to things, start tuning them out. I do, most of the time. But this car smells exactly like the police car that took me away. Except I smelled more gun oil in the Minneapolis car. Like it had gotten smeared on something besides the officer's pistol."

"Maybe he had just cleaned his weapon."

"Maybe."

Maude's proved to be nearly empty, and soon they were faced with coffee.

"I need to eat," Nora said shyly. "I'm supposed to eat six times a day until my appetite improves. But I can't eat much at once." Mainly because they'd had to sew her stomach back together, along with a few other parts.

"Anything that looks good," Jake said, passing her the menu. "My treat."

"That's not necessary. I got a job today."

"Still my treat. I asked you out. So tell me about the job? And please tell me it's not with your father."

"I don't think I'm up to that kind of work yet." She looked away for a few seconds, staring at the black window glass, beyond which the lighted street was dimly visible. "I don't talk about it that much, Jake. I don't. But I needed seven operations. I'm a mess of scars. And it'll be a few months or so before I get my strength back. So I can't stock shelves or stand at a cash register at the pharmacy."

He nodded. "So what are you doing?"

"Miss Emma offered me a job. I guess I'm an archivist. I stopped by today, because the library was one of my favorite places. Always. And the next thing I knew she put me to work on the county history, cataloging all the stuff people have donated." She turned her face back to him. "It's fascinating, and I don't have to work any more or any faster than I can."

"Well, that's great!" He wondered if Gage had talked to Emma about that or if it had been Emma's idea. Not that it really mattered.

"My dad won't think so," she said. But she closed the subject by picking up the menu. "Something not too heavy," she murmured.

"In this place? Good luck."

That caused another smile to dance across her face, and he was happy to see it. She finally settled on half a steak sandwich. Maude objected.

"Girl, you got to eat more than that!"

"I can't, Maude, I'm sorry. Right now I just couldn't. I'll be lucky to eat even half a one. Don't take it as an insult."

Maude put her hands on her hips. A stocky woman, she could be quite imposing. Jake tensed for the typical confrontation, but it never came.

"All right," Maude said finally. "We'll get you fattened up eventually."

"That's the plan."

"Just as long as you ain't being one of them girls that wants to look like a boy."

"Just recovering. Little by little."

Maude nodded, took Jake's order then stomped back to her kitchen. At this time of night, she did everything from waiting the tables to cooking. Or one of her daughters did—both of them were Maude clones.

"God, she's mellowing," Jake remarked with a half smile. "For you anyway. I wondered if it would ever happen."

Nora surprised him with one of those smiles he remembered from high school. It was almost shy, and yet it lit up her entire face. For an instant it was possible to see the woman she had been becoming, not the one shrunken by horror and hardship. His chest tightened unexpectedly.

Opportunities lost and wasted. He'd had plenty of time to reflect on them, especially after his marriage fell apart. With a sense of surprise, he wondered if Nora had been one of those missed opportunities. He sure as hell knew he regretted the way he had treated her that last time.

God, he'd thrown everything but the kitchen sink at her, and there she'd been, as vulnerable as a girl could possibly be. What the hell had he been thinking?

He'd been asking himself that for a long time. He knew she was attracted to him, but a lot of girls had been attracted to him in high school. He'd been one of the lucky guys that way. He hadn't paid it much attention once his own interest had settled on Beth. And he'd totally forgotten about it two years after graduation, when he'd been working to save up for an engagement ring so he could ask Beth to marry him.

Twenty years old, focused on one goal apart from working the ranch, and then a very vulnerable young woman had asked him to take her to the prom. All she wanted was to go to a prom. And she'd even felt herself so unwanted that she had offered to have sex with him as an inducement.

God, it killed him to think she had valued herself so

poorly, and then he had added to it by blowing up at her and throwing out all those insults she had heard growing up, and a few more besides.

What the hell had been going on in his mind?

Maude slammed their plates down in front of them, Nora's meal a half sandwich as promised, although Maude had included fries and a salad. Trying to fatten her.

Jake looked down at his plate and tried to pull himself out of memory. Either that or pull out an answer for his behavior. Not that he'd managed yet.

"Are you all right?" Nora asked.

He looked up, realizing he'd been ignoring her. "I'm fine. Just thinking about something. Let's eat." He offered a smile and picked up his burger, biting into it as an excuse for continued silence.

The question of why he had reacted so unkindly to Nora seemed to be taking center stage in his mind. He needed a moment to put it off and find safer territory to discuss. But danged if he knew what that was. He couldn't bring up her attack, or much of what happened. He couldn't discuss the past. What did that leave? He hardly knew her now. Then a thought occurred to him.

"Do you ever think you'll go back to counseling?" he asked.

"I'm not sure," she admitted. She was picking at her sandwich, taking tiny nibbles interspersed with an occasional small mouthful of salad. "I've got my own head to sort out first."

"Are you getting counseling to help with this?"

"I did, briefly, but when I was asked to resign, I lost my insurance. But I know all the techniques. I should be able to put them into practice."

He nodded, and didn't mention that there was a reason

most doctors didn't treat themselves. "And your dad. He hasn't changed much from what I can see. Has he?"

"Not a bit. I'm going to have to get out of there." She frowned faintly. "He's going to be mad that I got a job. He was trying to get hold of me all day because he needed me at the pharmacy. It makes me wonder if that's the only reason he told me to come home."

He was wondering about that himself, and his conclusions weren't any prettier than hers. Even so, he still had questions. "Why *did* he ask you to come here?"

"He said it was the least a father could do. I'm getting the feeling that didn't come from the heart but rather because of how it would look. Not that I really expected otherwise." She sighed. "I was panicking, Jake. That guy had called me again. I'm not sure if I was foolish enough to hope that Dad gave a damn, or if I just needed to get the hell out of there."

He shook his head a little. "You'd be a very unusual daughter if you didn't cherish some small hope. Well, I can see why you didn't want to stay in Minneapolis, but wasn't there somewhere else?"

"Not immediately. I needed to get out of there. And I was foolish enough to seize on his offer like a lifeline."

He nodded and took another bite of his burger. "Understandable," he said after he swallowed. "You haven't seen him in a long time, have you?"

"Not since my mother's funeral."

"He could have changed."

Nora's mouth traced a bitterly humorous curve. "I don't think that's possible."

"It must have been hard growing up with him. Harder than any of us guessed."

"Let's just say his public face isn't as harsh as his private one."

Jake swore silently, beginning to imagine the full extent of her childhood. Ugly clothes, ugly glasses, scoliosis, merciless classmates and a father even more merciless. Now this. He didn't often think of life in terms of fairness, but Nora had certainly met more than her share of unfairness.

Her eyes averted a little and he studied her, thinking that she looked almost ethereal right now, a mere wisp of a woman who had been on her way to beauty but now looked as if she might blow away in a strong wind. Her face, however, was already less pinched than when he had picked her up in Denver. Maybe getting that job today had been the best possible thing for her.

"So what hours are you working?" he asked. "Because I promised Daisy you'd be back for another ride."

Her head turned toward him, her eyebrows lifting. "You promised *Daisy?*"

"Of course. She liked you."

He was delighted when she giggled. "I'm sure she hardly noticed me."

"On the contrary, she noticed you a lot. Horses are very sensitive creatures. It's been a while since a woman has ridden her, and she always preferred my mother over every other rider. You filled a gap for her."

Nora looked as if she didn't quite believe it, but was at least considering it. "Miss Emma told me to work whatever hours I like. She was awfully kind about it."

Why wouldn't she be? Jake thought. Emmaline Conard Dalton had been through this particular hell herself, and was probably better equipped than anyone in this town to help Nora. In fact, he ought to try to talk to her himself to see if there were any guidelines he should follow, anything he should avoid like the plague. This was like walking on eggshells he couldn't see.

Finally he decided to take the bull by the horns, at least

a bit. For a fact, they were never going to get even so far as friendship if they couldn't discuss important things.

"Why did they ask you to resign?"

She pushed aside her plate instantly, and he wanted to kick himself for killing her appetite.

"Surely you read about it," she said tautly. "It was a damn scandal. I was arrested. Then I was released. I was accused of having an affair with my attacker. He pointed the finger at his wife, saying that's why *she* had attacked me. He wasn't too bright. Forensic evidence didn't bear him out. But no one believed that I could have been counseling his child yet never have met him. But it was *true!*"

"I believe you," he said quietly.

"Anyway, I was ill, it was taking a long time for me to recover, the parents were worrying about all the stuff they'd read about the case and whether their kids would hear about it and finally whether I'd be qualified to counsel anyone after what had happened. Good question. Even I couldn't answer that."

He pushed his own plate aside, leaned forward on his elbows and waited. She was talking, and he wanted her to talk as much as she needed, painful as it was to hear.

She rested her hands on the tabletop, spreading her fingers, staring at them. "I don't even know why he picked me," she said, her voice trembling a little. "I'd like to know why, but I guess I never will. Anyway, I was between operations when they put me in a jail cell. Can you believe that? I still needed more operations and they carted me off."

"Somebody was a total idiot." Anger edged his voice, but she didn't seem to hear it. She had gone back in time, and he had sent her there. Fool!

"I've been trying to figure out that part," she continued, her voice little more than a whisper. "As soon as I could, I gave them a description of the man who attacked me. I helped with that computer thing where you put together pieces...."

"Identi-Kit," he said.

"Yeah, that thing. It wasn't a good description, though. He was wearing a ski mask and I'd never seen him before. I just want to know why I would claim I was attacked by a man if a woman did it, the way he claimed."

"You wouldn't," he said quietly.

"I don't know what anyone was thinking at that point. I was pretty much wrecked myself. But they figured I'd given them a bad description on purpose once they fingered him. I don't get that, either. I'd lie about who attacked me, why? To save my career because I didn't want to admit to an affair? I'd pretend it was a stranger when it was my lover?"

He hesitated, then said, "Some women do things like that because they're afraid of retaliation."

She blinked, seeming to see him again, to land firmly back in the present. "You're right," she said, her voice strengthening. "Of course, you're right. But he damn near killed me. He left me for dead. I wouldn't have lied."

"I believe you," he said again.

"When they started zeroing in on him, I guess his wife helped them." Nora shook her head. "God, it was so surreal. The two of them pointing fingers at each other. But she was the one who got me out of the cell. She swore under oath that I'd never met her husband. That he'd never participated in any of our sessions with their child. That he was abusive to her and violent. Apparently she had the hospital records to prove it. I don't know what to believe about any of it, but I do know I never met that man before the night he grabbed me. Never. And I don't care what the police believe."

"Somebody really screwed up," he told her as firmly

as possible. "You should never have been charged with anything. Period."

Her chin quivered a bit, then she steadied herself. This woman, he thought, had a whole lot more strength than appeared on the surface.

"Thank God for DNA," she said finally. "I guess he thought I'd never be found because he left plenty of evidence. Unfortunately, it took a while to process."

"I know. It's complicated and they have to be careful."

"I get it. Anyway, it's still all mixed up in my head. All of it. I may never get it straightened out. I don't even know how much of what I think I remember is true. Between my injuries and all the operations, and the trauma, it's a whirl of disconnected thoughts and memories, a puzzle I can't quite piece together. I'm not sure I need to or want to. I just want to get *past* it."

"That's going to take time."

"Yeah." She shook her head, then lifted his mood a bit by reaching for her sandwich again and taking another tiny bite. "But I feel mostly better being here. I really needed to get away." She cocked her head. "Does that sound like running?"

"Not to me. I'd be antsy about that guy being out on bond, too." He didn't tell her how easy it was to get rid of a tracking bracelet. Or that it sometimes took days to find the perps afterward. This guy must have planned it fairly well, though, to get at his wife before he was caught. That worried Jake more than he wanted to admit.

"Next," she said with the greatest firmness he'd heard from her yet, "I need to move out. I can't stay with my dad. He'll drive me nuts. I don't even want to go home tonight."

Jake stilled the immediate impulse to tell her she could stay at his place. She'd be trapped out there without a vehicle, dependent on his schedule. Besides, he didn't think she wanted to share quarters with him any more than she wanted to share them with her father.

It also occurred to him that she had left here to become an independent woman. Returning her to dependency of any kind might not be a good thing right now.

Much as she seemed to be putting their unpleasant—okay, ugly—past behind her, he doubted it was that easy. Mistreatment had hit her from every direction. He hoped she'd had at least a few years in the past ten when life had been good to her.

He decided it might be best to change the subject to something more positive. Anything to get her looking forward beyond going home to Fred Loftis and then the struggle she'd undoubtedly face over her new job and moving out.

"What is the one thing you'd like to do tomorrow if you could?" he asked.

She didn't even hesitate. "Ride Daisy again. But I've got to work."

"We managed to fit in both things today, didn't we? And you said Emma was letting you set your own hours. So how about I pick you up in the morning and I'll get you back to the library right after lunch?"

Her face brightened so much that she no longer looked like the pale waif he had picked up just yesterday. "You really don't mind?"

"Not in the least. I'd enjoy it, too. So consider it settled. I'll get you around eight, if that isn't too early. Maybe you can ride Daisy a couple of times before lunch."

What killed him, though, was seeing those moments of beauty and happiness fade as he drove her home. He could almost feel her shrinking beside him.

So while he was worried about that lunatic from Minneapolis finding her, he became more immediately concerned about Fred Loftis. But what the hell could he do about the woman's father?

Nora had not the least doubt that there was going to be a big scene with her father when she got home. She had broken all the old rules, and she seriously doubted he had changed them in her absence. She had gotten a job, she had refused to go to work for him, she had gone out without telling him where and she hadn't been home to serve him his dinner after he closed the store. The rules had been engraved on her at an early age.

She just hoped her dad didn't blow up before Jake left. She had never, ever, wanted anyone to see how her father treated her. It always made her feel small and somehow shameful, and even though she'd been through her own therapy as part of her training, coming home had reawakened all those feelings as if she'd never dealt with them.

Well, darned if she would take it this time. Fred Loftis might be in for a bit of a shock himself.

She felt herself stiffening in anticipation of a confrontation. She had grown up hating fights and arguments, and it had taken her a long time to learn to stand up for herself at all. A long time to imagine that it was possible to ask for anything, a reluctance that still hampered her.

Damn, she wished she had more energy, but as the anticipation of trouble began to run through her, she felt her adrenaline surging. She sat up a little straighter and fixed her jaw. She was not going to take any trouble from that man. She was grown up now, thirty, able to make decisions for herself. She had proved that a hundred times over since she had walked out that door to go to college.

When they reached the house, Jake turned off the ignition. He walked around, helped her out and escorted her to the door. A gentleman. But this time he didn't leave her as she inserted her key in the lock. He loomed behind her and she couldn't imagine why. She'd already told him she couldn't ask him in.

But he waited, and was there when she opened the door. She turned to say good-night, wanting him to leave before her father began the expected eruption, but he didn't budge.

"Thank you," she said. "I enjoyed that. I'll see you in the morning?"

He nodded, but still didn't move away. What was going on? She started to step through the door, with the strange feeling that the coming battle might emerge from any direction. She glanced over her shoulder. "Jake," she said quietly, "please."

He just shook his head. "Seeing you safely home doesn't end at the door."

Oh, God. The anticipated trouble had just multiplied, and she didn't know what to do about it. She tried to run back over the evening, to remember what she might have said to turn him so protective. Something about a house rule, that was all. Surely?

Before she could find any other reason for this odd behavior, her father came out of the living room. In the background she could hear some sports announcer. He must have moved up from basic service to some cable plan that would give him more sports to watch. An irrelevant thought.

"Where you been, girl?"

Before she could answer, Jake did. "Out for dinner with me, Mr. Loftis."

"We had food at home. Sorry I had to eat alone." As if he hadn't been eating alone for years. "Gadding about gets you into trouble, girl. You ought to know that *now.*"

The way he said it tightened everything inside her. She felt her hands clench until her nails bit into her palm. He was blaming her for what that crazy man did to her? Blaming *her?*

"How dare you," Jake said from behind her. His voice carried the edge of steel.

"You get out of here. I'm talking to my daughter."

"Like hell I will."

"You got no part in this. I warned her about going to the city. I warned her about living alone. Now she's under my roof again, and she's going to live my way, the right way."

Loftis turned toward Nora again. "What's this about getting a job when you won't come help me out? Well, if that's the way you want it, you can pay rent. I ain't got no cause to support a grown woman."

"No, you haven't." Nora's own voice sounded far away, even to her. She seemed to be floating above it all somehow, suddenly free of the tethers of emotion that had nearly bound her with fear on her way home. "If you want rent, Dad, I'm not cooking for you. I'm not cleaning for you. I'm inviting my friends over when I choose. I'm through with your rules."

"Then you got no place here!"

"I never did."

The unwanted weakness was overcoming her again, and she reached for the doorjamb. What she found instead was Jake's arm.

"I'll get your things," he said.

"In just a minute." She felt like she was looking at her father from a long way away. "You deprived my mother of any joy or happiness she might have had in life. You will not do the same to me."

"Jezebel," he said, practically spitting the word.

"You are a hateful man," she said. "Now move out of the way. I'm leaving."

"To go live with a man you hardly know!"

"It's none of your damn business now."

She stepped forward, half expecting to get hit, as she had so often in childhood, but evidently with Jake standing there, especially in his uniform, he wasn't going to take the chance. He backed away.

On shaky legs, Nora made her way to her bedroom, feeling Jake's hand on her elbow every step of the way. Blackness seemed to be creating a tunnel around her vision. When she got to her room, though, she collapsed on the bed and put her head between her knees. *Don't let me pass out. Please don't let me pass out.*

"Keep your head down," Jake said gently. He pressed the back of her neck lightly. "Where do I find everything I need to pack?"

"I hardly unpacked. There are a couple of things in the closet. Except for my bath supplies, everything is still in my suitcase."

The tightening tunnel of blackness began to recede. Her heart was hammering as if she had just run a marathon, and her limbs were shaking. Nothing new, really, since the attack. Weakness had become her frequent companion.

Maybe she'd feel better about all of this tomorrow. Right now she just felt sickened. "I can't just move in with you," she protested faintly.

"You can look for a place if you want. No biggie. But you can't look at this hour of the night. And you're not staying here."

She heard hangers scrape against the closet rail, then from the corner of her eye saw him fold the dresses into the suitcase. "I guess not. But I could stay at the motel."

"Over my dead body." All of a sudden he squatted in front of her. She lifted her head enough to meet his gaze.

"He used to hit you, didn't he?"

She squeezed her eyes shut, not wanting to answer that

question. Why it should shame her so, she didn't fully understand. They'd worked on that in her therapy, how nothing her father did was her fault, but she felt the hot, miserable wave of shame anyway.

"I always wondered," he said. "He sure looked like he was about to, tonight."

Then he was gone again, moving around the room. "Your bath supplies. All girlie stuff?"

"Mostly. It's all in a flowered bag."

"Got it. You wait here."

She heard him open, then close the door. Then the most astonishing statement.

"You're kidnapping my daughter, Madison! You got no right."

"She's an adult choosing to leave of her own free will. Now step aside or you'll be the one arrested for unlawful imprisonment."

Wow, Nora thought. Wow. Could this really be happening? The surreal feeling she had experienced so often since the attack was claiming her again. This must be someone else's life.

But a minute later Jake was back with her flowered makeup bag, and he dropped it in the suitcase.

"All done, I think," he said. "Do you want to check?"

But she really hadn't unpacked much. She hadn't had the energy, or the desire, to settle in here. "That's it."

"Do you feel strong enough to walk out of here?"

She was determined to walk out of here, with her head as high as she could hold it. The last time, she had left in anger after their fight over her mother's death and her supposed responsibility. This time she would leave like ice. How much sweeter that would be.

She marshaled herself and stood. Jake was right there, ready if she needed aid, but she was grateful that he waited to see. She'd managed to sacrifice enough of her independence and sense of self-worth over these past few months. Even little victories had become important to her.

God, to feel that way after more than a decade of becoming a new and stronger woman. It was pathetic how fast she had slipped back into the ways of thinking she had learned in childhood. Fear. Living in constant fear of everything. Endless self-doubt. Endless feelings of inadequacy.

"I hate myself," she muttered as she started toward the door.

"Whoa there," Jake said quietly. "None of that."

"It's true."

Thank God he didn't argue. She needed to get out of this house, to breathe some different air, before she'd have the energy for anything. Coming home hadn't helped her. In some ways it had sapped her.

Survival demanded that she get out of here now.

It was as if something important was changing deep inside her, as if some cloud were lifting. For the past few months she'd been in survival mode, intensely focused on fear, rage, pain and recovery. Now she felt an urgent desire to focus on finding herself again, looking forward again.

She hoped it lasted.

If nothing else, seeing her father again, living in his house however briefly, had made her realize that there was no way she wanted to slip back down the rabbit hole of time.

Loftis was standing in the doorway of the living room as she emerged. Behind her, Jake carried her bags. Her father looked as if he wanted to erupt. The desire was fairly written all over him. His fists were clenched, and for an instant, just an instant, she saw him as the paper tiger he was. He couldn't control her anymore. He couldn't threaten her anymore.

Her head lifted and she shifted her gaze from him to the front door. Deep inside her grew the certainty that she would never come back to this house. Never. Its walls held years of pain, self-disgust and self-loathing. Just being here was causing the poison to seep back into her.

She lifted her head another notch and forced her step to grow firmer. Done. Finished. She should never have allowed herself to think that she had no choice but to return. Messed up as her life had become, sick as she still was, she shouldn't have given in to the craven impulse to hide and lick her wounds. Not with that man.

Just after she and Jake crossed the threshold, she heard him call after her, "That man's coming, girl. You're gonna be sorry you don't have me to protect you."

Her step faltered. Jake shifted a suitcase and grabbed her elbow. "Keep going," he said in a low voice.

But she didn't. Instead she turned and looked back at her father. "Protect me? You never protected me. Not once."

Then, before she could say more, Jake let go of her arm and slammed the door behind them. "The car," he said. "Can you make it that far?"

She damn well would, even as her legs began to feel like overcooked spaghetti. Reaction, she told herself. It was just reaction setting in. Down the short, bumpy sidewalk to the curb. Jake dropped her suitcases and opened the door for her, helping her into the cruiser.

Her hands had begun to shake so badly that she couldn't even manage the seat belt. He leaned in, snapped it into place then loaded her suitcases into the back.

She let her head fall back against the headrest, and for the very first time thought that at least one police car didn't smell that bad.

Moments later they were pulling away from the curb. She scarcely paid attention as Jake radioed to say that he needed to head back to his place. The voice of the dispatcher told him someone would cover him. Then he pulled out a cell phone and she heard it dial automatically.

"Rosa, I'm bringing Nora back with me. The guest room is ready?"

She couldn't hear the answer.

"Okay. Spray some of that air freshener around it. Nora likes it."

That got to her, that he remembered that silly comment. She crumbled then, quietly, a few silent tears running down her cheeks. No one, not ever, had given that much of a damn about her.

Chapter 5

Maybe it was Rosa's TLC, or all the excellent food and fresh air, but a week later Jake hardly recognized Nora as the woman he had picked up at the airport. She was striding around the ranch with a firmness to her step. She rode Daisy without a lead and was planning to join him on a short trail ride that weekend, probably the last weekend before the weather turned completely into winter. She went to the library every weekday afternoon, and her afternoons were growing longer.

The only problem he had was her desire to rent her own place. With Langdon still on the loose, he didn't like the idea at all, and so far he'd been able to scotch every rental possibility by pointing out all the problems, until finally she had looked at him with wry amusement and asked, "Do you really think I'm going to find something perfect?"

Of course he didn't, but he didn't want her that far away.

He didn't want her to be by herself. Especially not with Langdon out there somewhere.

He was also troubled by Loftis's threat as they had left that night, about that man coming after her. Did Loftis know something? Probably not. The cops were keeping mum. None should have revealed that they were watching for the man. The owner of the truck stop? Not likely. Hasty could be garrulous, but he also knew when silence was golden.

So maybe it had been an empty threat in an attempt to intimidate Nora. He wished he believed it. He and Gage had talked about it, but Gage had no ideas, either.

But he should have known secrets didn't remain secrets forever. Not in this town, not anywhere. And he should have guessed that sooner or later Nora would call one of her friends back in Minneapolis and get the news.

He was out in the barn in the early morning, forking some fresh hay into the stalls with Al's assistance. At this time of year the nights grew cold enough that he preferred to keep the horses inside. They probably could have huddled together in the paddock and kept themselves warm enough, but he didn't see the point in putting them through that when he could get them out of the wind and into a warm space. Their shaggy winter coats were thickening nicely, though. They'd probably make it through a blizzard outdoors.

But he was thinking about more than horses. He was thinking about Nora, too. A thought had been dancing around the edges of his brain, and he wondered if he was tinkering with memory. As a cop he knew how unreliable memory could be.

But as Nora strengthened, he felt the pull of an undeniable sexual attraction to her. Feeling that, and remembering how she had looked in high school, despite her hideous clothes, he began to wonder if the whole reason he had erupted at her as he had that shameful night was because he was promised to Beth and he really wanted Nora.

She had offered herself to him, and that made him mad for her sake, certainly, but maybe it had made him uncomfortably aware how much he'd wanted to take her up on that offer. Maybe his cruelty to her had been defensive denial. Or maybe not. Maybe he'd just been a stupid twenty-year-old who for some unknown reason had blurted a whole bunch of cruel stuff.

It wouldn't have been the first time in his life he'd acted on an idiotic impulse he couldn't explain. Probably not the last, either.

But regardless of what had been going on in his head twelve years ago, he knew what was going on in there now. And in his body. As Nora's health returned, he wanted her more and more. Not because she was prettier, but because she was stronger. He didn't feel quite so guilty about the yearnings now that she didn't look fragile enough to break.

Not that he should act on them. Not after what she had been through.

But he was growing increasingly uneasy. He couldn't imagine how Cranston Langdon had managed to evade both the Minneapolis police and the Minnesota state police. A lot of people slipped their bracelets every day, but most of them wound up back in custody within seventy-two hours. Mainly because they were stupid and didn't leave the area. This guy either had a great place to go to ground, or he hadn't stopped moving and wasn't using his own vehicle.

It was the latter idea that increasingly worried him. Initially he'd been certain that Langdon would be under wraps in a few days. It had been over a week now and he seemed to have dropped off the radar.

He was just emerging from the barn, covered in hay dust, when he saw Nora marching across the yard his way. His heart lifted a little at the firm determination of her step. She was coming back fast. She came to a halt about six feet away, putting her hands on her hips. Her blue eyes were shooting fire. Another time he might have liked seeing this burst of spirit.

She didn't even need to open her mouth for him to realize what was coming. He braced himself, suspecting this wasn't going to be pretty. Worse, he suspected he may have utterly sacrificed any trust she had begun to feel for him. Probably deserved to, too.

"Why didn't you tell me that man was missing? You knew, didn't you? Hell, that's what my father meant when he said the guy was going to come after me. Everybody knew but *me!*"

He hesitated, unsure of the best way to give the story to her. His mother used to tell him, when he was young, that it was all in the way you said something. He still wasn't sure he'd mastered that arcane piece of advice. "I knew," he finally said, with customary bluntness. "Usually they pick these runners up in a couple of days."

"Usually. *Usually?* At what point did you think I might need to know about this? When I was facing him in another ditch?"

"Nora…"

"Or did you think that because you're chief of this Podunk police force that you'd be able to stop him at the county line?"

"Everybody's watching out for him. We posted a BOLO."

"That's supposed to make me feel better? That you and a bunch of other cops are keeping an eye out? What about me? Don't I need to keep an eye out?"

She paled suddenly. "That's why I'm here, isn't it? Because this way you can be sure I'm never alone. If it isn't you, it's Rosa, or Emma at the library."

"Now, wait…"

But she wasn't waiting. She turned to storm back toward the house, although he couldn't imagine what she would do there except slam some doors, but then he noticed a slight stagger. The fury had drained her. Hell, maybe it had even set back her recovery.

Didn't he feel like something that ought to be on the compost heap?

Reason argued he should let her be, but emotion was having none of it. It pained him in an unexpectedly deep way that she felt angry. Pained him that he had once again hurt her and it didn't matter that he'd done so with the best of intentions. Hell, he'd thought he had the best of intentions last time when he'd turned down her offer, being promised to Beth and all. It wasn't turning her down that had caused the pain. It was the way he had done it.

That appeared to be the same problem now. The way he had handled this was clearly wrong.

"Nora!"

She kept right on walking, although her step was a whole lot less firm then when she had come at him. That tore it. Giving no thought to what was the right thing to do, he ran after her, caught up and wrapped her in his arms.

Then he felt a terrible stillness go through her, a shocking stillness as if she had turned to marble. Oh, God, he had just grabbed a woman who had been recently assaulted.

He didn't know what to do. He had no idea if she was locked in some cell of memory, if she might collapse if he let her go. But holding on to her seemed like a bad thing, too.

"Nora?" He gentled his voice almost to a purr. "Nora, I'm going to let go and step back. Will you be okay?"

After a few seconds he felt a jerky nod. Moving slowly, afraid of startling her or unwittingly frightening her, he loosened then dropped his arms. When he was certain she was steady, he stepped back.

"I'm sorry," he said. "I shouldn't have grabbed you."

Maybe what killed him most was the way her gaze had gone from furious to almost hollow. She stared at him and he could almost feel the effort she was expending to pull herself back from wherever she had gone. As if she couldn't quite focus on him.

Little by little, she seemed to visibly reassemble herself. "You shouldn't have done that."

"No, I shouldn't."

Then she said something that tore at his heart. "I'm not sure I'll ever be normal again."

"Eventually," he promised her. "You're already getting better day by day. It'll come." Mostly, he amended silently. He doubted all the scars would ever be gone.

Then she ripped at him even more. "I'm sorry."

"Sorry? For what? Nora, there's not one damn thing you need to apologize for. I'm the one who should apologize for grabbing you like that. I'm not long on finesse, as you well know, and I was just so disturbed that I'd upset you and you were walking away, I did the stupidest thing possible. I physically stopped you. That was wrong, no two ways about it."

"You hugged me," she said quietly.

Well, he had, sure enough. But he still didn't have the right to lay a finger on her without her permission, attack or no attack. His own ham-handedness appalled him.

"Nobody," she said, sounding choked, "has hugged me in forever."

Aw, man. That hurt to hear. His chest squeezed so hard he could barely breathe. No hugs? "Can I hug you? Now?"

She gave a jerky nod.

He approached her again, moving slowly, gentling every touch as he wrapped his arms around her, feeling as if he were dealing with a skittish mare. He felt the stiffness seep out of her until at last, ages later, her head came to rest in the hollow of his shoulder. Only then did he tighten his hold, making it a true hug.

A tremulous sigh escaped her, followed by the most miraculous thing: he felt her arms lift and tentatively wind around his waist. Turning his head, he pressed his face to her hair and smelled baby shampoo. It was an aroma he had always liked.

Eventually, though, reluctant as he was to disturb these minutes in which she seemed to have given him her complete trust, he murmured, "It's chilly out here. Do you want to talk inside?"

Some of the softness left her, an infinitesimal pulling away that he felt in the furthest corners of his being.

"Yes," she said quietly. "We need to talk."

No question of that now. He stepped back gingerly, regretting every inch of space between them. Together they walked toward the house.

Passing through the mudroom, they doffed their boots. Rosa was somewhere upstairs, cleaning a bathroom to judge by the sound of running water. Jake stopped to get two cups of coffee, then led the way to the living room. He considered closing the pocket doors to give them complete privacy, then wondered if that might make her uneasy, so he left them open. She took a gooseneck chair, saying as clearly as words that she wanted space, that she didn't want him close.

She opened the conversation. At least he hoped it would be a conversation. "Why didn't you tell me?"

At least she didn't sound truculent. That was a better start than he had hoped for. Of course, a lot of his conversations with Beth after their marriage had generally started with her mad about something. "Gage and I talked about it. We were pretty sure they'd pick the guy up in a day or two. We also wondered how likely it was that he would follow you here, or that he even knew where to look. We've been keeping in touch with the Minneapolis police, though."

"They haven't found him. And he attacked his wife."

"Unfortunately true on both counts. But the fact is, we put his photo out there to all our officers, and at the truck stop. Anywhere else in town, strangers will be noticed. You know that."

"That doesn't make me feel any safer." She pulled her knees up and tucked them under her chin, wrapping her arms around her legs. She seemed to have shrunk again.

"You've been through hell," he said bluntly. "It's going to be a long time before you feel safe again. Even after they put the guy away."

"If they can find him."

"They will," he said with a certainty he was far from feeling at this point. "How many people know you come from here? Apart from your immediate friends, who probably wouldn't mention it to anyone."

"I don't know." Her chin quivered, then steadied. "It's not like I made a big secret of it, but I didn't exactly bandy it about, either. It was in my employment records. My college records, but I don't even know if the police asked for it or looked it up. They wouldn't talk anyway, would they?"

"No." But he didn't mention that all the information would be available to Langdon's lawyer. *All* of it. He could have sighed when it hit him how many possible ways someone could find out where she lived. Loftis wasn't an uncommon name, but combined with her first name, that would narrow a search considerably. So far this guy had eluded police, which meant he wasn't your typical dumb criminal.

Of course, going after his wife wasn't exactly genius. Now he was up for two major felonies. So the question was, would he still have it in for Nora, enough to hunt her, or was he making his way out of the country to escape prosecution?

"Nobody ever figured out why this guy attacked you," he said.

"Not really. I never even knew who it was until they caught him, and then all I could tell them was that I'd never met him. That's when they got the idea that I was obstructing, trying to conceal an affair with him. But I told you all this, didn't I? Then when they arrested them, he claimed he'd blown his cork because I was having an affair with his *wife*. Maybe going after her was a way to bolster his story." She spread her hands, her eyes huge and sad. "I just don't know, Jake. I still can't believe most of this, let alone understand it."

He nodded encouragingly. When life changed so completely and totally, you could feel as if you'd been transported to a different planet where almost no landscape was recognizable. Feeling safe would be a hard commodity to come by.

For him, though, it was like looking through fractured glass, past and present leaving scattered pieces all over the place, and he wasn't quite certain how to put them together. There was that long-ago time when he had hurt this woman so deeply he'd forever lived with an awareness that he, too, could be immeasurably cruel, an awareness that stained his conscience. And there was now, a woman who had suffered a terrible attack, false accusations, intolerable pain both emotionally and physically, and she, too, was like shattered glass that needed to be put back together.

And her assailant was out there somewhere and nobody could guess if he might be a threat to her.

He was accustomed to moving through life in a pretty straightforward way. As a youngster and young man, he'd known his course: take over the ranch, marry, have a family. Well, Beth hadn't gone according to plan, but it was still straightforward: work the ranch. Then he'd added working part-time as a deputy to make ends meet better, with a little slack for the unexpected.

Basically a very ordinary life and path.

But when he looked at Nora, he saw a path full of knots and nooses. Yes, nooses. All the years she had suffered under her father's thumb, and from the taunts of her peers. All the years she must have felt like the ugly duckling watching swans through a window she couldn't get through. Followed by her leap for freedom and a new life, an adventure that most of the people he'd grown up with hadn't even attempted, whether they'd thought of it or not. She had guts. She'd reached out for the brass ring and built a new life. Then it had all been snatched from her in the most horrific way.

While he'd been sailing through, she'd been struggling, and in desperate need of a life preserver that no one would throw her. The clarity of that image was enough to twist *him* into knots.

And now she had reason to fear that the worst demon of any of her nightmares might be coming after her. He wished he could promise her that wouldn't happen, but he couldn't. Nor would she believe him if he did.

"So," she said after a little while, "that's why you've

objected to every place I thought of renting. You don't want me to be alone."

He couldn't deny it. "That's part of it. The other part is that I'm enjoying having you here."

Did her cheeks pink slightly? He couldn't be sure. Given their history, he decided it wasn't likely. She had no real reason to trust him. Not after that long-ago night. Although he was cherishing a small hope that they were becoming friends of a sort. And she *had* let him hug her.

But, God, how alone she must feel! She'd given up the home she had built, the friends she had made, to come running here to recover, only to find that the beast might be following her, that her father hadn't softened one iota over the years, and now she was utterly rootless, staying with a man she had ample cause to loathe, one who, over the past twelve years, had become a stranger.

Lovely.

"He'll find me," she said suddenly.

"What makes you think that?"

"Because he's crazy. Crazy enough to have wanted to do all that to me in the first place. Because of his daughter."

"What about her?"

"In some of our sessions, I talked about my childhood here. Told some stories to get her to open up."

He hated to imagine why it had been so difficult to get a child to feel safe enough to open up. Probably a childhood much like Nora's. "So you mentioned you lived here?"

"Yes. And I'm sure her mother knew, too. She was in on some of the early sessions."

"Damn," he said quietly. Uneasiness began to crawl along his nerve endings. "What were you seeing his daughter for, if that's not confidential?"

"It is, so I can only give you a bare-bones idea. Let's just say she and I had a lot in common."

That was enough. Apparently Langdon hadn't just suddenly gone off his rocker, but had been abusive to both his wife and child, enough so that someone felt the daughter needed counseling.

"You worked for the school district?"

She nodded just briefly. "You'd be amazed how many children need some counseling. Someone to just listen, if nothing else. We tried to get to as many as we could in elementary school in hopes we could forestall some of the problems later. Unfortunately, you can't always identify them."

"But this guy's daughter was identified?"

"By her mother." Nora froze. "I don't think I should have said that. I can't talk about any of that."

"Sorry. Moving on." She gave him a faint smile of gratitude. "So basically you were providing a whole bunch of kids with something you never had yourself?"

Her gaze clouded and the corners of her mouth seemed to droop just a tiny bit. "I guess that's one way of looking at it," she said finally. "I just wanted to help."

"That's the best reason in the world."

She nodded, seemed to let go of an inner tension, and leaned her head back, closing her eyes. "So he'll come. He didn't finish what he started. I'm supposed to be dead."

To hear her say it so calmly chilled him. He would have loved to have an argument for that, but there was none. From the reports he'd read, she was supposed to have been dead, all right. The guy had probably assumed she was dead when he dumped her. Or that she wouldn't survive even fifteen minutes. Instead she had survived for three hours and made her way out of the undergrowth to the highway just as the morning traffic started passing. God, he wondered how many people had spied her and just passed by in a panic, frightened by what must have looked like a bloody caricature of a human being. At least some of them had cared enough to call for help. Finally a woman had stopped, wrapping her in a blanket until the ambulance arrived. He hoped Nora didn't remember much of that night. He hoped the trauma had stolen most of her memory.

"I can't live with you forever."

"You're no problem, Nora. I'm enjoying the company. You can stay as long as you like. The real question is where you would feel safer. Here or someplace in town. I get that there are more people in town. So if that would help…"

Her eyes snapped open. "Nothing is going to help until that man is behind bars." She shook her head sharply and the fire returned to her gaze.

"Do you know what the district attorney told me? They can't charge him with murder because I'm still alive. So it's attempted murder. But even then there's the question of his intent. Did he *mean* to kill me? So anyway, she's going to pile on several felony charges, but he'll still probably be out in less than twenty years. How is that going to make me feel safe from him?"

She shook her head. "Did he mean to kill me? I can't believe anyone could wonder. And after all that, to think he could be a free man again while I'm still alive… Jake, that doesn't seem right!"

He couldn't argue with her about that. His time with the police had opened his eyes about a lot of things, and how crimes were charged was a big one. "It doesn't seem right," he said heavily. "But maybe they'll stack the sentencing."

"Stack?"

"You know, twenty years for attempted murder followed by twenty years for rape, followed by ten years for aggravated assault. The judge could give maximum penalties and have the sentences run consecutively, so he *might* be put away for the rest of his natural life."

"Right. Assuming he gets convicted on every charge they throw at him. Assuming the judge decides he should never walk the streets again. Assuming a whole lot."

"Well, he went after his wife, too, so I guess he'll be facing another trial after yours." It was the only comfort he could think to offer.

"Yeah, I guess." She put her chin in her hand and looked glum. "I'm trying not to be a big baby about this. I get that laws are written to cover a broad variety of individual circumstances, things that can vary from case to case. I'm not stupid. But after what that man did to me, it was hard enough to take him getting bail. Now look what he's done." She closed her eyes and her next words came out on a whisper.

"I'm scared to death of having to testify, too. I'm going to be asked about every detail I can remember. I can't remember a lot of it. Thank God. Then they're going to wonder how I can remember *him* and whether we were involved, which would explain the DNA evidence, and what I did to provoke him…." Her voice trailed away until it became nearly inaudible.

He crossed the room to squat in front of her and take her hand. "Nora. Nora, don't think about all of that now. We'll take it one day at a time. Just one day at a time."

"I know. I know. That's the right way to think, but sometimes I get overwhelmed. It's like there's this huge mountain lurking out there and I'm going to have to climb it all by myself. Nothing will be finished, not one thing, until after the trial and sentencing. This could drag on for a very long time, and I'm dreading it. I admit it."

He was relieved when at last her fingers curled around

his and clasped him. "If you want, I'll go back with you when it's time. You don't have to face the trial alone."

"You always were the protector."

The words stung, especially when he remembered the time he had been anything but a protector. Reluctantly, he looked into her face, but saw no bitterness there. She squeezed his hand briefly, then released it. He interpreted that as a sign to retreat back across the room. She had to be the one who set the boundaries, at least for now.

And he still wished to hell that he could figure out what had gotten into him all those years ago. It would be nice to understand for his own sake, if nothing else. Even nicer if he figured it out in some way that would help *her* to understand. Some way to clear the table, as it were. To bury at least one wound.

God, he doubted he'd ever felt as helpless in his life as he did right then. He couldn't take back a long-ago mistake, and he couldn't do a whole hell of a lot to help her right now. Sharing his roof was far from enough. He wanted— needed, perhaps—to make her safe and he couldn't do that. He could try, but there was no guarantee.

"Don't move into your own place just yet," he said finally. "Wait a little longer. I'm sure they'll catch the guy before he gets to the state line."

"Maybe." She fell silent again then sighed. "I wish you had told me. I wish you had trusted me enough to be honest. I get that you were trying to protect me, but there are things I *need* to know. Don't protect me like that again, Jake."

She was justified, he thought. Totally justified. She wasn't a kid, she was an adult, and keeping her in the dark wouldn't protect her in the end. It might only make her more vulnerable.

"I promise," he said.

"That's all I can ask."

She could ask a hell of a lot more, he thought. Because he owed her a hell of a lot more.

Once he crossed the Minnesota state line into North Dakota, Langdon felt better. He figured they wouldn't expect him to head north, because it wasn't the most direct way to Wyoming. Nor would they expect him to head for Canada because the minute he showed his ID at the border, they'd have him. Two good reasons to head west on a more northern route.

But he wasn't in a hurry. Not at all. The Loftis woman must have heard by now that he had escaped, and he enjoyed the thought of how she must be sweating. Sweating and frightened. Maybe even terrified out of her mind, because he'd given her plenty of reasons to be terrified.

But she shouldn't have survived. That hadn't been part of his plan at all. He'd figured they wouldn't find her body until the scavengers had scattered her bones, leaving nothing to tie him to her murder.

Instead she had defied him. He never allowed anyone to defy him, not even his wife or daughter. Defiance had a price, a heavy one, but he could sure as hell take his time collecting it. He would disappear for long enough to convince them all he was on the way to Brazil or something.

But he would be right here, waiting, and Nora Loftis would know. She knew his determination. She knew that once he made up his mind he followed through.

It was only a matter of when.

Chapter 6

Nora felt worn out again. Her ire at Jake had taken a toll, and as she sat in the armchair in the living room, with a fresh mug of Rosa's hot chocolate beside her while Jake went to deal with something, she felt a piercing frustration with her own weakness. She ought to be able to handle her anger. She shouldn't feel drained by a simple emotional burst. God, she wished she could heal faster.

Especially now that she knew she might be in danger from that man again. She couldn't rely on anyone else to protect her. She had to get strong enough to deal with him on her own somehow. But that needed time.

While she could see some of the improvement she had made just in the time she'd spent here at the ranch, it was clearly nowhere near enough.

It was then that she remembered her father's parting shout, about how that man was going to follow her. How could he have known that? *Did* he know that? At the time she'd hardly heeded the words. Fred Loftis often said the worst things he could think of when he was angry, making empty threats, trying to intimidate or scare.

At least with her and her mother, that's how he had behaved. The man most people saw at the pharmacy and the church was very different. Almost Jekyll and Hyde, although she'd gathered over the years that some had figured him out.

Regardless, she needed to remind Jake of it. It might mean something, or it might not, but Jake could probably find out.

The thought of calling her father herself made her insides curdle. If she hadn't been in the very pit of hell when he called and offered her shelter, she never would have come here. Given time, she would have found another solution to escape the area. As it was, she had seized what looked like a life raft, only to find out that—as usual with her father—it was anything but.

If she'd had to sort through his motives in making that offer, love would never have entered into it. No, he'd do it so he could look like a good man and father around town and most cspccially at the church. Oh, most especially at his church, because he'd no doubt spent years painting himself as the patient man with the ungrateful daughter. Or something like that. So he could polish his halo by bringing her here.

Then, of course, there was the store. Nothing to ramp up your profit margin like replacing a paid employee with an unpaid one, which she'd been from the time she was twelve.

A wave of weary bitterness passed through her. After all these years, she didn't have to look far into her mind to remember living at home. Her own therapy experience had helped her to a mcasurc of acccptance, if not understanding, but it could still hurt when she remembered how she had so often felt. Kids had an unerring instinct for someone who was different, and the one who could easily be hurt by their words. She'd practically worn a kick-me sign, she supposed, and had never learned to stand up for herself in any way. Instead she had shrunk back as far as possible, keeping her own company except for Jody, another outcast. Making herself as small a target as possible, yet still not safely escaping notice. Not entirely.

But inside a flame of determination had begun to burn. She'd had a need to leave all this behind and move on, to remake herself in a new image among people who didn't know what a sorry person she was.

She had succeeded, too, to a large extent. No one at college or in Minneapolis had known the old Nora. She'd worked hard at recreating herself, from her appearance to her behavior. Little by little, acting as if she were a bolder person had made her one, and the change in her appearance had given her the all-important self-confidence from which to start.

She'd even dated a few times, basking in the first male approval ever in her life. Nothing had become serious, but she didn't care. Her view of marriage had been soured by her parents and she rather liked the idea of remaining single and independent, answering to no one except an employer.

She'd made huge strides, and then that man had come and erased them all with his inexplicable cruelty.

Shivering horror trickled icily throughout her body, because she had not the least doubt he was looking for her right now. Unfinished business. It wouldn't do him a damn bit of good, other than the satisfaction of completing what he had started, and he had certainly enjoyed her terror and pain. Yeah, he'd come back for seconds.

The question was what woman would he meet when he found her. The whipped one she thought she had outgrown but had rediscovered immediately when he attacked her? Or a stronger version?

She had control over very little, but that was one thing she could be in charge of: herself. Her reactions. Whether she would become a quivering mess again or give him no satisfaction at all.

The problem was, as she had discovered, that she had a tendency to revert to type, to become the girl she had once been, rather than the woman she had created. She needed to do some heavy-duty work on that, and fast.

Then there was Jake. Did she want to stay here because it felt safer? Did she want to stay with Jake? The scar of that one encounter still hurt after all these years. Jake, the one guy she had known in the old days that she had trusted to at least not hurt her, even if he turned her down, had savaged her with words.

But he seemed to have changed. He'd even made an oblique apology. Maybe she should readopt some of the characteristics of the second model of Nora and come right out and ask him why the hell he had done that.

Or maybe she should just let it lie. He seemed to be a good man now. Why bring up something from so long ago that might bother him as much as it bothered her? Disturbing old wounds didn't seem kind, and maybe it wasn't even necessary. What would it accomplish anyway? It wouldn't take away the pain or the memory.

She sighed, and finally reached for the cocoa, hoping it was cool enough to sip now. She half wished she could talk to Rosa. The woman had a lot of life experience behind her, some of it obviously unpleasant. But what she hoped she could learn from Rosa, she couldn't imagine.

She guessed she just needed someone to talk to, to use

as a sounding board. Sometimes when you spoke your thoughts out loud, they became a whole lot clearer, and Rosa seemed nonjudgmental.

She could also talk to Jake, but for some reason she felt reluctant. Part of her felt that she could trust him absolutely, but another part remembered how he had turned on her in the worst way, and without warning.

That Jake would not quite vanish from her memory.

Finally she decided that sitting by herself wasn't wise. Awareness of *that* man being out there somewhere was like a burning black cloud surrounding her awareness of everything now. The more she tried to divert her thoughts from the threat, the more she felt its pressure. He would come from her. She knew it in the depths of her heart and soul, beyond reason.

So sitting around wasn't helping. Instead it had her thoughts tracking through every corridor they could find that might allow her to escape that awareness even briefly.

It sure wasn't working.

She picked up her mug and set out to find something to do. Someone to talk to. Anything to take herself out of her own head.

Jake turned out to have some ideas about that. He was just coming back into the house as she reached the kitchen. "Wanna take a trail ride?" he asked her.

Her heart leaped at the thought of riding Daisy outside the corral. "Really?"

"Really. I think you're up to a short one, and it's getting warmer out there. I can show you a few of the sights and Daisy is getting antsy in the corral."

She had seen him and Al ride the other horses out to various places around the ranch, so she was sure they were getting their exercise. "Why don't you ever take Daisy out?"

"She's getting up there, so I take it easy on her. But a short trail ride will be good for her and I think you're ready for it."

It was amazing how good that made her feel. Just a few minutes ago she had felt herself tumbling backward into the old Nora, and doubting her own physical recovery because she'd become so worn out by her anger. But he was telling her otherwise. She was certain he wouldn't have suggested it if she didn't think she was strong enough, and that felt great. "I'd love to!"

"Then get your boots on. And your jacket. It'll still be chilly in the shade."

Oddly enough, even though the day had warmed, she could almost smell snow in the air again. Not that it had grown *that* warm, but this was the second time since arriving here she had detected that particular scent, and for the first time she wondered if the trauma she had experienced had thrown off her sense of smell.

It was possible, but she hoped not. Over the years, she had come to rely on her unusually sensitive nose in so many ways, even though it wasn't always pleasant.

She waited while Jake saddled the horses, listening attentively to his explanation of everything he was doing but knowing she was in no way ready to help lift one of those saddles or do much else that required real strength. Enough for now that he apparently thought she could grip the horse well enough with her thighs.

"This is crazy," she said as they rode out across some open rangeland, past a handful of cattle and sheep amicably grazing in close proximity, "but I smell snow."

"Amazing nose you have there," he said. "It snowed

higher up the mountains last night, and there's a possibility that later we might see some."

"Really?"

He glanced at her as she rode beside him. "Really." He smiled. "It won't be much, but if you look over there—" he pointed west to the mountain peaks "—you can see a dark fringe of clouds. They're supposed to reach us this evening."

"That would be nice. I like snow."

"I would assume so, since you moved to Minnesota."

She gave a little laugh. "Warm climates never called to me. What about the sheep and cattle?"

"I've sold off everything ready for market and I'm down to mostly yearlings and breeding stock. If you're still here in the spring, you'll see us get really, really busy. But they winter pretty well. We bring them in close. And you see the hay bales? We feed them all winter long."

"That must be a lot of work."

"Not as much now that I have help."

It seemed overwhelming to her, most likely because she wasn't familiar with any of it. Still, since he managed to keep Al pretty busy, he must have had his hands full after his parents retired.

"Why did Beth leave?" The question popped out of her before she knew it was coming. Quickly, she added, "I'm sorry. It's none of my business."

He rode silently beside her for several minutes. The trees slowly surrounded them, and a clear trail guided them. "We fought all the time. She claimed I wasn't the man she thought I was. I was damn sure she wasn't the woman I thought she was. Somebody told me that marriages fail because roles, and thus expectations, change."

"That's true." She had learned all about that in the course of her studies. "It's most commonly seen in couples that live together first. They're essentially still dating, but the day they get married all of a sudden one is husband and the other wife, with all the baggage that may entail for a couple. Expectations change."

"Well, something certainly changed for us. The honeymoon didn't last long, and being a rancher's wife didn't seem to be at all what she expected. I get it. It's a lonely life out here unless you're really into the work and solitude. She wasn't. Note to self—don't marry a townie if you're a rancher."

A quiet laugh escaped Nora. "That might not always be true."

"Probably not, but it was in this case. If it's hard in these days when we have cars to get around in and phones to talk on, what must it have been like in the days where you had to travel on horseback or in a wagon? When you could only have a conversation with someone who didn't live on the ranch once a week or once a month? Less often in the winter. Anyway, I worked longer hours than she probably appreciated, and I wasn't as keen on heading into town to go dancing or take in a movie as she would have liked. Even going out to dinner at Maude's meant I had to be able to get away. So I can see her side of it."

"Apparently. But what about you?"

"I was raised to this life. I knew what it would be like, and by the time I'd been out of high school a couple of years, I'd adapted. I didn't expect to climb on a bus every day and spend my time with a whole bunch of people anymore."

"Do you regret that?"

"Not at all. Animals are often better company than people."

She wouldn't argue with that.

"But," he said, "you made a life of dealing with people and their problems. Do you miss it?"

Surprisingly, she had to think hard about that. "Maybe not," she said finally. "Maybe not. I don't think I want to be a counselor any longer."

"Why not? Because of that guy?"

"No, because it's hard not to bring the pain home with you, especially when you're working with children. They're so defenseless and vulnerable in so many ways. I was supposed to keep my emotional distance, but I wasn't good at that part. I seemed to identify with most of my patients."

"I wonder why," he muttered.

"What?" She wasn't sure she'd heard him correctly, or exactly what he'd meant if she had.

"Doesn't matter. Just carrying on a conversation with myself. One of the hazards of being alone so much."

"Being a cop must take care of some of that."

"Not always for the best." He flashed her a sudden grin. "You should read our blotter sometime. 'Assisted man who could not unlock front door. Directed him to correct house and cited for public intoxication.'"

She laughed. The sound rolled out of her easily for the first time in forever. "That's Conard City."

"That's any small town. Anyway, I don't see too many things that give me a distaste for people, except domestics. Those are always upsetting, often infuriating."

He fell silent, and she watched his face darken a bit. She returned her attention to the trail ahead of them, to the surrounding furs and occasional aspens, which had lost most of their golden leaves. Either he was remembering something unpleasant, or he was afraid of following the conversation about being a cop any further. Given how she had initially reacted to him and his car, she could understand.

But that brought her back to the question she had been wondering if she should ask. "Jake?"

"Yeah?"

"What do you think my father meant when we were leaving and he yelled that man was going to come after me? Did he know?"

"I don't know how he could have. We'd only just found out ourselves that he'd ditched his leash. And we weren't passing it around widely. Probably an empty threat."

"I hope so. Not that it makes any difference. I'm sure he's going to come for me."

He drew rein and reached out to grip Daisy's bridle, halting her, as well. "Why? Yes, we're concerned about it, but why are you so sure?"

"I have only a hazy memory of everything that happened that night. But I remember one thing so clearly because it reminded me of my father. He must have said again and again, 'How dare you defy me?'"

"So he was hung up on defiance?"

"That seemed to be at least part of it. Yes. And what's more defiant than surviving when he meant for me to be dead?"

He swore quietly and released the bridle. When he urged his mount forward, Daisy fell in beside him. "We were hoping he'd just skip out."

He fell silent, but she filled in the blanks of what he wasn't saying anyway. He was abandoning that hope, one she hadn't shared since she'd learned the news. That man would come. Only God knew when, but he'd come for her.

Jake seemed to have developed an instinct for when she began to tire, because a short while later he suggested they take a break before heading back. He chose a lovely glade with a stream tumbling through it, probably engorged with the recent snowfall at higher elevations.

He pulled a rolled blanket off the back of his saddle and spread it on an area clear of everything except pine needles and drying grasses. She still needed his help dismounting, mostly because Daisy, for all she was the gentlest horse in the world, was also a very big horse. She'd gotten used to the grip of Jake's hands around her waist as he helped her slide down. Panic no longer struck her.

She only realized how much she needed the break, though, when she felt her thighs quivering. Sinking gratefully onto the blanket, she looked around, admiring the peaceful beauty that wrapped them. An owl hooted, as if wakened from slumber, and at a distance she could hear something moving through the woods. Probably deer or antelope.

But mostly she filled herself with the rich aromas of loam and pine and even the running water. Decay and life commingled into scents that identified the woods even with her eyes closed. Pine sap dripped golden down some of the tree trunks, occasionally glimmering in an errant sunbeam.

"This is a piece of heaven," she remarked.

"I always think so." He joined her on the blanket, sitting cross-legged.

"Right now," she said, "I could imagine building a lean-to and staying here forever."

"Until the winter settles in," he said with light humor. "A cabin would be a whole lot better. Feeling like withdrawing from the human race?"

"I've felt that way more than once," she said, letting the painful honesty slip past her usual guard. "Often as a child. Then lately."

He nodded. "I'm not surprised. I'm sorry, Nora."

"For what?"

"For not being more aware of what you must have been going through when we were younger."

She shook her head a little. "Kids are born with empathy, you know. Really. Then they get into groups and other things become more important. They create in groups and out groups and everything changes. It's normal."

"Maybe, but not fun when you're the one in the out group."

"You tried to protect me when you saw it happening."

"That was little enough. And what I did later..."

She bit her lip and averted her face. "Someday maybe you can tell me why. I know I was out of line..."

"You weren't out of line. I was." He spoke firmly. "Of that there is no question. The question is what got into *me*. I'm still not sure. But all those things I said? They weren't true. I was fighting something inside me, not you at all. That much I *am* sure of."

She looked at him then, drinking in his strong features, enhanced by the past decade, thinking that time had only made him much more attractive. But he was not for the likes of her. That was clear.

Then she caught herself. Falling into old thought patterns, she realized. Running mental audiotapes that had been instilled in her by others. It was one of the first things you did in therapy: catch those tapes when they popped up, and shut them down. Don't let them run on and on about how worthless you were, how ugly you were and all the rest. She had eventually learned to stand fast against her father's voice in her head, but she seemed to have slipped again.

Maybe it was partly the attack. Maybe partly coming home again. Like taking the cork out of a bottle. But she'd been a therapist long enough to know that some things had to be fought forever. One trigger could set them all off again, and she'd had more than one.

She sighed quietly, the sound lost in the rustling of the trees and the song of the stream. "In a way, I'm glad I came back here. I guess I wasn't finished with this place."

"Do you want to be finished with it?"

"With my father, at least. Sometimes I think of him as an evil genie who just keeps popping up out of the bottle. He managed that feat even when I was far away."

"Some things are pretty much indelible."

"He seems to be. He accused me of killing my mother, you know."

For a long time, Jake didn't respond. Then he said, his voice taut, "I seem to remember she committed suicide."

"She did. But it was my fault because I wasn't there to look after her and make her life easier."

All of sudden Jake was beside her, and without warning, his arm draped heavily around her shoulder. He pulled her close, and after an instant, instinctive resistance, she yielded and leaned into his side. God, he smelled so good and felt so strong beside her. And it was heaven to be held again and yet feel safety. It had been so long.

"Did it ever occur to that man that *he* might have been the reason? Or that there was no reason at all other than that she got too depressed to take it anymore? Life with him must have been a real grind."

"He got a dishwasher," she said.

"What?"

"Mom wanted a dishwasher for years. He didn't get one for her. Too expensive, he said. Waste of money. After all, there were two women in the house to wash up. But he's got one now."

Jake swore.

"I know," she answered. "I couldn't believe it when I saw it."

"It speaks volumes, doesn't it? But trust me, Nora, she didn't kill herself because you weren't there. She'd probably been working up to it for a long time. You can't blame yourself for her decision."

"I know all that. I'm a counselor, remember?" She sighed again and leaned her head on his shoulder. "It was our last big fight, right after her funeral."

"Did that man ever take responsibility for anything?"

"Sure," she said bitterly. "The state of our souls. His business. What more was there?"

"Plenty. Like the happiness of his family. Did he miss that part? His duty to care for you well, not just judgmentally?"

She shook her head a little. "I don't know. He's a hard man. I've never seen any other side of him."

"I'm certainly not old enough to remember any more than you do. Do you remember your grandparents?"

"Only a little. They were gone by the time I was seven or so."

"So you have no idea if they raised him that way."

"What difference does it make? Every parent makes decisions about how to raise a child. I've seen plenty of them decide to do things differently because they felt their parents made serious mistakes. But everyone decides for themselves. I'd never raise my kids the way I was raised. If I ever have any."

"I honestly don't think you have it in you to raise a child the way you were raised."

"How can you say that?" She tilted her head to see his face.

"Because you know that pain and it didn't harden you. You wouldn't do that to anyone else."

She liked his confidence in her, but as she thought it over, she knew he was right. She would never treat a child, any child, the way she had been treated. "There's one disadvantage to becoming a counselor," she remarked.

"What's that?"

"You know how many things are abusive that aren't intuitively obvious. I treated a lot of abused kids, and you'd be surprised how often the abuse wasn't even intentional. People just didn't realize the impact they were having on their kids."

He fell silent, thinking she assumed, then said, "I guess I can see how that would happen. Simply not understanding would be enough."

"Exactly. Sometimes I wonder if my father has any capacity for understanding. For putting himself in someone else's position."

"Do me a favor?" he asked.

"What's that?"

"Don't make any excuses for that man. Please."

"I'm not. I'm just wondering."

"Wondering is okay. Excusing him isn't. One of the things about life is that we're supposed to learn. As far as I can tell, he never learned. He had ample opportunity to figure out that he must be doing something wrong when you left and then when your mother died. Instead he's blaming everyone but himself. That's not productive. He should at least be asking himself some questions."

The thought of her father ever questioning himself might have made her laugh if it hadn't been so unamusing. "He's always right."

"Yup. So it seems."

"How well do you know him?"

"Let's just say I've been keeping as much of a distance

as I could for years now. I honestly never guessed just how badly treated you were, though."

"Baggy long dresses and thick tights hide the bruises," she said in a burst of weary bitterness.

He swore with quiet fury. "Nora, if anyone had guessed…"

"Why would anyone? What's in the family stays in the family. I learned that very early."

His arm tightened around her shoulders. "I just wish someone had guessed."

"Maybe they did, but a guess isn't good enough to act on. He had plenty of ways of dealing with me, though, ways that wouldn't leave marks. Have you ever had to kneel on rice for an hour?"

She heard his teeth grind. "No," he said shortly. "What else?"

"Tabasco sauce on the tongue. Oh, there were all kinds of ways. At the time I thought it was happening to everyone. I thought I must deserve it. It's only in retrospect I understand how bad it was."

She had just told him more than she'd told anyone except the therapist she had been required to see during her training. Surprise filled her, that she had been able to voice all this to him. Then she realized she didn't want to go any further. "Can we talk about something else?"

"Sure. Anything you like. Horses, ranching, how you like working at the library?"

That brightened her mood a bit. "I never thought I'd get into being an archivist, but I'm loving going through all the old papers people have donated. There's some fascinating stuff in there. Old newspaper clippings, diaries, wills, divorce papers. It's like putting a big puzzle together."

"By the time you get done you'll know this county better than Miss Emma, and she was always a font of knowledge on local history."

"I doubt that I'll reach her level of expertise, but it's really absorbing. I never knew that there were once range wars here, for example. Or that the gold-mining boom created so much trouble."

"Claim jumping?"

"Some of that, yes, but a lot of fighting. It sounds like it was a rough place to try to live up there. I'm surprised anyone brought a family to a place like that."

"Maybe standards were different then."

"Sort of like the ones I was raised with, maybe." That made her pause. "Maybe that was it exactly. Women and children were chattel. Possessions. Property."

"I can't imagine thinking of another human being that way. But I get it. That's how they grew up back then."

"Yeah." She fell silent for a few seconds. "I've been reading this one woman's diary. You know how you mentioned that it must have been hard out on these ranches in the days before cars? It was. This woman's diary is like reading a descent into insanity. All alone, cut off from other women, raising nine kids, losing three in infancy, working dawn till bedtime, getting old fast, turning as much as she could over to her daughters as soon as they got big enough to help, and it still wasn't enough. I'm not sure what got to her most, the unceasing work or the unending loneliness."

"Or the perpetual pregnancies."

"That, too. It takes a lot out of a woman physically. Anyway, as time went on, her entries got shorter and less coherent. You can almost feel fatigue in the pages."

"Makes you wonder how they did it at all."

"The same way most of us live, putting one foot in front

of the other. Taking one step at a time. Looking too far ahead can be dangerous."

He shifted a little, turning so that he could see her better. In the process, he pulled away so that she was no longer leaning on him. She missed the contact instantly. Heavens, after all these years she still had a case of the hots for him? Still wanted him? Now, wasn't that stupid? Here he was just being a friendly protector, and once again she wanted more than he was prepared to give. Not good. She mustn't fall into that pit again. She didn't trust herself not to act the fool once more. Not when it came to Jake.

"Someday," he said, "I hope I see your eyes bright with excitement about the future, glad to look forward, no longer looking back."

Before she could respond to that astonishing statement, he asked, "Feel ready to ride back?"

She nodded and let him help her to her feet and back onto Daisy. As she did so, she had the unhappy feeling that she'd revealed too much about herself, and now he just wanted to escape all the ugliness that surrounded her.

She couldn't blame him for that.

Chapter 7

She woke sweating, icy and shaking all at once. Vestiges of the nightmare clung, horrific, terrifying. All the elements were there, from running and being unable to escape her pursuer. Except this time her pursuer had a face.

She reached around desperately for the switch and turned on the bedside lamp. At once the room evolved into familiar territory, wood beams overhead, papered walls surrounding her and a window covered by heavy drawn curtains. A cheerful room, warm in the bath of lamplight.

God, she had thought she was done with the nightmares. At least it had been weeks since the last one. Her daytime fears were enough, she didn't need them while sleeping, too.

It must be because that man had escaped. He was once again a threat. Even rest would be denied to her now.

Still shivering, she climbed out of bed, jammed her feet into warm moccasins and wrapped a fleece robe tightly over her flannel nightgown. She crept across the wood floor and pulled the curtain back just enough to give her a slit to peer through. The night was moonless, pitch-black, except for a few snowflakes that glistened in the little bit of light that escaped through the crack in the curtain. If there was anything out there, she would never see it.

She closed the curtain carefully, and stood with her arms wrapped around herself. Rosa was fattening her up, she thought irrelevantly. She could still feel her ribs, but they no longer protruded as much. That meant she was regaining her strength.

About time, she thought. She'd even gone on a short trail ride today, and riding a horse took more energy than she'd expected.

But none of that helped with the terror. Being alone in this room wasn't comforting, either, pleasant though it was. Maybe some milk would help her get back to sleep, because she certainly felt entirely too wide-awake now. Although getting back to sleep apparently no longer promised escape.

God, she hated that that man had turned her into a wuss again. Surely she had grown tougher than this during the years since she had left home. She couldn't possibly let that awful man turn her back into the old, frightened Nora. That would be handing him a victory even if he never came near her again.

Feeling a burst of determination, she decided to head downstairs to the kitchen. Warm milk. A book. Jake had plenty of books lying around, from nonfiction to fiction. And ranching magazines. Something ought to distract her. At the very least maybe she could learn something about what he was doing so that she could be more than a cipher around here. Carry on a conversation with him about something besides herself.

She rummaged in the kitchen until she found a small saucepan. She poured a cup of milk into it and turned the gas flame on low. It made her a little uneasy that the kitchen window wasn't covered, merely framed by a cascading curtain in bright colors, but it did have the advantage of letting her see the slowly falling snowflakes. They were beautiful. When she'd lived here, winter had merely meant cold and drudgery for her, and one cold after another as sick people came into the pharmacy.

But in Minnesota, she had learned to love it. Back there she'd splurged on cross-country skis and had loved to go out on some of the groomed trails, along with her friends or alone. There was something so soothing about swishing along on the snow in regular, comfortable movements, pausing frequently to admire the sights.

Those skis sat in her storage room now, a room on which she was paying rent. Most of her things were back there, and while part of her resented the hell out of having to leave her life behind, right now she was very, very glad she had. At the time she had accepted her father's offer, all she'd been concerned with was getting away from the nightmare and taking time to regain her health.

Well, she hadn't escaped the nightmare. But she figured Jake was doing more to help her back to health than her father ever would have.

She looked back to that encounter, so long ago now, and realized that whatever had possessed Jake to react that way, she had forgiven him. They had been so young, after all. Only youth and silliness had pushed her to ask such a thing of him, and his reaction had probably been born of the same youth. Plus, there was Beth. Even when she had asked him, she had known he was seeing Beth. How was he supposed to respond?

More kindly, perhaps, but there were enough years

behind her now to see all the times he *had* been kind, even when it meant facing down his friends and other students. He could have been ostracized for that, but he hadn't seemed to care. He'd stood up for her, whenever he'd happened to witness her being bullied or picked on.

That should count for more than a few minutes when shock had probably goaded him.

Regardless, he hadn't wanted her then and probably didn't want the ghost she had become, the one with all the emotional baggage. They could be friends, nothing more, and she felt she ought to be adult enough to deal with that.

Her milk was ready, and she poured it back into the mug she had used to measure it. She put the pan in the sink and ran cold water into it to soak it, then sat at the kitchen table, cradling the mug and sipping slowly.

She still felt that attraction to him. More than she'd ever felt for any man. Maybe that was why her relationships had never gone very far. At the back of her mind, she'd always been measuring the guys she dated against Jake.

They'd lost. The thought brought an almost impish smile to her face, even as her heart ached a little about what that might mean. Getting over Jake hadn't happened in all these years, and now being with him all the time wasn't going to make it any easier. With each passing day, she liked the man he had become more and more. What had been a childish crush based mostly on how handsome and kind he was to her seemed to be blooming again, and was based on a whole lot more. Not that she would ever act on it even if he showed interest. Her body was so scarred now from the attack and all the operations that she couldn't even bear to glimpse herself in the mirror.

Oh, well. She'd deal with that mistake when the time came. For now she had bigger concerns. Like that man finding her again.

She felt her shoulders sag, and a chill ran through her. God, would this never end?

"I thought I heard someone stirring."

At the sound of Jake's voice, she looked up, rattled that she'd been so inattentive that she hadn't heard his approach. He stood in the kitchen doorway, bare chested, hair tousled, jeans zipped but not buttoned, barefoot. He looked as if he had leaped out of bed to investigate.

She caught her breath, whether from being startled or from being greeted by a sight that would have done well on a cheesecake calendar. "I'm sorry. I didn't mean to wake you."

"I wasn't sleeping well." He must have caught something in her expression because he looked down at himself. "I'll get a shirt."

"Not on my account," she hastened to say. "Your house. Be comfortable." And she didn't mind the sight in the least.

He did reach down and button his jeans, though, maybe one of the sexiest gestures she had ever seen a man make. She closed her eyes a moment, telling her heart to still.

"What woke you?" he asked, moving into the kitchen and starting a pot of coffee.

"Nightmare," she admitted.

"Do you have a lot of them?" His back, broad shouldered and well muscled above narrow hips, was all she could see as he scooped coffee into the brewing machine.

"I did. I thought I was past them."

"This news must have brought it back. I'm sorry."

"You have nothing to apologize for. Besides, that may have had nothing to do with it. Maybe I was wrong to think because I hadn't had any in a few weeks I was over them. Maybe I'll have them periodically for years."

"I wouldn't be surprised." He turned and leaned back against the counter, folding his arms and crossing his ankles. She took a mental snapshot, feeling almost helpless before the force of the attraction she felt. She needed to squelch this. Life was complicated enough.

She tore her gaze away and stared down into her mug of cooling milk. "Coffee at this hour?" she asked, hoping to divert the conversation.

"It won't keep me awake if I get sleepy again. I can drink it any hour of the day or night."

"Oh." Any hope that the milk would put her back to sleep was rapidly fading. Maybe she'd have coffee, too. In fact, staying awake seemed safer than risking another nightmare.

Silence reigned except for the hiss of the drip coffee-maker. Finally it popped a few times, and he turned to get a mug out of the cupboard. "Would you like some?"

"Yes, please." Stupid, but maybe not so stupid.

The coffee smelled far better than the milk when he placed it in front of her. She pushed the milk to one side as he sat across the table from her and raised his own mug to his lips.

"It's snowing," he remarked.

"I saw. Not very much."

"Not yet. I don't think we're supposed to get more than an inch. It'll look pretty for a while."

"I love snow."

"I guess I need to find a way to appreciate it. For me it just increases my workload, both here and as a cop. The first snow is especially bad for car accidents. It's like everyone has to learn to drive on it all over again."

"I've noticed. It's amazing how fast you get used to dry roads."

"So what is it you like about snow?"

"Honestly? I didn't learn to like it until I moved to Minnesota. I go cross-country skiing all the time there. It got so I was impatient for winter to begin."

"What about camping?"

"I liked that, too, after the summer bugs let up. The mosquitoes up there are awful, but once bug season passes it's gorgeous. I loved going to the Boundary Waters area, I loved going to the shore of Lake Superior. It's a beautiful state."

"This must seem awfully bland after all that."

"Not really." She lifted her gaze cautiously, trying to focus on his face and not his chest. "I missed the mountains here. Missed watching them change with the seasons. Some people get addicted to the water. I was addicted to the Rockies."

"Really? I wasn't aware you got much time to go hiking up there."

"I didn't. But I still loved being near them."

"You were pretty hemmed in, weren't you?"

She just nodded. "But you must have been, too. I worked at the pharmacy. You worked here."

"Not all the time. My folks made sure there was time for fun. You remember that hayride, right? And other times some friends and I would go hiking and camping over a weekend. Horseback riding. We did a lot of things."

Staring into her mug seemed safer just then. Her therapy had taught her how much she had missed. In fact, the therapist had once remarked that she had been denied a childhood. Perhaps. But as she had discovered while working with kids, an awful lot of children missed what most people called a childhood. Sometimes she wondered if that was all just a myth, if any child really lived out those golden days or if people simply remembered them that way.

"They way I grew up," she said finally, "would have seemed perfectly normal in another century. Childhood,

at least our current notion of it, is a relatively recent in-
vention."

"Maybe so."

"No, really it is. Working-class families put children
to work as soon as they were able. Upper-class families
turned the kids over to nannies, saw them once a day then
sent them away to boarding school. I don't think the way
I was raised was unique."

"Except in comparison to something else."

She nodded. "Only then."

"So you're excusing it?"

"No. Because the level of abuse I endured sometimes
went beyond simply asking me to earn my keep. That was
where it crossed the line."

"Way across the line," he answered. "And this isn't a
happy path for you to be following."

"I don't seem to have one right now. Sorry."

"Don't apologize. You've been through a hell I can
barely imagine. It's only natural you can't be brimming
with all kinds of happy thoughts. I was just looking for
some subject that wouldn't drag you down. If there isn't
one, just say so."

At that she managed a crooked smile. "I am so much
fun to be around right now. My friends don't know how
lucky they are that I decided to bail."

"But before all this, you were happier than when you
lived here, right?"

"Much. I wouldn't say… Well, no life is all perfect and
no one is happy all the time. But I was better. I felt better.
I laughed more often. Happy might not be the right word.
Contented, maybe. I felt useful, I had friends, I had things
I liked to do. What more does a person need?"

He frowned faintly and she wondered why. He didn't
illuminate her. "I always admired you for having the guts

to get up and leave. Maybe you don't remember, but a lot of us talked about it in high school. You were one of the few who actually did it."

"I don't know if it was guts or desperation," she answered honestly. "Did you think about leaving?"

"No. Never. I really like ranching. I like working with animals. I even like working in the dirt. I'm outdoors a lot, always busy. And then I discovered a taste for small-town policing." He smiled faintly. "Note that I said small town. I don't think I'd like working in a bigger place, but here I pretty much know everyone, and it mostly feels like helping out neighbors. Or occasionally scolding them."

She laughed, a quiet sound. "The scolding part could be interesting."

"Sometimes you gotta get their attention."

Her laugh grew a bit more relaxed. "Old joke."

"Very. And misogynistic so I won't repeat it. But yeah, sometimes I have to scold people for minor infractions. I'm sure that you heard enough about the occasional drunken brawls and things like that. We're not in a hurry to make arrests unless things get really bad. Most folks around here don't act up too much."

"So you wag your finger at them?"

"Metaphorically. The stern voice, badge and gun seem to do the job."

"I'm not surprised." She had to drag her thoughts away from her own arrest and all the anger and sense of injustice that went with that.

"I guess that's not a good topic, either," he said.

"I don't seem to have any good topics." A sorry thing to admit. She cast around, looking for something, anything, that wasn't related to the distant past or recent events. It was as if she had a brain lock, though. Nothing else seemed to want to come up.

"God, this is awful," she said.

"What?"

"I don't seem to be able to think about anything else. Or talk about it. I had a pretty good life going and then all this stuff happened, and it's like I'm stuck in it."

"Hearing that he's on the loose probably didn't help, either. You know we're working on it, both here and back there. And by now, maybe at a lot of points in between. There was some talk just yesterday of declaring him an interstate fugitive, which would put the FBI on his tail. For whatever that's worth."

"They're pretty good, aren't they? But they must have more important things to worry about."

"Every life is important, and yes, they're pretty damn good."

He surprised her by reaching out slowly and gently covering her hand with his. His touch was warm, his palm rough from work. It felt good, and didn't frighten her at all. Maybe she was getting past at least one hang-up.

Tentatively, she turned her hand over and their fingers clasped. Considering his musculature and all the hard work she'd seen him do, it was amazing he had a touch so gentle.

"He's coming," she said finally. But this time the fear didn't choke her. "He's coming. I want to be ready. Can you help me get ready?"

"Ready how? Do you want a gun?"

She shook her head. "I wouldn't know how to use it. I'm not sure I could. But maybe some self-defense moves? Could anyone around here teach me?"

"I know just the guy."

"Who?"

"Me."

When her eyes flew to his face, he was smiling. He shrugged one shoulder. "It was a hobby that somehow turned into teaching a few days of self-defense classes every semester at the community college. I can teach you enough to escape his hold, and even to temporarily disable him so he can't chase you."

"Do you think I'm strong enough? I mean…"

"This doesn't rely on strength. Even if you were completely healed, you'd have trouble beating a man on the strength front. No, there are other ways. Ways where being small can even be an advantage."

"An advantage? Really? How?"

"Surprise, Nora. Surprise. Of course, that makes a basic assumption."

"Which is?"

"That he'll get close to you."

She lowered her head a moment, then met his gaze again. "Nobody can protect me if he comes at me from a distance with a rifle. You know that. I don't think that's his style anyway. He gets off on this, Jake. He gets off big on a woman's pain and terror. Well, if there's one thing I can do, it's to never again show him my terror."

Brave words, she thought, even as she spoke them. But a resolve was building in her. She was getting awfully tired of being frightened. She didn't want to be frightened anymore.

He studied her, then nodded. "Okay, we'll start tomorrow."

"You're sure I can do it?"

"Nora, I think you can do a hell of a lot more than you've ever believed. Look at you—one of the few who packed up and left town to go to college, and without any help at all from your family. Then you went to a totally different place and built a life for yourself. You're stronger than you think, and you're determined enough for any two people. You got knocked down. Horribly knocked down.

But I'd be damned surprised if you didn't get up again and turn out even stronger."

She nearly basked in his words. No one had ever said anything as complimentary as that to her. What's more, they deepened her resolve. Jake had known her when she was nobody at all, a mere shadow trying to remain unnoticed. If he could see her that way... Well, maybe there was some truth in it.

She started looking at what had happened that night again, but this time, instead of reluctantly glimpsing it out of the corner of her mental eye, she stared straight at it. For a few moments, she had the courage to face her memories directly, those things she hadn't forgotten because of the trauma. A shudder ripped through her, but she refused to deflect.

"I've got to face this. I've got to face him. Here or in a courtroom, it doesn't matter. And I need to dissect him."

"Dissect him?"

She emerged from memory and met his questioning gaze. "Dissect him psychologically," she explained. "I need some kind of understanding. I need a *reason*."

"I'm not sure you'll ever get that. His lawyer is going to make him clam up. You know that."

"I don't care about what he says or doesn't say. I need to think about what he did and how he acted. As much as I can remember anyway."

"What will that tell you?"

"Just what kind of sickness is driving him. Whatever he might say, it wouldn't matter. Like most of his type, he's probably really good at rationalizing, and he probably believes whatever he's telling himself. He won't make sense that way. I need to come at him another way. Actions *do* speak louder than words."

"I suppose." But a frown had settled over his face. "Are

you sure you want to do that? To dredge it all up and ponder it?"

She shook her head slightly and sighed. "The thing about the mind is, you either deal with things or they haunt you. Some traumatic amnesia is good. Seriously. I would never tell a patient who forgot something awful that there was any *need* to remember. The mind has its methods. Sometimes just forgetting is the best thing in the world. But there are times when the mind finds ways to keep throwing it up, causing problems, making it clear that you have to deal with what happened. Because if you don't, you'll never heal and you'll develop other problems."

"Your nightmare?"

"It's a huge warning flag. This one is not going away. I never told anyone, but I've forgotten large parts of my childhood. They're gone, beyond reach. I don't need them. The bits I have are still big enough to make a complete picture. At this point if I were to forget ninety-nine percent of it, it wouldn't be a problem. I've dealt with the overall situation in the most important ways."

"You've forgotten your childhood?" He sounded a little surprised. "I mean, I know we don't remember everything, but you're talking about something else, aren't you?"

"Maybe forgetting isn't the right word. It's like I've walled most of it off behind bulletproof glass. I know it's there, but it can't touch me, and I have to work hard to reach it. Lots of it just seems to be gone. But this is different."

"Bound to be," he agreed slowly. "Are you sure thinking about this all by yourself would be wise? I mean… Do you need a therapist?"

"I went through therapy as part of my training. I was also seeing one before I left Minneapolis. I have the tool kit, which is the important thing. Most therapy is done by the patient, you know. The therapist helps you develop a tool kit, pulls you up short when you start to go off the rails, but mostly it's a solo project."

"You would know." He still sounded reluctant, though. "I'm here if you need a sounding board."

"Thank you. I mean that."

"Just explain one thing to me, if you can."

"Sure."

"Why is it so important to understand this guy? To have a reason?"

"So I don't see every man I ever meet through the lens of that attack."

He stiffened a bit, leaning back a little. "My God, I never thought about that."

"I was seeing you through the lens of the my arrest. Which isn't fair, is it, because cops came to my aid when I was first found by the road. Overall, except for that one aberration, the police were great. So I've been getting past that. But maybe you also remember how reluctant I was to be touched, even casually. I know you wouldn't hurt me, but my reaction was deeper than reason. So I need to work this through. I need to figure out, at least to some extent, what makes this guy different so I can move on."

He nodded, still not looking entirely happy. "Okay. Just let me know if I can help in any way. I mean that. I'm willing to listen."

She felt so grateful to him right then that she tightened her hold on his hand. Something in his eyes seemed to leap—an answering flame?—but she dismissed it quickly. There was nothing desirable about her, there never really had been. And even if he did find her attractive, there were so many hurdles to leap, from her fractured emotional state to the scars that tattooed her body.

But that didn't prevent the warm drizzle of desire that

slowly filled her, pooling at last between her legs. If it hadn't been so strong, she might have been startled by a feeling so rare to her, even before the attack.

Long ago, something had been broken in her. By her father's words, by the treatment of other kids, by the things Jake had said. She had never come to believe that she was sexually attractive, even to the men who occasionally asked her out.

But what she was feeling now took hold of her, reminding her that however she felt about herself, she still had a woman's needs. Burying them hadn't worked. They could come at random times like this, although not the way she seemed to feel them for Jake. Always, always, she pushed them back down, telling herself that wasn't for her.

But as the air seemed to drain from the room, as her gaze locked with Jake's, common sense and life's lessons vanished with it. She wanted him. It would never happen, but she wanted him anyway. Maybe she always would.

There had been times when she had wondered what had driven her all those years ago to ask him to take her to the prom. As if she were linked to him by some invisible cord and couldn't keep her perspective around him. Even then she had been in his thrall.

That hadn't faded one bit, it seemed. All the anger she had tried to harbor against him was gone, a vague memory of an ugly scene that, when she was honest to herself, she admitted she had caused. There had been plenty of therapy about that. Why she had reached for a man who was unattainable because he was already promised to another?

To confirm her own feelings. To prove to herself that she really was the ugly duckling no one would want. He'd played a role in her breaking her last ties with this town, and it was unfair for her to blame him for giving her a response she should have expected. A response that in some deep part of herself she had needed. The final punctuation mark to the lifelong battering she had taken.

Offering herself that way had been the means to cut away the only thing that made her want to stay here.

Now she was back, and she still wanted the same things. Things she didn't feel at all entitled to. Things that were making her body ache, her heart hammer, her mouth grow dry.

And something in his expression told her he could see what she was feeling. She hadn't moved a muscle. What was giving her away?

She wanted to tense, expecting rejection, but her body felt full of the molasses of hunger. The ache between her legs hung her suspended in a web of anticipation, hope and fear.

She couldn't possibly. She wasn't ready. He couldn't be interested. This could turn out badly. A million warnings, familiar from years past, shrieked in some tiny corner of her mind, but she couldn't hear them over the pounding blood in her ears. She felt transfixed.

Still holding on to her hand, Jake rose slowly. She followed his every movement with her eyes, drinking in his fantastic chest and arms, his handsome face. He came around the table, stood right beside her and tugged gently on her hand.

She didn't know if her legs would hold her, but she struggled to rise anyway. The thought of being closer to him seemed to take over, granting her strength even as she tried to find enough air to breathe.

Then, almost as if by magic, those powerful arms surrounded her, drawing her close until she rested against his chest and felt his skin, so warm and smooth beneath her cheek. With one arm around her waist, he held her. With his other hand he stroked her hair.

"Easy," he murmured. "Just be easy."

Easy? Impulses she hardly knew were pushing at her, demanding that she do things she could barely imagine. But he held her so gently, another part of her just gave in. He would decide, and she was grateful to be held.

She had no right to more.

After a minute or two, she even dared to raise her arms and wind them around his narrow waist. Her palms found the bare skin of his back, and it felt so good, so indescribably good to her. How had she missed discovering how wonderful a man's warm skin could feel?

"That feels nice," he murmured as her palms settled on his back.

The words gave her the most incredible sense of power. She could make him feel some of what he made her feel?

Emboldened, she began to run her palms over his back, stroking him as he was stroking her hair. She felt his muscles quiver beneath her touch, and a quiet sound escaped him, almost like a purr.

She leaned into him even more, loving it, loving it even if it never went a step further. She would at least be able to forever remember having held Jake, and been held by him, with an intimacy that had long been denied to her.

That seemed worth even the price of disappointment, and disappointment was something she knew all too well.

"I want to tell you something," he said softly.

"Hmm?"

"All those years ago, when I was so cruel? It took me a long time to figure out why."

She started to stiffen, not wanting the intrusion of that memory, but he simply tightened his hold a bit. "Hang on. This isn't bad. I'm not being an ass again the way I was back then."

Still, she was on edge now, as if waiting for a blow. Her

hands became motionless against his back, even though he continued stroking her hair, then letting his hand slide down toward her shoulder before bringing it back up again.

"You know I was all but engaged when you asked me to take you to the prom. I was saving for a ring. I felt... Well, a duty to behave. But it wasn't just that, Nora. I didn't get mean to be mean to you. I was furious at myself."

She waited a moment, then finally found a piece of voice to ask, "Why?"

"Because that was the instant that I realized I wanted you, too. I wanted to take you to that prom, I wanted to take you up on your offer to sleep with me. It made me all messed up inside, because it didn't seem right. I wanted to say yes, but that would have meant betraying Beth. I couldn't do that."

She didn't know how to take this. Everything inside her seemed to be jumbling as if she were in a cement mixer.

"But it wasn't just that. It was that it hurt."

She stilled, everything inside her going quiet. "Hurt?"

"Hurt to hear you think you needed to offer to sleep with me to get me to take you to the prom. Hurt to realize that I wanted to do it. I should have had the sense right then to realize that I cared more about you than Beth."

"You're just saying that." Her mind whirled, unable to believe.

"I'm not just saying it. I've had to live with that memory as much as you have, and I'm not proud of it. I spent a lot of time wondering how I could have been such a bastard, what drove me to say terrible things. My only excuse was that I was young and didn't know how to deal with all the mixed-up feelings that caused. I struck out at you when I should have struck out at myself. I'm sorry and I'm ashamed, but it's the truth."

"Let it go," she said weakly, feeling as if her world were turning upside down again. "Just let it go."

"I can't until I've finished. I've thought about it over the years, but I've been thinking especially hard about it since you came home. I wanted you and I retaliated against *you* because of it."

"Nobody wanted me," she said, a burst of pain adding strength to her voice. "Nobody!"

"That's not true! Maybe nobody else did. I'm not speaking for the whole world here. It was sure as hell obvious that your father wanted you to believe that. The other kids told you that often enough. But except for that one time, did I tell you that, Nora? Ever?"

She couldn't even manage a shake of her head.

"I just need you to know that. If I'd been a little older and wiser, I never would have gotten engaged to Beth. I'd have taken you to that damn prom. Hell, I'd even have bought you the prettiest dress you could find so you could feel like the belle of the ball, because, dammit, regardless of all those ugly clothes and glasses, I could see the beauty behind them. I *wanted* you. And to my everlasting sorrow, I didn't have the sense to realize it. So here we are, twelve years later, all water over the dam, nothing I can do about it to fix it, except be honest. I screwed up big time and hurt you in the process."

"Jake…"

"I know. It's too late. We're practically strangers now, and none of what happened then changes that. But the fact is I *still* want you."

A shiver of delighted, unadulterated longing passed through her, and she tightened her hold on him, even as long years of wounding made her say, "You didn't have to say that. It's okay. I put it in the past."

"I haven't," he said firmly. "I finally faced up to it.

I want you to know. I realize it doesn't change a damn thing, I get that things have changed… Hell, at this point you probably couldn't even consider such a thing after what you've been through. You're scared, too, justifiably so, and I wouldn't want to take advantage of you. But now you know. Now *I* know. It's done and over."

But it was far from over, she realized as she leaned into him, enjoying his warmth, enjoying the intimacy, enjoying the sizzling sensations that zinged through her body.

Far from over. She just didn't know where it could go.

Chapter 8

Langdon's impatience was growing. He'd found a cheap motel room that didn't ask for ID, only for cash, and had learned from a newspaper that his wife might be recovering from her coma. Even though she would need months of therapy, it remained: she had defied him.

That defiance maddened him. He was moving ever closer to Nora, and he'd figured that as soon as he took care of her, he'd be on his way, disappearing to some distant country where no one would ever find him. The escape route was planned, the money squirreled in an untraceable bank account.... Oh, he was ready to take off.

But now he sat between two women who had defied him by surviving. Some cowardly part of his mind suggested he should just skedaddle now, but he couldn't do that. Not with unfinished business.

At least as far as Nora went. Going after his wife again would mean returning to Minneapolis, too dangerous despite his fury. But finding Nora in the virtual middle of nowhere would give him plenty of opportunity to escape.

He could tie up one loose end. Teach one woman that defiance was the ultimate sin. With reluctance, he had to accept that maybe one of the women would escape him, at least for years to come.

But Nora wouldn't. He could at least take savage satisfaction in teaching her a lesson before he wiped the defiance out of her forever by killing her.

His hands clenched as he considered the sheer pleasure of the terror he meant to inflict, the pain he would show her. Damn, he could hardly wait.

Turning on the bed, he reached for his map and reviewed his route with an eye to getting there faster and settling one issue quickly.

Of course, he had to be careful. Chances were since she'd gone to her hometown—a piece of knowledge for which he thanked his wife, who had told him in the midst of his threats before he gave her hell—they might be expecting him on that end.

At some point they'd think he'd fled the country. He was counting on it.

Soon, though. The pressure inside him was building. He'd learned something about himself—that he couldn't wait too long. The only reason he didn't take out his frustration on some woman along the road was that he didn't want to leave a trail.

But it was starting to drive him nuts. He had to act soon, before the pressure drove him to complete stupidity.

He scanned the map again, calculating. If he were careful, he could probably take care of Nora in the near future. The thought left him nearly salivating.

It also began to compress his time scale.

* * *

Two weeks later, Nora was enjoying increasing health and increasing confidence. Jake had given her a half dozen lessons in self-defense, and while she wasn't trying to hurt him, he was teaching her things that *would* hurt if she used full force. Ways of breaking a hold, ways of making a man much bigger at least temporarily helpless from pain.

She especially liked the one about bending a finger or two back. She could do that, for sure.

Jake began to let her exercise all the horses in the corral, although he still had Al handle the saddling beforehand. A good thing, too, she admitted, once she tried to lift a saddle. Maybe if the horses hadn't been so tall, but she had struggled and been forced to admit she couldn't yet do it.

A small defeat, one she was determined to overcome.

In fact, determination was filling her. Her nights became less troubled, although the fear that nagged at her hovered around the edges of every thought. That man would come. She knew it in her heart, and it kept her alert every single minute, even out on the ranch, where she should have felt safer because she was never alone and she'd be harder to find.

But as her determination grew, so did her defiance. She went to town four days a week to work on the archives. She made herself leave the security of the library to walk to the diner for lunch.

But she had almost given up looking for her own place. Jake had made it clear that he was going to create reasons for her not to do that at least until her attacker was caught.

And there was the other thing, looming almost equally as large in her mind: her father. She didn't want to see him. Not even for a moment on the street.

Unfinished business, she thought one evening as she

and Jake curled up near the woodstove in his living room, reading. Lots of unfinished business, especially with Fred Loftis. All that therapy, and being around him could still turn her into the frightened, diminished, ugly duckling he had raised.

She didn't need that right now, and she was so grateful to Jake for giving her haven.

Then there was the unfinished business of Jake. He might have explained what had happened twelve years ago, but he had also said things had changed, they had changed and it was now firmly in the past.

She wasn't at all sure about that. While she had done a decent job of shedding the pain he had caused her and forgiving him, there wasn't one damn thing she could do about the attraction she still felt for him.

He had held her, surely to comfort her and for no other reason, but it remained that the feel of his naked chest against her cheek, the feel of his warm, smooth skin beneath her hands, had been branded in her mind and yes, dammit, in her groin. Trickles of desire plagued her every time she saw him, and she had to create swift diversions of some kind to distract herself.

He didn't want her. He'd said he had wanted her back then, but that was back then. How much clearer could he make it?

The weather had turned colder, a dusting of snow remained on the ground outside, but inside near the stove it was plenty warm. Warmer, perhaps, because of the direction her thoughts kept taking.

She couldn't prevent herself from looking up over the top of the book she was reading to study him as he sat in his own chair a few feet away, scanning a book or a magazine.

He kept up with a lot of stuff, from ranching to animal

husbandry to policing. He seemed to have an endless thirst to know all he could, and only occasionally drifted into a novel or some other subject.

He'd talk to her about it some when she could think of an intelligent question, but little by little she was coming to an appreciation of the odds he was fighting as a small-business owner. The world seemed to have little room for independent operations anymore.

But he never complained. He just said he needed to work harder.

Rosa interrupted her bouncing balls of thought by appearing with the nightly mugs of hot chocolate. Nora was certain they were slowly growing spicier with chili pepper, and she liked it. She never would have imagined combining chocolate and chili, but it worked.

"I'll say good night now," Rosa said as she always did. "Al is waiting."

Al came every night to walk her back to their little bunkhouse.

"Thank you," Nora said. "Can I ask a favor?"

Rosa lifted a brow. "Of course. But what could I do for you?"

"You could find some ways for me to help around here tomorrow. I don't have to work, and being a lady of leisure isn't what I'm used to."

Rosa smiled, a wonderfully warm expression that Nora was coming to love, and laughed with the comfort of someone who felt everything was right in the world. "Of course! It'll be fun to work together!"

"Wow," Jake said after Rosa departed.

"Wow?"

"She's always seemed to get offended anytime I try to wash a dish or clean the shower after myself. It's *her* job, she says."

"Well, it is. But maybe it's different because I kind of told her it would help me."

He winked. "Next week I'll have you pitching hay in the barn."

"Try me."

"I just might." A smile creased the corners of his eyes, and she felt punched by attraction to him. "It's good to see you regaining your strength so fast. When you first got here, I wondered if you ever would."

She lowered her book, thinking about it. "There was a lot more stress back in Minneapolis. A lot more. I was closer to the whole situation—there were the cops, the newspapers, losing my job, all of that. I don't think it helped."

"But here you can relax?"

"A whole lot more." She didn't mention the nagging terror she couldn't quite forget. Sometimes she wondered if that terror would ever go away, even if they put that guy behind bars for life. And she still couldn't bring herself to think his name, let alone say it.

"I'm sorry," he said suddenly. "I didn't mean to bring up bad memories. I'm just glad to see how much stronger you're getting. Even your hair is thickening."

She reached up self-consciously and touched it. "I don't know why it seemed so stringy before. And it can't have grown that fast."

He shrugged. "Who knows? Maybe when you're not well it just shows everywhere."

"Maybe."

Then out of the blue he said, "You know, you were pretty in high school, but you've grown into a really beautiful woman."

Her mouth opened in astonishment and disbelief exploded in her brain, yet at the same time she felt her cheeks grow hot as fire, as if his compliment had embarrassed her beyond belief. All she could respond with was a weak protest. "Jake!"

"It's true." His smiled widened a bit. "I just thought you should know. The ugly duckling you probably felt like has turned into a swan that would attract every guy with eyes to see."

Maybe, she thought almost desperately, guys with eyes to see were in some special class.

"Didn't mean to embarrass you," he said after a moment. "Someday I just hope you can see yourself through a pair of eyes other than your father's."

What a sweet thing to say, she thought as her eyes stung with emotion. What a very sweet thing to say. She didn't believe it for one minute, though. Maybe she had a pretty enough face now that she was filling out again, maybe her hair looked better, but she didn't even have to close her eyes to remember the angry red scars on her body. They'd repulse anyone, and it might be years before they faded to silvery, puckered lines.

"Thank you," she said finally.

"You don't have to thank me for the truth." He shifted, placing one ankle on his other knee. Then he put his magazine aside and reached for his cocoa. He looked so relaxed, so masculine in the way he sat, in his jeans and flannel shirt, that her heart skipped a crazy beat.

Oh, hell, she couldn't stop herself from reacting. All she could do was keep it to herself so she didn't suffer another massive humiliation.

Like the one this man had delivered twelve years ago. She might have forgiven him, might even believe the explanation he had recently given her, but the wound remained, a reminder of just how badly she could be hurt in ways beyond the physical.

And now her body was covered with other wounds, as well.

Hell, she thought again. Hell. Life could be such a bitch sometimes.

"I have to work tomorrow," he said. "Are you going to be okay out here with Rosa and Al? Or would you feel better in town with me?"

She'd always feel better around him, she realized uncomfortably. He seemed like a bulwark lately, but it would be foolhardy to rely on him. He was just being nice. Helpful. Maybe making up for his past sins, for all she knew.

Yes, she'd feel better at the library with Emma, but Emma wouldn't be there tomorrow and it wasn't exactly a busy place. Hiding out in the back office there archiving might be okay, might be out of sight enough, but...

She caught herself. Hadn't she been learning self-defense from Jake so she didn't have to live in constant terror? At some point she needed to stop letting other people and her fears dictate every moment of her existence. At some point she needed to take control again the way she had when she had left for college.

She had done it once. She could do it again.

"I'll be fine," she said.

But she didn't quite believe it. Almost as if there was some kind of timer or countdown clock inside her head, almost as if the very universe was conveying some kind of pressure, she could have sworn she felt that man drawing closer. As if she were a fly caught in a spiderweb and could feel the web tremble as the spider crawled toward her.

God! She put down her book and jumped up, overwhelmed by a sudden urge to flee, although there was nowhere to run to. What was she supposed to do? Get a car and drive endlessly around the country until they caught the guy? Her savings wouldn't last very long that way. This wasn't the only way to end this problem.

But sitting here waiting for something she was convinced was inevitable was like being constantly stretched to breaking on an invisible rack of terror. She might repress the feelings for a while, but they always returned, reminding her that she never, ever fully relaxed.

She couldn't. She even had to force herself to resume her seat.

So was she sitting here in some web? Unable to tear away in time? He would come. She knew deep inside that he would come for her unless they caught him first, and with each passing day hope that they'd find him was vanishing.

"Nora?"

She realized that panic must have blinded her, because all of a sudden she found Jake squatting in front of her, reaching for her hands to squeeze them firmly.

"Nora?" he said again.

"I'm sorry."

"Damn, I wish you'd stop apologizing. It's your first response to nearly everything. You're scared, aren't you?"

She managed a jerky nod. "Sometimes it swamps me," she whispered.

"I'd be surprised if it didn't."

He rose, then bent over her, scooping her up in his powerful arms as if she weighed nothing at all. Compared to one of those big bales of hay, she thought almost wildly, she probably didn't.

He pivoted, then sat with her in his lap sideways. One arm wrapped her shoulders, the other her hips. For a long time he just held her, as if willing his strength to fill her. Or as if his arms were a defense against the big, terrifying world beyond them. If only.

Once she had dreamed of him holding her this way, the innocent wish of a young girl. Now it was happening and she couldn't even enjoy it. Fear had once again pierced her too deeply.

"I wish I could make promises," he said, as her head rested on his shoulder. "I wish I could promise that he'll be caught before he gets within a hundred miles of you. I wish I could promise I'd find him before you ever set eyes on him. I wish I could promise you'd be safe forever."

"I wouldn't believe you," she whispered.

"Nor should you. I'm just wishing. If I had the power, I'd erase this whole thing from your life."

"I'd still be in Minneapolis," she murmured. For once, that didn't seem like such a good thing. As he held her, she knew that being here, just as she was, appealed to her more than recovering her old life. As if she could. Those days would never come back.

"I know. And I'd have been very sorry to have missed this chance to get to know you again. If none of those bad things had happened, I would have missed this."

At first the words struck her poorly, but then she realized what he was saying. He wouldn't have missed her if she'd stayed away, but now that she was back, he felt he would have missed something but for her return.

A little kernel of warmth sprouted in her heart, easing the icy world she had entered the night of the attack. "Thank you. I'm glad to be getting to know you, too. We've changed a lot."

"For some of that I say, thank God." His tone sounded faintly humorous. "Looking back at my teen years seldom makes me proud. Amazing how egocentric we are at that age."

"It's normal."

"I'm sure it is. But it's still amazing in retrospect. In

some ways we were so full of ourselves, so sure we were going to do better than our parents, create a better world, solve all its problems. I doubt you were part of some those conversations, but a gang of us would sit up late into the night, busy talking about how things should be. I don't rightly notice that many of us changed a damn thing when push came to shove."

"We're still young," she remarked.

"Yeah, but still. You at least helped little kids."

"And you keep us safe from drunk drivers."

"That doesn't quite measure up to creating world peace," he said ironically.

She tipped her head back a little but could only see his chin. Stubble had begun to sprout there, indicating that he had a heavy beard, one he seemed remarkably good at shaving away every morning. "We each do our little part," she said.

"I guess. And small enough it seems sometimes. But man, we used to dream big. Now I'd settle for just being able to keep one woman safe."

She turned her face into his shoulder and sighed, letting go of a piece of the perpetual tension. "You make me feel safer," she admitted quietly.

"I'm glad. I just wish I could guarantee it."

There was no answer to that. Not a one. She was still trapped in the web, and she could still feel it vibrating with threat.

"I feel," she admitted reluctantly, "as if he's getting closer. I know that sounds crazy...." She trailed off. It *did* sound crazy.

"I don't know," he said after a few seconds. "He might be smart enough to get the hell out of the country, but from what you said..."

She bit her lip, turning her head so her cheek once again

rested against his shoulder. "I studied serial-killer psychology in college."

"My God, why?"

"Part of studying deviant psychology. We had to know at least some of it in order to recognize warning signs. Anyway, we got into it some. They're compelled, Jake. They're not in control of themselves all the time. The need comes over them like an altered state of consciousness, and starts driving them. How long they have before they act can vary, but once that need takes over, they'll act eventually. Some killers pick their victims at random, strangers off a street, by the way they look, or move, whatever. But they start hunting as the need grows."

"You think this guy is hunting you?"

"I don't know that he's a serial killer. I don't know that his psychology deviates that way. But I know how he responded to defiance or any sign of resistance. My survival was defiant. That's how he'll see it. I'm sure of it. So yes, I think he's hunting me. I don't think he's going to leave the country until he's done teaching me his lesson."

Jake swore. "Okay, I'm going to tell Gage we need to get on even higher alert somehow."

"How can you? There are just so many cops and deputies around here, and a lot of wide-open space. This place is more porous than a sieve. You don't need me to tell you that."

For a long time he didn't say anything. "Then I'll keep you with me every damn moment."

"That's impossible and you know it. You have a job. Two, actually. But I can't ride patrol with you all the time. I have a job. I need that job. I've got bills, like everyone else. I need a car. I've got to work—my savings won't last forever."

Again he fell silent, his arms holding her a little closer

as if his embrace could somehow solve the problem. "I'm definitely talking to Gage in the morning," he said. "He knows people. All kinds of people. I'm sure there's something we can ramp up."

"Or I could be wrong, and he could be smart enough to run."

She felt him shake his head. "You're the psychologist. I'm betting on your instincts, not some pie-in-the-sky hope. Better to spend the resources and not need them than not have them and need them."

That seemed to close the subject. He was determined to do anything he could, and at some level that helped. Just knowing somebody gave that much of a damn helped. She wasn't alone.

It had been a long, long time since she had felt that way.

He surprised her by reaching up to tip her chin toward him with his fingertips. Then he utterly astonished her by kissing her, just a gentle, brief touch of his warm lips against hers.

Instantly every other concern flew from her head. That a kiss could have the power to fill her with heat, to expand the nagging need deep inside her into an aching pool of fire, amazed her. Every cell in her body suddenly seemed to want to reach out to him.

"You're not alone," he said, as if he'd read her mind. "And as long as I breathe, you won't be until this is over for good. I mean that."

It was a vow. She wasn't sure how he could keep it, but it felt good, settling into her like a warm, cuddly blanket.

Amazing to realize that never in her life had she felt as cherished as she did right then. Not her parents, not a boyfriend, not any friend, had given her the feeling that promise did.

She wouldn't hold him to it, but it still made her feel

so good in places that seemed to have been empty her entire life.

For a brief space, just a brief space, it almost all seemed worth it.

Jake held her on his lap for a long time. Some part of him didn't want to let go, as if he feared she'd slip away and never come back. Crazy way to feel. Maybe her fears were infecting him ever more strongly.

But finally he sent her up to bed, pausing to kiss her once more, gently, demanding nothing, asking nothing, even though he wanted to ask for everything.

It was an internal struggle, one she didn't need to know about. She had enough on her mind, and plenty of healing yet to do.

But he stayed awake for a long time, busying himself with carrying the untouched mugs of cocoa out to the kitchen and emptying them so Rosa wouldn't know they hadn't been drunk, rinsing them for easier cleaning in the morning. He knew better than to go beyond that.

He smiled wryly at his reflection in the dark window over the sink. Rosa had taken him in hand, and he had no doubt about who ruled within the walls of this house.

Al, on the other hand, took no such position in dealing with the ranch. He was a good man, capable of a whole lot, tireless and eager, but he was always careful of the boss-employee positions. He hoped someday that Al would get as uppity as Rosa.

But all of that was distraction and he knew it. What had started as a native impulse to help someone in trouble, a need to atone for his actions of so long ago, was transforming into something much stronger, and maybe that wasn't smart.

When they caught this guy, Nora would probably want

to rebuild her life in Minneapolis. She hadn't talked about it all that much, but he had gathered she liked it there, had liked her work. One crazy man had stripped it all from her.

Just as her father had stripped her of childhood. Damn, he got heartburn just thinking about Fred Loftis. Thoughts of Langdon filled him with fury, but Loftis gave him serious heartburn.

He couldn't imagine the cruelties, both major and minor, that Nora had grown up with and concealed from the world. He wished there was some way to make up for it, but he was no magician with a wand to wave.

Nora had been repeatedly hurt, and no amount of wishing or any number of magical incantations could wash that away. Tonight he had held one of the most damaged people he had ever known, and it had forced him to face his every shortcoming. He could never take it away, probably couldn't even make any of it any better.

No kissing away this boo-boo or putting a bandage on it.

But at the same time he'd faced his limitations, he'd recognized her inherent strength. God, she was strong. She had proved it beyond any question. He felt a huge admiration for her, and figured a lesser person might have been reduced to a puddle by all she had been through.

And now, as terrified as she was, she wanted to learn self-defense. She wasn't running, although the thought must have occurred to her, but was standing firmly in place, facing her terror, facing the possible arrival of her enemy.

She was magnificent, and probably didn't begin to realize it.

Nor was he going to ignore her evaluation of the guy. She alone knew him, knew the violence of which he was capable. She alone of anyone around here could evaluate that man. If she believed he wouldn't give up, then Jake believed it, too.

He stared out the window, looking past his own reflection, and for the first time in his life saw threat in the darkness outside.

He knew what was out there, every damn inch of it. He'd been walking and riding over that land his entire life. He knew every knoll, every dip, every tree, bush and sapling. He'd watched some of those trees grow from mere sprouts on the ground. He'd raised hay and alfalfa and stored it for long winters. He'd tended calves, cows and steers, and more horses than he had in his corral right now.

By closing his eyes, he could choose to see any part of it in his mind's eye, familiar as a photograph. And never had any of it seemed threatening.

The weather could sometimes be threatening, or a snake. Coyotes could be a pain. The wolves had left him alone and he doubted they were bothering some of the other ranchers as much as they complained. Coyotes and dogs were aggressive. Hell, he'd faced more trouble from feral dogs than the wolves.

But whatever problems had lain out there, from disease to predators, never had the darkness held a threat.

Now it did.

Darkness would provide the perfect environment for Langdon. As Nora had so correctly pointed out, no amount of law enforcement could make this county impermeable. These wide-open spaces, the endless square miles, could allow anyone to approach surreptitiously, either on foot or in a vehicle. If he avoided town, no one would notice someone who just appeared to be driving through. No one. Not even cops, unless Langdon came in his own vehicle. They could be on the lookout for that, checking every car of that description. But if he changed vehicles, and he probably had or he'd have been found by now... Well, he could sail into this county.

All his life he had thought of this as a safe place to live. Life brought the usual accidents and tragedies, but it was generally a safe place. Occasionally some creep would turn up, though.

A creep like Langdon, on a hunt. And when he thought over the cases he was aware of, he realized they'd been luckier than they probably had any right to be. None of these guys had succeeded in killing anyone.

Now they faced that possibility again.

Swearing, he turned and brewed a pot of coffee. He wasn't going to sleep tonight, work tomorrow or not. He thought of that fragile, lovely woman sleeping upstairs, and his gut knotted so tightly that it hurt.

His male urges paled beside his need to protect her from any additional harm. He couldn't make the fear go away, but he'd damn well die trying to protect her from that beast.

While the coffee finished brewing, he gave in to the need for action, pulled on his boots and jacket and stepped out into the frigid night. His breath blew clouds, and he stuffed his hands into his pockets.

Wasted effort, he was sure, but that didn't keep him from walking widening circles around the house, looking for footprints in the snow in places where he and Al hadn't walked. Playing sentry against a killer who was probably nowhere near. But he couldn't fight the need to make sure that this night, this darkness, was safe for now.

He even went into the barn, where the horses, surprised to see him at such an hour, opened lazy eyes to watch him. Would they alert at a stranger? He had no idea. They'd had little enough to fear in their lives.

Back outside, he looked up at a sliver of moon, then headed back toward the warm light falling from the kitchen window. In the morning he'd tell Al and Rosa to keep an eye out for strangers. They must have learned some of Nora's story by now and wouldn't ask questions. They'd simply take care.

He didn't feel good about leaving Nora here while he was gone, even though he had great faith in Al, but he couldn't see how it would be better in town. Every time he dropped her at the library to work, he knew that all that stood between her and trouble was Emmaline Dalton, the librarian. A brave woman, too, but a match for a crazy killer? He doubted it.

His only comfort was that if Emma called for help, half the sheriff's department would descend within minutes.

He knew, too, that Nora had taken to walking to the diner for lunch. Did she feel safe walking those few short blocks? Maybe too safe? Or was this another act of defiance on her part, a reclamation of some normalcy for her life?

God knew she must need it. He certainly didn't want to deprive her of any of the steps she was taking to reassert some control. While nobody was in control of everything, it was a basic need to feel you had *some* control. At least a little.

He shucked his boots and jacket, poured a coffee and headed back to his easy chair. He had a lot to think about.

Like what he was going to discuss with Gage in the morning. The sheriff must have noticed how much time had passed without anyone finding the least sign of Langdon's whereabouts. And while that might be good, they couldn't risk it. Maybe he was already beginning to think about how they could beef things up to protect Nora.

Maybe he'd been living in a fool's paradise, counting on this area's grapevine and locals to notice anyone out of place. Maybe he'd counted too much on Nora's being out here rather than at her former address with her father. Maybe he'd counted on her being hard to find out here. Maybe he hadn't gone on high enough alert.

Damn Fred Loftis. He wouldn't put it past the man, in his anger and self-righteousness, to tell a total stranger who knocked on his door in the late hours exactly where to find his daughter. Did the man grasp what was going on here? Had Nora even told him?

Somehow he couldn't imagine Nora telling that man anything she didn't have to.

So he'd talk to Loftis in the morning, too, make sure he didn't reveal where Nora was. He just hoped he could do it without punching the man in the jaw.

The little things Nora had let slip, combined with memories from their childhood together, didn't create a pretty picture of what she must have endured. A simmering anger had been building in him, and right now it was a white-hot flame in the pit of his stomach. How much could one person be asked to endure?

At least the flame of anger burned away the throbbing ache of desire in his groin that had been driving him crazy the whole time he'd held her on his lap.

That was going to have to wait. Maybe forever—he didn't know. But now was not the time.

However, coffee or no coffee, as he began to get drowsy his thoughts drifted to the woman asleep upstairs, drifted to the way she felt in his arms, drifted to the growing hunger he felt for her.

He had no difficulty imagining carrying her to his bed, imagining her shyness, her tentativeness, her inability to believe he found her both beautiful and desirable.

What he'd tried to kill twelve years ago hadn't died. Not

for him. And sometimes in her eyes he saw that it hadn't died for her, either.

Their bond might be hopeless, but it was powerful, and as he dozed, he let it consume him.

Chapter 9

Dressed in his uniform, gun strapped to his hip, Jake lingered in the kitchen, watching Nora nibble at the huge breakfast Rosa had made.

"You're going to be okay?" he asked yet again.

This time the look she gave him was almost ruefully impatient. "I'm going to be fine. Rosa promised to keep me busy, and I need it."

"I'll take care of her," Rosa said. She stood at the sink rinsing his breakfast dishes. She said it with such determination that Jake knew he'd better hush. The woman could have a real temper when she needed it.

So he grabbed his winter jacket and started pulling it on. Just then Al came in the back door.

"Boss? We got three pickups on the way up the ranch road."

Jake stiffened. Three pickups wouldn't be the Langdon

guy, but it might be trouble in another form, because they weren't expecting anyone.

"Stay in here," he said to the three of them. "You especially," he said, pointing at Rosa and Nora. "Al, you know where the shotgun is. Watch from the window."

"What are you expecting?" Nora asked, her face suddenly pale and pinched. "An invasion?"

"Actually, no, but this is unexpected. It could be anything."

"I'm sorry. Now I've got you uptight, too."

"Quit apologizing, dammit. When you live this far out, it just pays to be cautious. That's all I'm doing."

Then he went out front to meet his visitors.

He waited at the top of the porch steps, leaning casually against a stanchion as he watched the three trucks approach, their tires crunching on the frozen ground. Ah, that was Fred Loftis's truck, he realized when it got close enough. That explained the kind of trouble on its way.

He almost smiled, expecting to enjoy this.

The trucks pulled into a semicircle in front of him and stopped. Loftis was the first to climb out, and soon five others joined him, three men and two women dressed in the same drab way he'd made Nora and his wife dress, like something left over from the thirties and captured in a black-and-white photo. Both women had the same worn-out look he remembered from Nora's mother. The guys, on the other hand, looked like natural brutes.

What was it about this church? he wondered. They'd always stayed on the fringes locally, socializing only among themselves, but generally leaving their neighbors alone. Causing no trouble, but never really fitting in. Kind of interesting when you considered that Loftis himself was one of the most prominent businessmen in town. Jake wondered idly if he wasn't most of the force in this group, controlling it through the power of the purse. God knew the rest of them could probably barely meet their bills.

He waited until they were arrayed in front of him. No weapons that he could see, so it was a good start to whatever.

"Howdy," he said. "Something I can do for you folks?"

"I want my daughter back," Loftis said. "She's bringing shame on me by living with you."

"No shame," Jake said easily. "She has her own room, and she has a chaperone, my housekeeper."

"People are talking!"

"Maybe you are. I'm not hearing a thing from anyone else."

"She's my daughter and you have no right to keep her here, sin or no sin. And it looks sinful to me."

Jake straightened, careful to appear relaxed, although his anger was winding up again. "I don't recall that you were elected judge and jury. What's more, Nora may be your daughter, but she's an adult woman and can do as she chooses. You lost your right to say anything the day she turned eighteen. Get used to it."

"That's not the way we believe," Loftis thundered. "An unmarried woman should be in her father's care."

A murmur of agreement came from the chorus of crows he'd brought with him.

"Regardless of what you believe, I'm telling you the law. Didn't have a problem when she left home and made her own life, did you? No, you're just worried about gossip, and that disgusts me."

"You have no right!"

"No right to what? Offer my spare bedroom to a guest? Look after a woman who's been seriously wounded?" His pretense at relaxation seeped away, and his hands balled into fists he would very much have liked to use.

"I was taking care of her!"

"You weren't even giving her time to heal, you old jack-ass. You were insisting she come to work for you immediately."

"She was well enough. She took another job."

"Sitting at the library, not stocking your shelves. Now get out of here, all of you, before I get the sheriff to cite you for trespass."

"Not until I see my daughter!"

"Over my dead body."

Loftis took a step toward him, as if he were going to turn this into a fight. Jake was spoiling for it, but he didn't want to give Nora the inevitable grief. Damn, a rock and a hard place. The law would be on his side, but how would it affect Nora?

Then he heard the front door creak open behind him. He turned, half expecting to see Al armed with the shotgun, but instead Nora stepped out, wrapped in her jacket.

"Drop it, Dad," she said in a voice as flat and hard as steel. "Don't come any closer."

"Girl, you know better than this. I brought you up right, and you know the appearance of sin is as bad as the sin itself. A stumbling block to others. You come home with me now."

"I wouldn't come home with you if it were the last place on earth. I'm tired of you and all the misery you inflict. Go away and leave me alone. Don't ever come near me again."

Jake's heart swelled with pride in her, but his anger was still trying to take control. He stared icily at Loftis. "You heard the lady. Now get off my property and don't ever come back."

That was when Al decided to make an appearance with the shotgun. Perfect timing, Jake thought. Nora had had her say, and now they'd deal with the trespassing.

Loftis glared at Al, then included Jake and Nora in his fury. "You'll pay for this, girl."

"I've paid for sins I've never committed," she said quietly. "I've paid more than you'll ever know, some of it at your hands. Leave me alone."

Loftis took one step toward her. Jake threw back his jacket to reveal the weapon strapped to his hip, but made no move to unsnap the holster. It did have the effect of making Loftis pause.

"Now," Jake said quietly, "I'm giving you a second warning that you're trespassing. I'll speak to the sheriff about it today. Trust me, you won't get another warning."

If furious glares could kill, Jake figured Loftis's would have turned him into a cinder on the spot. The man stood there a moment longer, as if unwilling or unable to cede anything, but then he turned sharply and climbed into his truck. Like silent puppets, the rest followed him.

Jake remained where he was until the last dust of their passage made it clear the trucks were headed back to town. Then he turned.

"Let's go inside. I'm making a call before I go anywhere."

Nora had begun to shake. Even now, facing down her father frightened her. Like the man who had attacked her, Fred Loftis wouldn't tolerate defiance. He might not make another move out here on Jake's ranch, but what about when she was in town? What if he came after her in the library or walking down the street to get lunch?

That frightened her almost as much as being pursued by her attacker from Minnesota, even though she didn't think her father was capable of the same level of violence. He could be violent, yes, but that had usually been slaps and blows with a belt, not an attack with deadly weapons of any kind.

She tried to assure herself she could deal with it, but her rubbery legs barely carried her to the table before she collapsed back in the chair in front of her breakfast.

Jake grabbed the kitchen phone off the wall and dialed. Rosa came to give her a squeeze on her shoulder, as if offering reassurance. So many good people, she thought. So many. She needed to think of them, not the two men who had demonized her life.

They were outliers, she thought as she wrapped her arms around herself. Outliers. Exceptions. Of all people, she should know that. But her training in psychology wasn't helping much with her emotional response.

"Gage?" she heard Jake say. "I've had some trespassers this morning, and I may need your help. Fred Loftis and five of his cronies showed up to take Nora away. I didn't get the feeling they're ready to give up. You know she works at the library and she ought to be able to walk down the sidewalk to the diner without being molested."

A long silence. "Yes, I warned them against trespass, twice, but that doesn't take care of the time she's in town."

Another silence. "Okay, thanks. Now I need to make another call. Or you can just let my guys know I'm going to be a little late this morning. Thanks."

He hung up, and the next thing Nora knew he'd pulled a chair over to her side and wrapped his big arm around her shoulder. "You, lady, are about to become the most protected person in Conard County."

His arm made her feel so safe, as did Rosa's quiet clucks of concern and the fresh cup of coffee that appeared in front of her. "I'm causing everyone so much trouble!"

"You're not the one causing trouble at all," Jake said.

"Believe me. Your dad is causing trouble. That Langdon creep is causing trouble. You're not doing one damn thing wrong, except maybe breathing."

She gave a shaky laugh. "Breathing seems to be dangerous for me lately."

"Maybe all along," he said gravely. His arm tightened. "I really don't want to leave you here today. Not after that."

"I'd just be in your way."

"You mean you don't want to ride in a patrol car."

She flushed faintly, glad that her shakiness was receding. "That, too," she said in a nearly smothered voice. "But I'm getting used to your car."

"And me, too," he said warmly. "That's good. Little steps. But you can stay in the office. I'm sure we could put your talents to use there."

She thought about it. Pushing papers in his office all day or staying here to help Rosa with housework. Truth was, housework was a chore she didn't especially like, something she did because she had to, not because she wanted to. But would doing odd jobs at Jake's office be much better?

Probably. Making her mind up she said, "I'll go with you. Sorry, Rosa."

Rosa shook her head. "No apology. I'll work faster alone anyway."

Nora was sure she was right. She'd have only slowed the woman down and interrupted her routine. She almost flushed again.

"Help is always nice," Rosa said, "but some help is better. What is best for you is better. So go! We will have a nice dinner tonight."

Nora raced upstairs to get dressed, realizing that for some reason she was actually looking forward to the day.

It would at least be different, and she'd be behind a wall of cops.

Jake was beginning to make her feel very different about cops.

The new police department did indeed share facilities with the sheriff's office—right in the same building. Jake's office was in the back, next to Gage's, and cops in both uniforms came and went as if they were one big fraternity. They even shared the same dispatch.

"It really *is* a cut-rate operation," Nora remarked as she entered Jake's office. It was a tiny room, outfitted with a computer, swamped in papers.

"Believe it," he answered. "Basically they created a payroll and the county was kind enough to share facilities. God knows how they would have managed this if they'd had to supply offices and dispatch for us separately."

"I thought you said they got a grant."

"Not that big of one. The sheriff got a bigger grant so he has all the nice, shiny new equipment."

"Teetering on ancient desks," said a familiar voice. Nora looked up to see Gage Dalton. As a child she'd been fearful of his scarred face, but time had washed that away as she'd learned what a kind man he really was. "How are you doing, Nora?"

"Pretty well, Sheriff."

"Gage, please." He looked past her at Jake. "If ever we've coordinated, now's the time. Your officers are going to have to keep an eye on Nora while she's in town."

"You know I'm not going to squawk about jurisdiction."

"I know you won't. But how much arguing do you want with the council? Did I ever tell you how grateful I am they decided to make a police department?" Gage sounded wry.

"I have my hands full with the county commissioners. You took the council off my plate."

"At least somewhat. They're always trying to get their fingers in the pie somehow."

Nora had settled into a chair facing Jake's desk, and now Gage limped over to sit beside her. He looked at her, his expression kind. "Do you have a cell phone?"

"Yes, when it works around here."

"Is it preprogrammed with the emergency number? And does it have GPS?"

"I think so." She picked up her purse and pawed through it, then handed him the phone.

He scrolled through a few things before passing it back. "It'll work in town. Outside things get more problematic. A lot of companies aren't eager to build cell towers on millions of acres of basically empty ranch land." He looked at Jake. "Do you have a phone for her?"

"You bet. I started thinking about that this morning."

Gage nodded. He looked at Nora. "We have a satellite link for law enforcement. That should work almost anywhere, and it has GPS. Jake'll show you how to use it. In the meantime, I guess we need to start keeping an eye on Loftis and his friends."

Jake shook his head a little. "I don't want Loftis to become a distraction. Langdon is still out there."

"Oh, he's not going to become a distraction. I'm going to pay him a visit about trespassing at your place. I'm sure we can add some hints about what awaits him if he or anyone else bothers Nora in town."

"I can do that part. It's my job."

"I already think Loftis is angry enough at you. He'll probably be calling the city fathers before lunch. No, I'll put the bug in his ear. For example, he wouldn't want anyone to think he was colluding with Langdon, would he?"

Nora gasped, but Jake laughed. "I wasn't going to go that far."

"No, but you were never a fed. I know how to use these little things from long experience, and in that regard he's more likely to listen to me than to you. It's time he learned that he's not the only one who can intimidate people, and that you and I have the law behind us."

He rose and patted Nora's shoulder. "Jake's a good cop, Nora. A fine one. I was sorry to lose him even though I could understand why. Stay close."

Which was exactly what she was doing, she thought as Gage limped out. Staying close.

An hour later, Jake left on patrol, after teaching Nora how to use the satellite phone—which he referred to as "the brick." It was certainly bigger and heavier than any modern cell phone, but easy enough to use with some direction.

He'd also given her a stack of paperwork to file after a brief explanation of the filing system. He'd taken her at her word about keeping busy, and she was grateful.

There were times when thinking could be your worst enemy, and this was one of them. Not that she could entirely avoid it. Filing didn't require her full concentration.

She still couldn't believe her father had come after her like that. Had he really thought he could drag her home? Or had he merely been trying to impress some of his flock? Probably the latter, she decided. He must have known that short of physical force he couldn't take her anywhere, and must have realized after their first confrontation that Jake would intervene. Unless he had thought Jake wouldn't be there.

Unless he had thought she would give in to her old training and the pressure of six people. Something in her spine had stiffened in her years away from home, though. She wasn't nearly as easy to push around now.

She did feel surrounded. That creep was probably steadily making his way here, and now she had her father to contend with. Neither of them was likely to give up, because neither of them would tolerate defiance.

The thought caught her, freezing her. Had she misinterpreted Langdon, seeing him through the lens of her father? What if he were a different sort of beast altogether?

It was certainly important to know. Very important to have the measure of her enemies when so much hung in the balance. If she had misunderstood what motivated that creep because he'd reminded her in some twisted way of her father, that wasn't going to help at all.

For the first time she wished she could remember more about the attack. She'd been grateful for how much had been erased by trauma, but now it might prove to be her undoing. She sat down slowly and began to dredge the wisps of horrifying memory.

She wasn't sure this was wise. Not sure at all. The brain had its ways of protecting people, and trauma alone, the kind of physical trauma she had endured including blows to the head, could affect the brain's ability to create memories. Some of it would probably never, ever come back.

But if she could get at some of the remaining pieces… Well, they might be useful. Then again, they might tip her over another cliff of terror.

She sat there for a long time, wondering if she might be making a big mistake. A very big mistake.

Jake took his four hours on patrol in stride. There wasn't much to do, but he was used to that. Most of the time it had been quiet when he was working as a deputy, too. The scenery just changed more on the longer roads than it did in town. As he drove past the pharmacy for the third time, he saw Gage's vehicle parked out in front. Probably dealing with Loftis, and in a public venue. Unless Loftis was smart enough to take him into a back office.

Jake would have liked to be the one doing the dealing but he recognized the wisdom of Gage taking over. On the trespassing issue, Gage had jurisdiction. In town, though, Jake had it, and he was making sure his handful of officers knew what the threat was.

They were already on the lookout for Langdon, but now they had to make sure Loftis didn't accost Nora. The funny part was—and it struck Jake as funny—his guys looked delighted to have a big mission. Well, of course. They probably got awfully bored handing out parking tickets, pulling over a few drunks and making sure the kids got home from school safely.

It kind of amused him that they were so glad to have something new to deal with, but the cause of the amusement didn't make him smile at all. He almost felt as if Nora was dangling out there like bait on a hook between Langdon and her father.

It was important that she be able to have some kind of normal life. Absolutely essential to her recovery, he would think, but here she was dealing with all this crap. Too much.

He almost thought it was unfair, but he'd given up on that concept a long time ago. Life wasn't fair. Period. If there was any fairness, he had to make it himself, for himself and for others. People made things fair. Overall, the universe didn't give a damn. Random things happened to everyone, sometimes seeming to defy the odds, but they happened.

Fact: bad things happened to good people all the time. He didn't blame God for it; that was just the terms of life.

You took the cards you were dealt and made your best play with them.

But sure as hell, Nora had been dealt enough rotten cards. It was her turn for something good.

Big philosophical questions, ones he didn't ponder often because mostly life had been decent to him. Beth had been the major tragedy of his life, and her leaving hadn't turned out to be so tragic after all. Once he'd gotten past the sting of being rejected, he'd been relieved. No more fighting. Nor more complaining. No more demands that he change this or that about himself or the way he lived.

He'd been one of the lucky ones. Someday he'd get his share of bad times—it seemed everyone did—but he felt damn lucky overall.

Right now, if he could have, he'd have willingly shared a lot of his luck with Nora. Just a break, he found himself thinking. Just give the woman a break.

He hoped to hell he could help provide it.

"Well, that was boring as hell," Jake remarked as he returned to the office. Nora was stuffing some papers in a filing cabinet, trying to look as if she had been busier than she had been. Opening the can of worms about her attack had left her feeling drained, even though she hadn't come up with much more than she already recalled.

"What's wrong?" he asked almost immediately.

"Nothing really. Memories."

"I guess the filing wasn't enough to keep your mind busy. Not that it would have been much busier if you'd been with me."

She managed a smile. "I was doing it on purpose. Trying to get a better handle on that creep."

He frowned. "Want to talk?"

"Not now." Definitely not now, she thought. She'd tried

to worm her way down the rabbit hole and right now she just wanted to shovel the dirt back in. Forgetting had begun to seem wiser by the moment.

Before he could reply, Gage rapped on the door frame. "I had that discussion with Fred Loftis."

Nora froze, then turned, feeling her hands tremble a bit. Quickly she put the papers back on Jake's desk. "How angry did he get?"

"Nothing I couldn't handle," Gage said with a crooked smile. "That's one man who doesn't like being told he has limits."

"No kidding," Nora murmured. She leaned against the filing cabinet to steady herself, wondering just how much worse things had become.

"Anyway," Gage said, "I told him he'd already been warned twice about trespass at Jake's place. I gave him an official notice in writing. If he shows up out there again, he or any of his church followers, they're subject to arrest. But we went a little past that."

"Oh?" Jake said.

"Oh, yeah. I informed him that legally Nora is an adult. That if he bothers her verbally or physically he'll be subject to possible arrest for assault or battery. That if he attempts to coerce her against her will into coming with him, he could be subject to charges for kidnapping or illegal imprisonment."

"Oh, my," Nora breathed. "He must have been furious."

"He got a little red in the face. Then I told him your attacker jumped bail in Minneapolis, might be looking for you, and Loftis had damn well better make sure his nose stays clean and that he keeps his mouth shut about you. Wouldn't want it to look like he was an accessory."

Nora sucked a deep breath of air. All of a sudden she

couldn't breathe. "Dangerous," she gasped finally. "He's a dangerous man to make mad."

"Maybe for you," Gage said. "The man's a paper tiger. He didn't like the sound of that at all, and when I left he was swearing that he'd make sure that guy never found you, if he had anything to say about it at least. I advised him the best way to do that was to keep his mouth shut about your whereabouts and make sure anyone else who knows doesn't say anything. He seemed pretty eager to do that. He also agreed to keep an eye out for strangers."

Astonishment rippled through Nora. "When did he get so protective?"

"When his own butt looked like it might be on the line," Gage said. He shrugged. "We'll see. He knows I'm going to be watching, and so is Jake. Hell, all the cops around here are going to be watching."

Then he limped back to his office. The silence seemed deep, freighted with things Nora couldn't identify. She was frightened of her father, but maybe this once, to protect himself, he'd do the right thing. Maybe?

"Amazing," Jake said, "how a person can change their viewpoint when they feel at risk. Gage did a good job."

"I hope so."

He looked at her sharply. "Let's get you home. You look whipped. Want to get lunch at the diner or wait?"

She chose to wait. Jake's ranch had begun to feel like a haven. Eventually she'd lose that and have to move on, and she was aware that her feelings were likely to cause her pain, but right now she didn't care. She needed that feeling of security.

And while Gage might feel he'd put her father in the corner for now, she wasn't at all sure herself. Loftis didn't like to be thwarted.

She knew what that meant.

Chapter 10

Langdon had long since left his expensive car in an out-of-the-way ditch and had changed through two cars. Now he was driving an ancient pickup that wouldn't look out of place, and he'd also switched out the plates. Nobody was going to pick him out easily along the roads.

He took a dirt track across the state line from North Dakota into Wyoming and headed toward Conard County.

And nearly every damn minute he thought about the lessons he was going to teach Nora Loftis. Long, slow, painful lessons. More than he had given her last time, because that obviously hadn't worked.

He was going to enjoy every damn minute of it, too. He got hard just thinking about it. He hated her for the powerlessness she'd made him feel when he was arrested, as much as he hated her for surviving, defying him by living.

Endangering him when if she'd just died where he'd

left her they still wouldn't have found her remains. Of that he was sure.

So not only had she defied him, but she'd also threatened him. He was going to take his satisfaction, then move swiftly on. Even after Nora, he was beginning to realize the pressure would return, the need to take another woman and teach her would come back.

He wondered how he'd kept this in check for so long, this need. But he was going to control it now only until he got Nora. Then he was going to satisfy it all he wanted.

The power was growing in him, making him feel really good. He'd escaped, and they hadn't been able to find him in all this time. He could evade pursuers forever. He was invisible.

He turned that idea around in his mind and realized it was true. He had become invisible. And the next person he would allow to see him was Nora Loftis.

She was going to be one sorry woman.

A winter wind had swept in by the time they reached the ranch, bringing leaden clouds with it. Rosa had made a big pot of thick, rich potato soup and served them heaping bowls of it while Al assured Jake that he'd taken care of everything in case it stormed.

"I didn't hear about snow in the forecast," Jake remarked.

"No," Al agreed. "But to me it looks like it."

Jake nodded in agreement. He waved Al to join him at the table for lunch, and soon the four of them were gathered around eating together. To Nora it felt cozy and comforting. Ordinarily Rosa and Al ate at the bunkhouse, but had hesitated only briefly at the invitation this time.

Had something changed? Maybe this morning when Al had backed up Jake with a shotgun? Maybe they were feeling a little more like family and a little less like employees after that. Pure speculation on her part and no way to ask.

"So what was with that father of Nora's?" Rosa asked. "Is he loco? This is not the past century."

"Or even two centuries ago," Jake said. "He acts like it is, though."

"He's always been like that," Nora volunteered. "His word is law."

"Not around here," Jake said. "I hope he got the message this morning."

Nora wondered. Her father had never been one to back down when he believed he was right, which was most of the time. But maybe Gage had successfully scared him.

Not that he was the biggest of her concerns. No, that sense of being caught in a web that was trembling at the spider's approach still nagged at her, keeping her on edge. And nothing she had managed to think about today had eased her fear at all. That man was going to come for her. She knew it all the way to her bones. Despite all the protection Jake offered, despite the self-defense he was teaching her, she was still terrified. He was strong. She remembered that. Strong and savage. Facing him down wasn't likely to succeed for long.

She ate her soup because she needed to build her strength. She complimented Rosa on it even though she could barely taste it. Fear crept along her nerves like skittering cockroaches. The more time passed since that man had escaped, the more her terror grew because it meant he must be coming closer.

Even if Conard County had been protected by an army, one man could slip through if he was careful and determined. This was one man.

"Have you ever fired a shotgun?" Jake asked suddenly.

Nora looked up. "I've never fired a gun at all."

"Maybe we need to remedy that."

"I don't like guns."

"I'm not crazy about them myself, believe it or not. But when you live on a ranch, you need them. Plus, I'm a cop. I don't keep an arsenal, but a shotgun is essential out here, and you need to know how to use one. Are you game?"

"Why do you need a gun? Trespassers?"

He shook his head. "No, but I have to protect my livestock, and sometimes, if an animal gets badly hurt, I have to put it out of its misery."

"Oh." She shook her head a little. "That must be awful, putting an animal down."

"It's not my favorite part of life, I can tell you. But having to wait on the vet would mean a lot more suffering for the animal. So…" He shrugged. "You do what you have to. Thank God it's rare."

When she thought of the horses she had come to love, or even the dogs that had the run of the place and seemed to mostly do their own thing among the other animals, she was glad to know it was rare.

"Your dogs aren't pets," she remarked, trying to get her mind away from the darkness that loomed.

"No, they're not. Good for protecting the herd, good watchdogs, but they're working dogs. It's a different kind of relationship."

"They seem happy."

"They are. They're not hemmed in."

At that, a smile broke through her cloud. "Not stuck inside by the fire."

"Nope." He returned the smile. "I'm not opposed to having one as a pet, but I think it would be jealous of the freedom the others have."

"It's possible," she agreed. She'd never had a pet, so she could only imagine. "Someday I'd like to have a dog as a pet. I didn't feel it would be right when I was working, though, because it would be alone all day. That seemed cruel."

"Well, adopt one of mine," Jake suggested. "They may like pretty much running free, but there isn't one of them that wouldn't be happy to be petted or put his head on a warm lap for some scratches."

"I'll think about it." Somehow she couldn't imagine making a long-term plan right now, or getting emotionally involved with anything. Or anyone, she reminded herself, although she seemed to be developing an attachment to Jake. Rosa and Al, too, but especially Jake. If she survived this, she suspected that was eventually going to hurt, but despite the walls she had been putting up all her life against emotional pain, there seemed to be a few remaining chinks, and Jake had definitely slipped through one.

"Back to the gun," he said. "It wouldn't take long to learn to handle a shotgun."

She put her spoon down. Her heart beat nervously as she considered the question. The way she had been seized last time... "No," she finally said. "No gun."

"Why not?"

"I won't have a chance to use it if he comes for me again. And I'm not sure I could anyway."

"Not even in self-defense?" He seemed a little incredulous.

She shook her head. "I'm not saying for sure I couldn't. Most people probably would, and I can understand it. The thing is, there's a price for that, even when you do it to save your own life. I'd have to live with it. I already have enough to live with."

He looked flummoxed, but there were some things she knew about herself, and she knew she was capable of carrying huge burdens of guilt even when she had had no other choice. Imagine knowing she had killed someone. She wasn't sure she could learn to live with that, whatever the circumstances.

"Okay," he said slowly. "You're probably right. And if you're not sure you can use it, all you might do is arm him."

Rosa nodded vigorous agreement.

"But," Jake said almost gently, "if you're walking around with a shotgun, he'd probably not bother you."

At that, with a spontaneous burst of humor that surprised her given how gloomy her thoughts had been running, she replied, "Then he'd just wait for a moment when I don't have it. Walking down a street, sitting in the library. Can you imagine Emma's face if I walked into the library armed?"

At that even Jake cracked a smile, and a quiet chuckle escaped him. "You win, Miss Nora. Okay, no gun. But more self-defense lessons."

Nora nodded her agreement, surprised to realize she felt a bit better. She had settled something within herself, even though she wasn't sure exactly what it was. Nonetheless, her terror eased and a sense of peace edged in, just a bit.

She guessed deciding her limits made a huge difference. And she had just made them.

Jake spent the remainder of the afternoon outdoors. Apparently he agreed with Al that they had some bad weather on the way. Rosa turned on the radio, and soon there was talk of snow moving in over the mountains. There wouldn't be a heavy accumulation but the winds would cause whiteout conditions.

"Not good," Rosa remarked when Nora came into the kitchen for coffee. "They need to finish soon."

Nora looked out the window and saw what she meant. It wasn't bad yet, but already snow was beginning to blow.

"Of course, it will keep that man who hurt you from coming closer," Rosa said reassuringly. "You can relax."

Nora flushed. "Is it that obvious?"

"You're tense. Why wouldn't you be? I heard what happened, I heard that man escaped. I understand why you are afraid. You don't think he'll just keep running?"

Nora shook her head. "No. He won't."

Rosa sighed and surprised her with a hug. "We all take care of you, okay? But for now, no worries."

"Yes." For now no worries. Trying to move in a white-out was a recipe for serious trouble. Even that creep had to figure that out. And it wasn't like he wasn't familiar with winter weather.

She returned to the living room with her coffee, aware that the day was darkening into early night, and tried to read.

But Rosa's well-intentioned remark had brought it all flooding back. The brief escape she'd been enjoying since she had made her decision about the gun now deserted her, leaving her on the knife-edge of anxiety again.

She heard Jake come in through the mudroom and speak to Rosa. Moments later, he poked his head in and told Nora he was going to shower and be right back.

"Rosa is insisting on serving us dinner on trays in here. I don't know why, maybe she thinks it's festive." He winked then headed for the stairs.

She listened to his feet hit the steps as he ran upstairs, then came the unmistakable sound of the shower being turned on.

He was back in the house. His mere presence seemed to drive the night back. God, she had it bad, and it worried her that she was becoming so dependent on him. She'd moved away to become independent, and now here she was again with few choices, no place of her own. A backward step on a huge order.

Yet what choice did she really have? He was right— living alone in town would put her at risk. It wouldn't be long before everyone knew right where she was, and the most innocent slip of the tongue could bring that creep right to her door.

Damn, she wished this was over for good, one way or another. That man had wrecked her entire life, and was still wrecking it. Caught in a spiderweb indeed. Nor did there seem to be any way to cut herself loose, short of spending her life on the road always one step ahead of him until he managed to get himself caught.

Maybe that's what she should do. But once again she faced the limitations of her finances and wondered how long she could manage it. Skipping from town to town trying to find temporary jobs as a waitress or clerk until the fear overwhelmed her and she had to move on again?

That was no kind of life. None at all.

Inwardly she stiffened a bit. No, she wasn't going to run any farther than she already had. Come what may, she was going to settle this here. Either they caught the guy or she'd face him again, but at least it would be over.

And sometimes she didn't even care if she died in the process.

She wouldn't let those thoughts take over, though. She knew better than to give in to depression. It would weaken her, make it harder to act. She needed to be able to act when the time came.

Jake returned, clad in fresh jeans and a black sweater, in stocking feet. He set up the TV tables, and soon Rosa appeared bearing steaming plates of freshly cooked chicken with yellow rice and sides of creamy broccoli. The aromas made Nora's mouth water, a good sign considering how she had reacted to lunch.

"I go home now," she said. "Call if you need me."

"Have a good night," Jake said. "You may need to thaw Al out."

Laughing, Rosa departed.

"It's getting bad out there," he remarked as they began eating.

"Rosa had the radio on. She remarked that it would give me at least a day when I didn't have to worry."

Jake looked up from his plate. "Why do I think that was the wrong thing to say?"

"It wasn't, exactly. It's just that I had managed to forget for a few hours."

"I'm sorry."

"No need. She's right. Nobody's going to be moving in this. So I can go back to pretending."

"Can you?"

Damn him, sometimes he saw right through her. "I never really do," she admitted. "I won't until he's safely in prison."

"I can promise you he won't get bail again."

She nodded, and tried to pay attention to dinner. It was delicious, and it would be a shame to eat it as if it were sawdust. "Don't you wish I could think about anything else? Talk about anything else?"

"It's pretty hard right now, but I understand it. I'm not thinking about much else, either. And since we're on the subject, why did you look so pale when I came back to the office earlier?"

She started to shake her head, then decided to just spit it out. Maybe he could clarify her thoughts. "I started to wonder if I was evaluating that creep through the lens of my father. You know how much my father hates defiance.

I got to wondering if I'd mixed up his motivation with…
Langdon. God, I hate to say his name!"

"Then don't. 'Creep' will do just fine. So you were wondering if you'd misjudged the creep, he might not come
for you at all."

"Call it a hope. Anyway, I was trying to remember more
about the attack."

"Oh, God," he said quietly. "Are you sure you should
do that?"

"No. It didn't work anyway. I still have the same bits
and pieces to work with, but going through them… Well,
it upset me more. Maybe not my brightest move. Regardless, I'm left with this certainty somewhere inside that the
creep isn't going to quit until I'm dead. And the conviction that I won't be his last. I can't tell you exactly why,
except I guess that's the impression he left me with, and
it's sticking."

"I'm going with your gut instinct. It's the safest position to take under the circumstances. What's more, it's
probably right."

She looked at him, feeling her eyes widen. Only as a
professional had she experienced having her judgments
accepted so unquestioningly. "How can you know that?"

"I don't *know* it, but I suspect things you've forgotten
have added to your evaluation of the guy. The fact that he
may resemble your father in some way is probably irrelevant. Very different people do have similar traits. Say,
after we eat, wanna play a game?"

He was trying to distract her, and she grasped at it.
"Sure. What do you have in mind?"

He wiggled his eyebrows. "Strip poker?"

She flushed a bright red and he laughed.

"Just kidding," he said.

"I wouldn't play anyway," she blurted, even though the

suggestion had lit a bonfire at her very core. God, with each passing moment she wanted him more, and she was as terrified of that wanting as the creep who was probably hunting her.

His smile faded. "Shy?"

She shook her head and looked away. "Too many scars. Ugly scars. I...couldn't."

She didn't see the change come over him, but knew it had happened when her table was whisked from in front of her.

"We need to have a talk."

"Huh?" She looked up, utterly confused.

"Well, more than a talk. I already told you I wanted you back in high school. That hasn't changed at all. I want you even more now. And if you think some lousy scars—"

He broke off suddenly and tugged her up from her seat. "There's one thing we can deal with right now. One hangup we can get rid of. Much as I'd like to, I won't make love to you unless you want it, but we're going to get rid of one bogeyman *now*."

She stumbled a little as he tugged her toward the stairs, fear and anticipation warring within her, making her weak, filling her with so much contradiction that she didn't know what to do. She just felt she shouldn't do this.

But he settled the matter, sweeping her up into his arms and carrying her up the stairs, this time to his bedroom. He set her on her feet, then turned on every light and drew the curtains against the night. In the corner stood a full-length mirror.

"You know what your scars look like, right?"

She nodded. She'd looked at them often enough, hating them.

"Well, I don't. So I'm going to look. And then we're both going to find out how repulsed I am."

"Jake…" Her heart began to hammer wildly. She couldn't do this. *Couldn't.*

"No. This is something we can deal with, and while I don't know about you, I do know that I have a desperate need to settle *something* in this mess. This is it."

He turned her back to him. "You don't have to look at me, you don't have to look in the mirror, but I'm going to look at you, like it or not. Then we'll both know."

She wanted to protest, but the words wouldn't come. She was certain he wouldn't get very far, certain that he'd find her so repugnant he'd have to stop. He was right about one thing: it would be settled for both of them. Then maybe she could stop this constant mooning for him.

She couldn't believe she was going to allow this. Panic fluttered wildly in her stomach. This was unthinkable.

But she closed her eyes anyway as she felt him begin to strip away her clothing. She didn't want to see herself or, worse, the expressions on his face. He was going to be sickened. Absolutely sickened.

There was something else, too, something she'd never been fully able to explain. She was ashamed of those scars, as if she had somehow inflicted them on herself. They humiliated her.

Her shirt and bra vanished quickly. Chilly air met her skin, but not too chilly. She didn't have to open her eyes to know what he saw: the curving cuts on her breasts and abdomen, some inflicted by the creep, some inflicted by the surgeons who'd helped put her back together.

Then he put her hands on her shoulders so she could steady herself while he tugged away her pants and socks. No secrets left.

Except behind the closed lids of her eyes rested secrets: secret terrors, secret embarrassment, secret shyness, secret self-loathing. She hid in her own internal darkness.

"You are beautiful," he said. There was no hint of uncertainty in his tone.

She kept her eyes closed. "I'm ugly!" The cry felt as if it was ripped from her very soul.

"You're beautiful. Every one of those scars is a badge of strength. Do you ever think of them that way? They show strength and determination. You should be proud."

Proud? Proud of what that man had done to her? Proud that she looked like... "Frankenstein's monster," she blurted.

"Oh, sweetheart, no. Not at all. You're a survivor. You're determined. And you're gorgeous."

She didn't believe him, but then she felt the most incredible thing: something warm on one of the scars tracing her breast. Warm and moist. Her eyes popped open and she saw the reflection in the mirror.

She saw the full length of herself. The worming red scars, the straighter surgical scars, all of it looking as if she had been tattooed over most of her torso and upper thighs by a madman. But she also saw something else: Jake bent to kiss the scars on her breasts.

He didn't shy from them, just sprinkled them with kisses as if to say they didn't repulse him at all. As if he wished his kisses could heal.

Terror eased a bit, just a bit, and warmth slowly began to take its place. She could tell he wasn't even closing his eyes, but looking straight at the scars he kissed.

A kind of amazement filled her when she realized how far she had come. She was letting a man touch her again, unlike when she first arrived here and was leery of the merest touch.

What's more, she was naked with one and allowing him to kiss her body. She was healing, and God, it felt so good to realize that creep's hold on her was slowly letting go. Not entirely, not yet, but it was easing, or by now she would have fled out into the frigid night.

Maybe someday she could be whole again. As whole as possible anyway.

Hope flickered in her heart with each touch of his lips. Warmth and need began to seep into cold places that she'd thought would never be warm again. Could she trust this much? Yet she was doing exactly that, and with a man who had once wounded her so deeply that she had been reluctant to ever seriously try another relationship.

It seemed to come suddenly, but perhaps it didn't. She was entering a hazy land of warring need and fear, and then she felt his lips on her belly, her abdomen. Her eyes snapped open, meeting her ugliness in the mirror, but she barely saw it as she realized that Jake was now kneeling in front of her.

She felt his hands cradle her hips as he leaned toward her, still sprinkling kisses on each and every wound. Making them as memorable to him in a different way than they were memorable to her. Changing her perception kiss by kiss.

Oddly, a kind of magic began to envelop her. Something she had never experienced before. But it was as if each simple, gentle touch of his mouth was healing something within her far beyond the reach of any surgeon, touching upon deeper wounds left by her attacker.

It wouldn't last, she told herself. In a few minutes he would stop, and all the old wounds would ache again. But for now…for now…

Daringly, as warmth began to turn hotter, she lifted a hand and touched the top of his head. His hair was soft, welcoming the tentative touch of her fingers. He was kissing the hideousness of her body and seeming to rain mercy where there had been none before.

He was kind. Kind beyond belief. But that's all it was…
kindness. But a kindness she desperately needed. Her head
fell back a bit, her eyes still closed, as the sprinkling kisses
moved down to her thighs, deepening the sense of healing.

And the sense of yearning. Longing. Desire for things
she thought she would never have.

Illusory? Maybe. But she accepted what he was offering because she was so desperate for it. Reassurance when
she had been able to find none for herself. A forgiveness
she wasn't supposed to need but still needed desperately.

When he reached the last scar, she almost cried out as
she felt him stand. She never wanted it to end.

But then he was behind her again.

"Look," he murmured in her ear. "Look in the mirror."

She feared what she would see, but she already knew
what was there. Battling her own cowardice, she opened
her eyes to view her hideous tattoos of scarring again, but
this time she saw more than herself. She saw him standing right behind her, eyes wide-open, looking at the same
image in the mirror that she saw.

But his eyes were alight, and not with horror or dismay
or scorn. Something hot was there, reaching out to her. She
felt her insides quiver with painful need.

"You are beautiful," he said, staring straight at her reflection. "Absolutely beautiful. I see you and you are beautiful."

He did see her, and he wasn't recoiling. Far from it. The
magic he had woven around her deepened. Then, to her
dismay, he drew away and reached for her clothes.

"You're getting cold," he said quietly. "And I made a
promise to you."

"But…" The protest died because she couldn't find the
courage to say it.

He tilted her chin toward him as he tugged the shirt

over her shoulders. "You're not ready for what I want to do to you, all the ways I want to love you. And I do want to make love to you. But not yet. It wouldn't be right."

Disappointment filled her even as she recognized the justice of his decision. She wasn't ready. And for him to have given her such a healing experience and then taken advantage of it to make love to her might have undone some of the beauty he had just given her. She might have felt that he'd kissed her that way simply to get what he wanted.

So she finished dressing herself, remaining mute, battling down needs that would go unsatisfied. At least for now.

Because he was right. To do more might distort the magic of what he had just given her.

Five or six hundred miles left. Langdon had to take a room, and it infuriated him, but the snow was blowing so badly that he knew better than to drive through it. It wouldn't get him there any faster if he went into a ditch, and he might wind up with some explaining to do. He'd been able to change vehicles and plates, but not his driver's license. At least he could find fleabags along the road that didn't ask for anything other than cash up front, and little enough of that.

A year ago he wouldn't have believed that he would ever stay in a room so repulsive that he was afraid to remove his clothes, but here he was, settled on a bed he wouldn't pull the spread down on, his jacket covering a pillow he didn't trust, staring at a ceiling and trying to focus on his plans for Nora.

Except she kept slipping away. The impulse was growing stronger, and a few miles back up the road there'd been this waitress he would have loved to snatch when she came off shift. She was a little uppity, a little less than great at her job, making him feel like a nobody. She needed to learn a lesson.

But he'd forced himself to pass on her, because he'd give away his whereabouts. Maybe not immediately, but eventually. What if he didn't get to Nora before they found out he'd been through this part of the country?

But hanging on to his self-control was getting harder with each day. He had a desperate thirst he needed to quench, and the number of miles remaining between him and Nora had become a mantra that held him in check.

He just hoped the reminder would continue to control him because getting Nora, teaching her a lesson, had to be more important than satisfying his need on just the next handy victim.

That could come later. Nora. He had to think of Nora. Once this storm blew through, he could make it in two days. He wasn't going to shoot for one because he didn't want to get sloppy, maybe get a ticket.

So two days, then maybe part of a day to find her, and part of a day to snatch her.

He could hold on that long. He *had* to.

He reached out for the bottle of whiskey on the bedside table and took a couple of swigs. It would ease the pressure a little bit.

He had to remain in control. That was the whole point, wasn't it: that *he* be the one in control.

Chapter 11

Downstairs, Jake reheated their dinners, remarking that Rosa would probably not be happy about her cooking being wounded in the microwave.

Nora was surprised by her own trill of laughter. Her mood had begun to shift so rapidly and radically that she wondered if she should worry. "We won't tell her."

"Damn straight. She swears the microwave ruins food. Not sure I always agree, but I'm not going to argue with the woman who makes me fabulous meals three times a day."

"Smart move."

She wandered over to the window and was glad to see in what little light poured from the house that the white-out was complete. "How long will this last?"

"Probably most of tomorrow, according to the latest weather."

"It makes me feel safe."

"I imagine so." She saw his reflection in the glass, then

felt his arms wind around her waist. His chin rested on the top of her head. "Let's pretend we're on another planet. Out of time, in a different world. Imaginary escape, I know, but it might be a fun way to take advantage of the safety the storm is giving you."

"How should we do that?"

"We start by finishing dinner. Then we can play games, watch a movie or just gab. Up to you."

The storm outside was indeed freeing her from the web of fear she'd been living with for so long now. It would come back, but not until that snow had settled enough to provide visibility again.

Might as well enjoy it, she thought. In whatever way enjoyment presented itself. She'd known little enough pleasure in months. Even simple ones seem to be denied to her most of the time.

"God," she whispered.

Behind her, the microwave dinged.

"What?" he asked.

"I'm just wondering if I'm ever going to be able to put the shattered pieces back together again. It seems like forever since I've enjoyed almost anything. Even food tastes flat most of the time. I've been afraid to go out, afraid to… Well, I barely even read anymore because the memories get in the way."

"I think you enjoyed our little exercise in front of the mirror, or was I mistaken?"

Her cheeks flushed. "I loved it," she admitted, her voice thickening. Just thinking of it made her glow with wonder and heavy desire.

"Good. That's a start. I think the rest will come, Nora. Honestly. It's just taking time."

"I enjoy riding the horses," she said after a moment. "Okay, that makes something else."

"See?"

She turned within the circle of his arms. "I'm enjoying the work I do with Emma."

"That's three."

Then he bent and kissed her lips, a slightly deeper kiss, demanding nothing, but almost seeming to make a promise. "Now we'll spend the evening finding something else for you to enjoy."

He turned to pull the food out of the microwave and she was astonished at how bereft she felt. Going rapidly over the cliff edge for this man wouldn't be wise, but it seemed to be happening anyway. She wanted him. She wondered how long it would be before she felt he wouldn't hurt her in some way. Or if he'd ever get to that point. Or even, come to that, if *she* would.

Or if he even really wanted her, despite what he said. Words from the past still burned a bit, engraved on her mind forever, despite his explanation and apology.

Smothering a sigh, she accepted her plate and walked into the living room. She hoped he came up with something sufficiently distracting, because right now it would be easy to spiral into places she didn't want to go, places that had nothing to do with the creep and everything to do with Jake.

"Will the animals be okay in this?" she asked as they resumed dinner.

"We've got windbreaks for them. Al and I took care of everything else this afternoon. Come morning, though, we'll probably have to break the ice in troughs and ponds so they can drink. But they're okay for the night."

"I'm glad. I wouldn't want to be out in this."

"It's not going to get too cold, so as long as they shelter from the wind, they'll make it. They're better suited to this climate than we are."

"That's not hard to believe."

"If they weren't," he said wryly, "I wouldn't have any animals at all."

"And the dogs?"

"They'll bed down in the midst of the crowd. They'll probably be warmest of all."

At that she laughed again, feeling her mood rise once again. "What about cats? Don't you need mousers?"

"The dogs take care of that, too, believe it or not. We're surprisingly vermin-free."

Distractions. She knew next to nothing about how all of this worked, despite having been here for so long now. She'd expressed little interest, hadn't really asked him to open up about ranching. Had she lost her native curiosity, too?

"Do you like card games?" he asked. "I'm not talking strip poker here."

"We already did the strip part," she said a trifle tartly, even as her cheeks heated again. God, what a memory! She wondered if it would embarrass her for years to come or always remain a secret delight. The man had literally worshipped her with his mouth, despite her scars. Amazingly, given the condition she had been in so recently, she had let him. And she was glad she had. The warmth, the glow, the sweet honey of need that filled her didn't approach the sense that something previously broken had just been mended. At least as far as he was concerned.

"You did anyway. The thing with cards is most games are better with more than two players. We can find something, though. I have word games you might like. And a collection of movies if that suits your mood."

"Let me think about it." What she wanted was just to be with him, talking. About what she wasn't sure, but she had come to love the sound of his voice, no matter what he talked about, and the animation he brought to most subjects once he got going. The boy had truly become an enticing, intriguing man. Yet she still knew so little about him, really.

Kind of astonishing when she thought about it. She'd grown up with him, moved away for twelve years, and yet she'd never really known him in any meaningful way. He must have hopes and dreams like most people. Things he wanted to do.

A thought occurred to her. "How about we play Twenty Questions or something like that?"

"Meaning?"

"I ask a question about you, you answer. Then you ask me one."

He hesitated. "I think I'm an open book, but what about you, Nora? What if I ask the wrong question? Not that I would want to, but I might not know."

He had a point there. She pushed some food around on her plate. Finally she said, "I'm game. If it's something bad, I'll just say so."

Again he hesitated. "Okay, but let's try to keep it light."

"Fair enough. If you could go anyplace in the world on a vacation, where would it be?" Safe. Very safe. And not what she wanted to know at all.

"That's a tough one," he admitted. "I'm pretty well nailed here because of the ranch."

"You have Al and Rosa. So say you could get away for a week."

"Well, that opens up the entire world. I used to dream of traveling, even though I knew I probably never would. I wanted to see damn near everything."

"Have you gotten more selective?"

He laughed. "I've had to. So a one-week vacation any-where in the world?"

"Yeah. No limits. This is pretend, after all."

He tilted his head a little, staring into space. "Dang. Only *one* place?"

She giggled. "You're the one who limited yourself by remembering the ranch. You can take off your own restrictions. Say you didn't own a thing in the world, but had all the money you wanted and could go anywhere."

"Now, that boggles my mind. In the first place, I've never been able to imagine having so much money. Like everyone else around here, my means have limits and they're so ingrained I can't imagine being without them."

"Now, that's interesting." And it was, because it said something about the way they had grown up, and their expectations of life. Reality always limited dreams. "I guess I'm the same way. My goals were always small ones. Get to college, get a job, have a little place of my own. I never dreamed any bigger."

"Isn't that big enough?" he asked, surprising her. A smile seemed to dance around the corners of his mouth. "Who needs more?"

"We're not talking about need here."

"I am. Maybe I can't dream like a billionaire because it's pointless. I think about what I want, and what I want is to keep this ranch going, making it break even if it can't be profitable, having a family eventually, hoping maybe I'll have one kid at least who'd like to take over from me…." He stopped and his eyes seemed to twinkle. "Those are actually some pretty big dreams. No travel."

"How about a trip to Yellowstone?" she suggested, still smiling.

"That I might be able to fit in. Now your turn. Where would you travel?"

Once upon a time, long ago, she'd dreamed of travel, but she suspected a lot of it had been born of a desire to escape her father. Since she'd left home, her travel desires had narrowed for the most part, but perhaps that had been limited by her budget. But what wasn't? "I don't know. I used to have a hankering to seen Mayan pyramids."

This was beginning to seem like a poor topic. Considering the vastness of the world, its many beauties and its many cultures, how could she pass up even just dreaming of visiting some exotic location? There was so much out there to see and do, and just thinking about this was beginning to make her feel parochial.

"How many pyramids could we do in a week?" he asked.

She started to laugh, then caught on a realization. He had said *we*. Surely he couldn't mean that. "Not very many," she said finally. "But I'd be happy to see just one."

"That's doable," he said as if it were decided. "Next question?"

Just then the wind strengthened, keening around the house like a banshee, and window glass rattled behind her. She couldn't help it. She jumped.

Keening wind. That was all she had heard that night when she had wakened in the woods near a road. Wind keening in the treetops. Naked, cold, weak, forcing herself to crawl and inch her way to where the night seemed brighter, which turned out to be an open road.

"Nora?"

She slammed back into the present as Jake's arms lifted her and settled her onto his lap.

"Nora?" he repeated.

"The wind," she whispered. "That night… The wind."

His arms tightened around her and he began to rock her as well as he could in an armchair. "I'll put some music on. Loud."

"It's all right," she whispered. "It's all right."

Music wouldn't help. In an instant she had been cast back, and the memories still darkened her thoughts. Music wouldn't wash them away now, even if she didn't hear the wind again.

"I crawled," she whispered. "It seemed like forever. There was a moon, I crawled toward the light. I was so cold and it was so hard…"

He didn't speak, didn't offer false reassurance, simply kissed her forehead and continued to hold her and rock her.

"I dragged myself. I don't know how long it took but it seemed like forever. Inching on the ground. I seemed to fade in and out, but I knew I had to get to the light. I *had* to."

"And you made it." He spoke quietly. Gently.

"I should have died."

"I'm glad you didn't."

She gave a little shake of her head, still caught in the nightmare. "No, they said I should have died. I lost so much blood…."

A shudder passed through him and she felt his muscles tighten, but he didn't say anything.

"Sometimes…sometimes I wish I *had* died. It would have been over. All of it. Is it ever going to be over?"

"Probably not completely. Ever. But it will get better. You know that. You're a psychologist. You know that with time things fade, even terrible things. That you still have a right to find joy and happiness, and you'll find them again. Because you're still alive, for which I am so thankful."

Then he kissed her, really kissed her, a lover's kiss, full of yearning. He ran his tongue over her lips, sending skitters of delight running throughout her, dragging her by that simple act out of the nightmare, right into the present.

She'd have missed this if she had died, and that kiss,

that single kiss from lips she had so often wanted to really taste, was enough to make her grateful. At least for now.

As his tongue danced over her mouth, she eased into the moment and finally parted her lips, offering entry.

He didn't hesitate. His warm tongue plunged into her, tracing the contours of her teeth, her cheeks, wrapping around her tongue in an ancient dance of seduction. She'd been kissed like this by her few boyfriends, but none had felt like this, none had swept her away to mindlessness. Her hand lifted and she gripped his shoulder, as if afraid he would slip away or pull back.

But he didn't. He kept right on exploring her mouth, then began to stroke her along her side with his hand, almost petting her, but so much more arousing.

Finally, though, he did pull back. He sprinkled kisses all over her face. Her hand clutched him, trying to pull him back again, but he wouldn't yield.

"I don't want to be a momentary escape," he said huskily. "Not with you, Nora. I need to be more than that."

The justice of his words hit her hard. She turned her face into his shoulder, tears suddenly hot in her eyes. Too wounded to even make love because she might do it for the wrong reasons. Unfair to them both.

Her hand tightened until she clenched his shirt into a knot, and the tears turned into sobs. Her own brokenness overwhelmed her.

He resumed rocking her, stroking her hair. "Cry, sweetheart. Cry. Let it all out. When you're smiling again, we'll revisit this, I promise you. Because I want you more than I can say."

But as her sobs eased, something else began to replace them, a need that had been with her for as long as she could remember. Her fist still clutched his shirt, and she pounded it lightly on his shoulder.

"Stop it! Stop it," she demanded brokenly.

"Stop what?"

"Stop pulling away. I've had it. I don't know if I'll be alive next week. That creep could find me and finish the job!"

He didn't argue with her, although she had no idea whether it was because he wouldn't offer false reassurances, or because he didn't know how to respond.

"Nora?" he questioned finally.

"Don't you get it, Jake? When I asked you to take me to the prom, that wasn't some wild impulse. I've wanted you ever since I was old enough to understand what that meant, and even before when I didn't know what it was. All along I've wanted you, and now you keep saying you want me, but pull away."

"Nora…"

"I know you think you're protecting me. Maybe you are. But can you promise me tomorrow? Nobody can promise tomorrow will come. What if it's this night and no other? What if there's never another chance? Stop protecting me from myself!"

He was silent for so long that fear began to replace the desire that pulsed, growing stronger, then weaker but never, ever dissipating, not even all those years she had been in Minneapolis. Had she done it again? Pushed him into a position where he would reject her? Perhaps not so brutally this time, but rejection all the same.

But she needed this settled. He'd reawakened hopes she'd been trying to bury for so long. He'd brought them all the way back to life. She needed a damn answer, at this point *any* answer, no matter how painful.

She felt him draw breath, and she tensed, expecting a blow.

"All those years ago, like I told you, I was cruel because

I was protecting myself and the commitment I'd made to Beth. I was trying not to do something wrong. Instead I did the worst thing possible. I lashed out at you. The things I said still keep me up some nights."

She drew a ragged sigh, but refused to say any more. Let him say what he would.

"Maybe," he continued slowly, "I'm not just protecting you. Maybe I'm protecting myself again, too."

"From what?"

"From how I'd feel if I took advantage of you in some way. Truthfully, Nora, what if it turns into a one-night stand for some reason? Would that wound you? Would it wound me if we made love tonight and you decided I wasn't all that and it was time to move on? And for God's sake, can you please tell me how you can still want me after what I did to you back then? You ought to hate me forever."

"But I don't," she said quietly. "I've learned something about myself over the years. Yes, I was an abuse victim as a child. Yes, it made me more inclined to accept abuse as normal. Yes, I was wounded by what you said, hurt to my very core. But I have to own up to something."

"What's that?"

"I realized that I set that up. You were the last and only reason I had to stay here, and even though I didn't consciously realize it at the time, I was cutting that tie. I knew you were going to tell me no."

"But I didn't have to be so brutal!"

"It helped me pack my suitcase and leave. It propelled me in a way all my dreaming didn't. So you weren't solely responsible for what happened. Honestly, Jake, embarrassing as it is to admit it, I never for a moment thought you were going to say yes to me, not to take me to the prom, not to sleep with me."

"But…"

She stirred and he fell silent again, waiting. "At the time, I was crushed. I admit it. Hopes died, but other hopes took over. It required a lot of therapy and a long time to realize I had set myself up for that so that I wouldn't waver in my decision to leave. As a therapist, I have to say, sometimes we're smarter than we realize. It was a dumb move, I didn't get why I did it back then, but in the end it turned out to be just what I needed."

"I'll still never really forgive myself. No matter what you say."

"I wish you would. I'm not sure it would have worked as well if you'd been gentle. I was cutting the last tie that held me here."

"Me."

"You."

"Wow," he breathed.

"Yeah." She ducked her head a bit, not wanting to even glimpse his face after that admission. "Anger took over from hurt, and kept pushing me to achieve other goals in other places. I had to do it one way or another. I did it. I'm not proud of it, and even less so when I realize you're still beating yourself up over it. But there it is."

"But you were still so angry when I picked you up in Denver."

"I nursed my anger against you for a long time. But by the time you picked me up, that was a minor thing compared to everything else that had happened. And yes, I was wounded. I won't deny that. But I put myself out there for it."

"I still shouldn't have said those things."

"I shouldn't have put you in that position. So maybe we should both forgive each other and ourselves. When you look back on it, remind yourself that you were my escape module. My rocket pack. Whatever."

After a few seconds, he began to stroke her side again, and she felt him relax. "Okay. I'll accept that, but I'm still not happy with the way I behaved."

"All of us have those moments and regrets." As he relaxed and continued stroking her side, she relaxed, too, into his embrace, enjoying being held by him. Her earlier frustration had seeped away, a necessary confession had been made and she'd already had time to accept that her own behavior back then had probably been necessary to her survival. She needed to give him some time, too, no matter how much she wanted him this very moment.

"Just suppose," she said, "that you had said yes. It wouldn't have worked for us back then at all. We both know that. So it might have been an even worse wound if you had been kind. Let's just let it go."

But he didn't quite do that. "You really wanted me all those years?"

"I don't think it ever stopped," she admitted. "I was always attracted to you. But then, so was half the school."

"I doubt that. I was just another rancher's son. Nobody special."

"Hah!" A short laugh escaped her.

She felt more than heard the chuckle deep in his chest. "I guess we didn't see things the same way."

"Apparently not."

"But I *did* see you," he offered. "I felt an attraction to you, too. I still don't know why I was stupid and ignored it."

Some questions had no answers, so she didn't even try.

"Maybe I was just too busy growing up and I was a typical teenage fool," he said presently.

"We all were."

"No kidding. But I also know I admired the way you left and moved on. I think I told you before, but while a lot of people I knew back then talked about it, almost no-body but you managed it."

"I had more reason than most to leave." It was as sim-ple as that. She didn't think of herself as courageous or admirable. She'd needed to escape her father, and she'd used Jake to give her the final push. There was nothing in that to create pride.

"What about now?" he asked. "Do you still hate it here?"

"I never hated this town. I hated the way I was treated by the other kids and by my father, but I never hated this place. I actually missed it while I was away."

"But Minnesota must be beautiful."

"It is. Gorgeous, but different. I'm glad to be back near the mountains."

"But you'll want to get back to Minneapolis, I assume."

She wondered if that was more than a simple question, but she couldn't tell and did ask. His gentle stroking of her side was beginning to heat the fires that never quite went out, and a slow, deep throb, though still gentle, had begun between her legs. "I don't think so," she said finally. Why did it feel as if all the air was draining from the room?

"Somewhere else, then?"

"I doubt it. I'd like to find a way to come back here, I think."

Then he asked, totally out of context, "Can you forget the creep tonight? Just tonight?"

"Of course. With that storm blowing out there..."

It had made her feel safe, and she had actually been doing a pretty good job of not thinking about him at all.

But her statement seemed to unleash him. All of a sud-den he was holding her tighter, tipping her face up and diving in for the deepest kiss she had ever experienced.

When he tore his mouth from hers, he said, "You can stop me at any time. I promise."

Right then she didn't want to stop anything. The sky could have been crashing down and she wouldn't have wanted him to stop. She had only the vaguest idea of what she was asking for, but she had wanted it for so long she wasn't going to pass up what might be her only opportunity.

But she also understood his point. She might discover hidden land mines after what had happened to her. She might find she was broken in ways she hadn't really pondered. He was telling her it was okay if she did.

God, how could she have ever believed this man to be cruel because of one thing he had done when he was little more than a child?

She knew a lot of nice men, but few had struck her as being as kind and gentle as Jake. When she thought about his life, about him being a rancher and a cop, that gentleness amazed her all the more.

Not that he didn't have a tough side, as well. It had come out with her father, a steeliness she wished she could emulate herself.

But not right now. Steeliness wasn't a part of what was happening inside her now. No, she was melting, beginning to understand how a warm puddle of honey could feel as everything inside her softened in ways she had never dared to soften before.

Letting go. Letting go of everything except the sweep of his tongue in her mouth and the sweep of his hand along her side. Every last bit of tension seeping away in the most delightful of heats.

A vast yearning built alongside the heat. Yearning for Jake, but also yearning for a real, normal life. To be a normal woman with a normal man, with normal hopes and dreams.

Jake had figured in those hopes and dreams for a long time, and now he was starring in them again. Right now she didn't feel like arguing the wisdom of those feelings. All she wanted was the experience of being with Jake as she had once imagined it. Imaginings that clearly didn't approach reality.

He rose from the chair, still holding her in his arms. She missed his kiss, but before that could settle in, excitement began to rise in her, roaring as strongly as Niagara Falls. He walked toward the stairs and began the climb, each step bringing them closer to a dream fulfilled.

Her entire body began to throb in time with her heart. At last. At long last.

Jake was losing his mind. He knew it and didn't give a damn. This was a huge risk with a woman so wounded. He could give her new hurts without meaning to. He could pick up a few himself if she rejected him for any reason.

But he was past fighting the battle. He'd fought his attraction to her once before, and the price had been heavy for both of them. This time only she could stop him. He sure as hell wasn't going to stop himself.

His groin felt heavy. He had already stiffened inside his jeans and couldn't wait to shed their confinement. There was only one place his manhood wanted to be now, and that was buried in Nora's warm depths.

He had to fight down the deafening drumbeat inside his own head, get a rein on the desire that pulsed through him, so heavy and demanding. Had to find some shred of control over the ache that wanted to turn him mindless in its search for satisfaction.

He wanted this to be perfect for her, but damned if he

knew how to accomplish that. It was a sorry thing for a man of thirty to admit he'd had only one lover in his life: his ex-wife. But in a place this small, scattering wild oats could be dangerous, and there weren't a lot of opportunities.

Nor had he really wanted them. Beth had burned him badly. Climbing these stairs with another woman, especially one he had already hurt, might well be the act of a supreme fool.

But need drove him. Every rational thought he tried to summon got washed away in the growing tide of hunger.

He ached. He nearly trembled with anticipation and thirst for this woman's body, for their union.

Common sense played no part in this. He felt the same kind of anticipation he'd felt his first time, perhaps more so because he knew some of the pleasures he would find.

He felt as randy as an eighteen-year-old in the backseat on a warm summer night. And as nervously hopeful. Would she let him? Just this one touch? Just this one pass at fondling her breast? Would she slap him down?

God, it would have been funny if he weren't so driven.

But he remembered her allowing him to kiss her from head to foot essentially, standing there shivering. He wondered if she had even realized how badly she had been shaking when he'd started showing her that her scars didn't repel him. They angered him, but he felt no repulsion at all.

When they reached his room, he was careful not to put her anywhere near the mirror. He didn't want her to see herself again for fear that not even his earlier actions had been reassuring enough.

He cupped her face in his hands as she stood by the bed until she opened her eyes sleepily. "You're sure?"

He hated to ask that question, didn't want to ask anything at all, just act, but he owed them both this.

"Yes," she breathed. "Oh, yes."

Then she astonished him, reaching up to twine her arms around his neck and lean into him. The feel of her pressed to him hit him hard with strengthening need. "God," he muttered, "I want you so bad I'm going to rush my fences."

A sound that was almost a purr escaped her. "I like that." Her voice hitched as her breaths grew shorter.

He was almost panting like a runner at the end of a race, and this had barely started. He was sure in a blinding instant that he had never wanted Beth the way he wanted this woman. Never.

God, he'd been a damned fool.

Then astonishment nearly froze him. Quiet, restrained, fearful Nora began to tug at the buttons on his flannel shirt. If ever life had given him a green light, this was it.

Filled with impatience, encouraged, he swept her hands aside and yanked the shirt over his head. He watched her face for clues, but all he saw was the faintest of smiles around her mouth, as if he had just pleased her. Then she pressed her palms to him.

"You feel so good," she whispered.

He forced himself to remain mostly still as her small hands ran over him, tracing contours of muscles all the way to the tops of his jeans. His blood pounded, his body ached in every single cell.

But he didn't want to scare her, so while she petted his chest, he reached for the snap on his jeans and tugged the zipper down slowly.

Her smile widened a shade and she looked down. "Fair's fair," she said, and grabbed his waistband to tug it downward.

His shaft sprang free, ready and hard. A quiet sound escaped her, then she wrapped her hand around him and squeezed.

"Oh, sweetie…" It was all over then. He kicked away his jeans as quickly as he could, loving the way her hands kept reaching for him as if she didn't want to break contact for even a moment. He felt her light touches on his back, his butt, his staff, everywhere she could find.

Then he turned to her and reached for her clothing. Damn clothes anyway. Who the hell had invented them?

She was as eager as he was this time, pulling her own shirt and pants away along with them.

Until finally, finally, after what felt like an eternity but could only have been a couple of minutes, they stood naked, facing one another.

"You're beautiful," she said huskily, still smiling. "The most beautiful man I've ever seen."

Not as beautiful as her, but he was in no mood to have a conversation. Nor, apparently, was she. She leaned forward, found one of his small hard nipples and drew it into her mouth.

She taught him something he'd never known about himself before when she did that. A torch seemed to light every nerve ending between his nipple and his groin. He groaned and pulled her closer, only dimly thinking that somehow they had gotten this backward. He was supposed to…

Enough thinking. He gave himself up to sensation and tried to give her the same feelings in return.

Her breasts were full, and he filled his hands with them. Apparently the nerves hadn't been damaged, because when he brushed his thumbs over her pebbling nipples, she arched away from him with a cry, almost as if offering herself for more.

The ability to stand was escaping him. In one swift movement he carried them both down onto the bed, half covering her body with his, tangling legs with her, finding every possible place to kiss and touch. He paused only once, to roll on a condom. His last sane thought.

He claimed her mouth again, but only briefly. This time when he kissed her breasts, it wasn't on the scars. He sucked her nipples deep into his mouth, reveling in her groans, in the way her hips tried to buck.

Sliding his fingers down while his mouth continued to torment her, he slid his hand between her legs and parted her moist petals.

She cried out and her whole body seemed to reach up for that touch. Over and over he stroked that most delicate of places until she was calling his name on nearly every breath.

He loved it. But his own body was refusing to wait. When her legs parted of their own accord, he took the invitation.

He levered himself over her, watching her face, and forced himself to move slowly, sliding into her warm, hot depths.

Coming home. It felt like coming home. Rocking into her, he lost himself completely. The explosion built and built, like igniting the rockets on a missile before takeoff. Then, with a final shuddering cry, he exploded into her.

Nora felt completion take him, and it was as if it were the last push she needed to tumble over the cliff edge herself. His paroxysms started her own, she was dimly aware of her cry joining his, then the Fourth of July seemed to happen inside her head, exploding with multicolored lights and sparklers as her body shuddered to completion. As the ache changed from compulsion to satisfied need.

Reaching up, she hung on to his shoulders, never wanting these moments to end. Never.

Then he astonished her by moving again, and a minute

later she once more toppled over the pinnacle into a pleasure so piercing she could hardly believe it.

He pulled blankets over them. He wrapped her in his
body. He held her and for a little while she wondered if
she'd lost consciousness. With her head pillowed on his
shoulder, she was sure she never wanted to move again.

She felt a sprinkling of kisses on her forehead but didn't
even open her eyes. She responded by tightening her arm
around him, spreading her palm against his back, drinking in the wonder of being free to touch him so openly,
the wonder of skin against skin.

Right then life seemed like a beautiful gift, more beautiful than she could ever have imagined it to be. She would
have lived in that moment forever, frozen in amber, if it
were possible.

"Wow," he whispered. "Just wow."

"Me, too," she answered quietly.

He surprised her with a laugh, a truly happy sound,
and squeezed her even tighter. "You're a firecracker, Nora
Loftis. Amazing."

"So are you. I never dreamed…" She left the thought
incomplete. He could probably finish it himself, and right
now talking seemed like an awful lot of effort.

Besides, talking might shatter the spell.

But spells don't last forever. The keening of the wind
reached her again, trying to stir the memories she wished
she could bury forever.

Almost as if he sensed the change in the mood, he left
her. She wanted to protest, but as reality returned, her courage seemed to be fleeing ahead of it. She heard him turn
on the shower and figured he'd be a while.

But then he amazed her by coming back, scooping her
out of bed and, with his arm around her waist, leading

her to the bathroom. He tugged her under the hot spray, reached for a bar of soap and began to wash her in slow, lazy, erotic strokes. He spared no part of her, to her astonishment, and seemed to be enjoying himself thoroughly.

She learned how fast desire could return. Learned that she had some sexual gumption after all, because after he had finished lathering her, she grabbed the bar of soap, treating him to the same delight, washing both his front and back until she was thrilled to see him hardening again.

A sense of power filled her, unlike anything she had ever known.

"Woman, you're going to bring me to my knees."

"I rather like that idea."

"So I gather." But he laughed.

Toweling off proved to be an equally erotic experience. Instead of silky touches, these were rougher, but just as exciting. Her skin glowed, and soon his did, too.

She expected to tumble back into bed with him, wet hair and all, but he helped her wrap a towel around her head, then went in search of one of her nightgowns.

A momentary disappointment filled her, but as he helped her into her sensible flannel nightdress, pulled slippers onto her feet and then donned his own bathrobe, she quickly realized this night wasn't over.

The anticipation would be allowed to build again. There was more to come, and absolutely no rush. How absolutely delightful.

Chapter 12

By morning Nora felt more sated than she could have believed possible. She ached pleasantly, and not even the sleep they had snatched during the night was enough to bring reality back into clear, hard focus.

Her mind was awhirl with a new set of memories and experiences that it wanted to play and replay as if she could ensure she would never forget a single instant of her night with Jake.

She stirred reluctantly only when she could hear him moving around downstairs.

Her skin tingled with new awareness, even of the brush of her clothing against her skin. Her mind brimmed with things that made her want to smile or sigh happily. Her body, sated though it felt, was already awakening to a day of new possibilities.

When had she last felt this way?

Never.

The whiteout still raged outside, giving her assurance that she needn't think about other things again, not yet. The vacation from her fears alone should have been enough, but now she had a whole new stockpile of things to think about, good things, memories to savor like fine wine.

Even as she began to make her way downstairs, she promised herself that she would treasure the night they had shared and not let it hurt if that was the end of it.

He had given her a great gift. More than one, actually. She must not let disappointment mar it.

To her surprise, he was cooking. He stood at the stove in jeans and stocking feet, a fresh flannel shirt hanging unbuttoned, as he made eggs and bacon.

"Where's Rosa?" she asked.

He looked around. "Well, there went my plan to bring you breakfast in bed."

She blushed faintly. "Sorry."

"That's okay. It'll taste just as good down here. As for Rosa, I called and told her to stay home. She could get lost just between here and the bunkhouse. Al and I have some work this morning, though."

"In *this?*"

"Animals must be cared for."

"But you guys could get lost, too."

He shook his head. "We'll use safety lines and work together. Want some coffee?"

Of course she did. She slid into a chair at the table while he brought her a mug. "Thank you."

"The pleasure is all mine." His warm gaze seemed to embrace her and promise more delight to come.

"I'm surprised this whiteout hasn't let up at all."

"Sometimes they blow for a while. Not uncommon, as I'm sure you remember."

"I lived in town. I heard about them more than I saw them."

"True." He slid some eggs onto plates, added toast and bacon, then carried them to the table. "Out here we're used to it for a few hours at a time. It's not unusual. One that lasts as long as this, though, might happen only a couple of times a winter."

He paused to pour two glasses of orange juice, then joined her.

He raised his glass in a toast. "To a gorgeous woman, on a perfect morning after an even more perfect night."

She felt color flood her cheeks and he laughed.

"I love that you can still blush," he said. "It's pretty, and it gives me a kick. You're special."

Then he started eating as if he hadn't just almost knocked the wind from her with his compliments.

Oddly, the things he said reminded her of Beth, his ex-wife. She had known Beth in high school, mostly from afar since she had been hanging on the fringes and no one had really ever wanted to get close to her.

But she remembered her impression of Beth, a very pretty blonde who had always struck her as slightly phony, as if she were playing life for an audience. She had often told herself not to be so unkind, and had blamed her reactions on the fact that Beth was dating Jake. But now she wondered.

"What ever happened to Beth?" she asked. "Is she still around?"

"She left before our divorce was final. She hasn't been back except to visit her parents every year."

"Where did she go?"

"She went to stay with cousins in Denver, met some guy and I hear they live in Dallas now. Plenty more to do there."

"Lots more," she agreed noncommittally. None of her

business really, and she had no right to say anything. But she wondered why Beth had married Jake if she wasn't going to be happy as a rancher's wife. Of course, how many people that age really had even a remote idea what they wanted for the rest of their days? Not many. And Beth, as she recalled, had lived in town, the child of two teachers. She might have had no idea what it would be like out here for weeks on end, especially in the winter.

Certainly Nora wouldn't have. Probably still didn't have the faintest idea even after several weeks.

But the difference was that isolation had been part of Nora's upbringing. She was used to being left to her own devices. Something of an introvert by nature. She enjoyed having a few friends, but too much socializing wore her out. She needed her quiet time to follow her own pursuits and interests. Recharge time, she thought of it, and that wasn't unusual for an introvert. It wasn't that she didn't like people, it was that she needed a certain amount of downtime. Still. Even after the years at college and working as a psychologist. It balanced her.

Beth, as she recalled, had never been without a coterie of friends, or Jake at her side. An extrovert. She needed the people, needed constant company.

"She wasn't the right type of person to live on a ranch." The words were out before she could stop them.

He looked up questioningly. "Psychological evaluation?"

"I didn't know her well enough to say that professionally. But I was just thinking back. She's the kind of person who was never alone. Life out here would be hard for her, for any extrovert."

"I wish someone had told me that before it was too late."

"Or that she had realized what she was getting into. But

most of us aren't that self-aware, especially when we're young and changing so much day-to-day."

"I certainly wasn't," he admitted. "So when do we stop growing up?"

At that, a laugh escaped her, and she felt her cheeks stretch with a smile. "Never. I felt so grown-up when I got my first job and apartment. Now I'm thirty and I can say I'm not finished growing up."

"Maybe not in some ways. In others, I'm sure you're quite the adult."

Color filled her cheeks again as memories from last night surged to the forefront of her thoughts.

His smile seemed freighted with pleasure and promise before he resumed eating.

She offered to do the washing up while he and Al went to check on animals. After he phoned Al and then stepped through the back door out into the hell of winter gone wild, she stared for a few minutes, hoping the two of them would be safe. She doubted either of them would be able to see more than a few feet in any direction. It just didn't seem safe to be out there at all.

The chill crept through the glass on the door and she shivered a little, thinking how much colder the wind must be making it out there.

Then she turned to washing the dishes. She hoped she did a good enough job for Rosa, who seemed to be something of a perfectionist.

But the time alone was good, too. She hadn't had as much of it as she was used to. Then she remembered she was supposed to be at the library today. She guessed Emma wouldn't be expecting her, but making a courtesy call seemed like the decent thing to do anyway.

"Of course you're not coming in," Emma answered. "Gage wouldn't even let me open the library, it's that bad."

"Then how did I reach you?"

"Call forwarding," Emma said, a smile in her voice. "A bit of extravagance I insisted on. Look, the schools shut down today. A lot of businesses aren't bothering to open. If you lived in town, you could get to the grocery for milk in a pinch, but that's about it. Safety first. Enjoy it, Nora. Give yourself a snow day. Remember when we used to love them?"

Nora never had, she thought as she hung up. Snow days for her had just meant extra hours working for her father at the pharmacy on the grounds that some of his employees would fail to show.

This was different. A whole day free. A vacation.

With Jake.

The idea that everything in town was pretty much shut down, too, added to the feeling of security generated by the whiteout. Nothing would be moving. The creep couldn't reach her, probably couldn't travel even a short distance to get to town, or if he were there, to leave it.

But after a couple of hours she was beginning to worry about something else: Jake. And Al. They'd been out there in this for what seemed an awfully long time, and she had no idea how she would know if they might be in trouble.

Rosa would know, she decided. Rosa must have been through this before, and would call if she suspected a problem.

That didn't prevent Nora's nerves from stretching as minutes continued to tick by. Nor did the keening of the wind help at all. Dark memories of that night began to hover around the edges of her mind. She tried to push them back with reminders of the night she had just spent with Jake, but their power was such that they remained hovering, like hawks ready to strike.

She paced the house, wrapping her arms around herself, becoming increasingly anxious. Snow day? Vacation? Hah!

But at long last, just as she was beginning to feel as if she could crawl out of her skin, she heard the back door open. She hurried to the kitchen and saw Jake, looking like a snowman, step inside the mudroom and begin shaking off, stomping his boots clear of snow.

"I was beginning to worry," she admitted.

"I'm sorry. It took longer than I expected. It's wild out there, and we kept having to huddle in wind breaks of our own to keep from getting too cold." He shucked his jacket, kicked off his boots then grabbed a handy mop to clean up what he could.

Moments later he stepped into the kitchen and pulled her into his arms. She could feel the chill on him as she returned the hug and accepted a quick kiss.

"Coffee," she said, pulling away with difficulty. "You need to warm up."

"I'll make it. I need to keep moving until I can feel my fingers and toes again."

"That's not good," she remarked, managing to keep the scold out of her voice.

"No, it's not," he agreed. "But animals first. And I'm getting hungry again. Could you eat, just a sandwich or something?"

"Let me make it for you. I need to do something other than pace and worry."

He paused after filling the drip coffeemaker with water. "Worry?" His eyes tightened a bit. "I really *am* sorry."

"You were doing what you needed to. I just had no idea how I'd ever know if you needed help."

"My fault. Rosa would know when to send out a flare. I didn't think about telling you. I should have."

She couldn't settle yet, so she waited while the coffee

brewed, watching him flex his fingers and rise up repeatedly on his toes, encouraging the return of circulation.

"I talked to Emma," she said finally. "I guess most of town is shut down."

"Yeah. It's bad, and nobody's moving. Not so bad there, I imagine. You must remember."

"I remember working at the pharmacy because so many employees couldn't make it in."

"No snow days for you, huh?"

She didn't answer directly. "How many did you actually get? Look at you now."

"Well, when I was younger, but yeah. Once I got big enough to be a decent help around here, I didn't get them, either."

"So it was ordinary. Nothing to feel bad about."

"Not for me. Of course, I didn't have to work with your father."

That at last elicited a laugh from her, and the laugh eased the remaining tension.

He stopped bouncing as he began to feel warmer. She went to the refrigerator and found cold cuts, mayonnaise, lettuce. A loaf of homemade bread was waiting to be cut in the bread box.

"Wow, Rosa makes bread, too?"

"Nearly every day. Al and I put it away like there's no tomorrow."

She made the sandwiches quickly, two thick ones for him, a half one for herself. It hadn't been that long since breakfast and she wasn't hungry, but she hadn't been out in the cold working for a couple of hours.

"I wish I could help out more around here," she remarked as they ate. "I feel like baggage most of the time."

"But you have a job."

"I'm not really contributing here, though. I want to

know more about how this place works, and find things I can do to help. Rosa obviously has the house, but there must be things I can help with."

"You were exercising the horses," he reminded her. "My mom used to do that. If you want to get into it, I can teach you how to train them, and we might be able to expand their numbers again. She had quite a nice little business going for herself, training saddle horses and selling them. But it's a lot more work than the training. She took care of them, too."

"Is that why you only have a few now?"

"There's only so much a guy can do. What she was doing took a lot of her day."

She thought about it and decided she would like working with the horses in bigger ways. Even the caring-for-them part. "Okay. After this other thing is over, if you don't want to see the last of me, I'd like to give it a try."

"See the last of you?" He caught on that, his gaze growing troubled. "Don't think that, Nora. Please."

She looked down, feeling oddly embarrassed and touched at the same time. "Okay," she said in a smothered voice.

Just then the wind howled like a banshee and snow rattled against the glass. It was different, but not different enough, and in an instant the nightmare came crashing back.

"He's coming," she whispered. It was as if she could feel his approach in her very bones.

Jake pushed back from the table. He seemed to be developing a habit of scooping her up into his arms. He did, then, and carried her to the living room, once again settling with her on his lap, wrapping her in the protective circle of his arms.

"Shh," he whispered, kissing her head, her face, anything he could reach. "We don't know that. But even if he is, everyone is watching for him."

Pointless argument. Sooner or later she would become an easy target again. He'd find a way. "If he gets me," she whispered, "I don't want to live."

"Nora!"

"I'm serious," she said tautly. "I can't survive that again. I *can't!*"

He tightened his hold on her but didn't offer any false platitudes. Once had been enough, and despite how much she had forgotten of the torture she had suffered at that man's hands, she remembered enough, and enough about her lengthy recovery. She couldn't do it again. Hell, she still wasn't over the first attack.

"He'll have to get through me."

"You won't always be there."

"If you want, I'll staple myself to your side until he's caught."

It was such a generous offer, and even in the midst of her terror, swamped by the dark memories, she felt selfish.

"You can't do that. It wouldn't be fair."

"What wouldn't be fair is something happening to you. And I wouldn't be able to live with the feeling I didn't do enough to stop it. Anything. So we're joined at the hip from here on out."

It took a while, but steadily she battled her way out of the horror and landed once again in the present, wrapped in Jake's arms, reassured by his strength, thinking that she could spend the rest of her life on his lap just like this, and then maybe she'd always feel safe.

But reality was reality. That man was on the loose, she had no doubt he would come and Jake couldn't possibly spend every minute playing her bodyguard. She didn't say so; she didn't want to make him feel bad. But it was the truth. She gathered as much courage as she could muster and acccptcd that she might well have to face the creep again. Alone. With only her own wits and skills to help her.

It was not a comforting thought, but a seed of determination, growing for the past few weeks as Jake had taught her self-defense, had given her a new reason to live, grew stronger now. She would survive. She *had* to.

"You never told me," he said after a bit, "what you were thinking at the office that seemed to get you down so much."

"Psychobabble," she said finally.

"What?"

"Oh, I think I told you I only remember snatches of the attack. A mercy, I guess. But I got to wondering if my interpretation of the creep might be affected by my father. He was never one to put up with defiance, either. So maybe I was misinterpreting his motives. Maybe he doesn't care that I survived. Maybe I'm scared for no reason. After all, his wife is still alive."

"And in a coma," he pointed out.

"Still?"

"Still."

"God." She shook her head. "I knew her. She was a nice woman, a good mother. She didn't deserve that."

"Neither did you. Bottom line, nobody deserves that."

The tension had begun to seep out of her muscles and at last she relaxed against him. "You must be so tired of my fears and moods."

"Hardly."

"Well, I am."

"With a lot more reason, I guess." He paused. "The wind sets you off, doesn't it?"

"Yeah."

"Well, all I can suggest is you listen to it now while

you're safe. To me it makes a cozy sound. I'm inside, warm and safe, and with you. It doesn't get much better."

A valid point. With effort, instead of trying to tune out the sound, she forced herself to pay attention to it and try to knit it into her current experience with Jake.

It wasn't easy. Paying attention to it brought the memories bubbling up again, but she battled them back, forcing herself to stay in the present. It stood among the hardest things she had ever done. It might even take months or years to achieve what he was suggesting.

But she had learned about desensitization during her education, and accepted the rightness of his suggestion. She needed to become desensitized to the wind, and there could be no better place than where she was right now.

And no better way than to not only feel safe but to feel again the slow, almost springlike emergence of desire once again.

Jake felt her relaxing, but he wasn't quite ready to, himself, yet. What she had said about not being able to endure another attack, about preferring to die, had struck him right in his heart and gut.

He guessed she had plenty of reason. He'd seen the scars, and he could still only barely imagine the depths of her suffering, horror and fear. For years to come this would haunt her, and his easy solution of trying to unite the sound of the wind to being safe in his arms right now seemed like a paltry offering.

But he hadn't been kidding. He was going to find a way not to let her out of his sight. He couldn't quite figure out how, given he had work to do, but he was going to find a way. Even if it meant tasking one of his officers to stay with her if he needed to be away.

He couldn't be 100 percent certain that Langdon would come for her, but he wasn't willing to risk being wrong about that. She, of all people, despite her memory blanks, probably had the best measure of that man of anyone on the planet. Even the judge hadn't taken Langdon's measure well enough to keep him in a cell, but had granted him bail.

This whole situation suggested that Langdon was an emerging serial killer, driven by impulses that sooner or later took control of him. The attack on his wife meant nothing if he removed that context.

The man would keep repeating his attempted murders. Sooner or later he would succeed. In Jake's mind it seemed clear that the compulsion would keep driving Langdon until he was stopped for good.

Unfortunately, Nora might be right: he might still be after her, wanting to complete the job. Whether it had to do with feeling she had defied him by surviving seemed the least of it to Jake. No, what mattered was Langdon's failure to fulfill his sick compulsion.

He could, of course, hunt another woman. But since his wife there had been no more reports of attacks. So it seemed likely he was going to take care of Nora, perfect his method and madness then move on to a new victim.

Jake could understand people getting mad beyond all reason and reacting violently. He understood how most people could kill in the right circumstances. What he would never understand was a mind that stalked and hunted victims for the sheer pleasure of it.

But from what little he'd read in the police and medical reports, probably far more than Nora remembered, at least in the medical descriptions of her injuries, he perceived that this guy got pleasure from what he did.

The most dangerous killer of all.

* * *

Gradually Nora felt her reaction to the sound of the wind changing. Maybe because it wasn't exactly what she had heard in the woods that night as she had made her desperate crawl toward the road. Maybe because Jake's hold was so comforting.

Regardless, the memories were fading away, and her awareness of the present intensified. Desire, at first a mere seedling, had begun to grow. She wanted him again, and she wanted him now. She wondered if he felt the same, then realized there was only one way she could find out.

Taking every ounce of courage into her hands, she murmured, "I want to make love with you."

"I thought you'd never ask."

She had sensed a somberness in him, but that vanished instantly.

"I was hoping you'd ask," he added.

"Then why didn't you say something?"

"Because," he said wryly, "sometimes a guy likes to be asked, too. Because I wanted it to be your idea. It feels good."

She got that instantly. She tilted her head back and smiled at him. "What are we waiting for?"

"You to get off my lap so I can chase you upstairs."

That was exactly what happened. She slid off his lap, and soon was giggling as he chased her up the stairs, his laugh following her.

There was little finesse as they pulled at each other's clothing, but a lot of laughs and smiles. A wholly different mood than before. No caution, no surprises, just an eagerness and sense of freedom as if she had cut loose from the darkness that haunted her days.

Such a short time ago she had believed she would never

have the guts to let a man see her naked body, or even the desire to, but look at her now.

They tumbled onto the bed, happiness still enveloping them along with the rising scents and heat of desire.

She could smell it. She had smelled it last night, but today she knew what that musky scent was, and it enhanced her pleasure. Life, she was sure, didn't get much better than this, and to think she had waited all these years to learn that.

But Jake was in no hurry despite their eagerness. He lingered over her breasts, driving her nearly insane as he licked and sucked her nipples until they engorged so much even the whisper of the air felt sensual, until they ached with their fullness. He trailed kisses all over her, much as when he had dealt with her scars, but he didn't just attend to her scars this time. And when he parted her legs...

Shock shot through her as he kissed her there. She wasn't a complete innocent, but it was an utterly new experience for her to feel his fingers stroke and part her petals, and then his tongue start flicking the nub of nerves. The first few touches were almost painful in their intensity, but after a few of them the pleasure overrode everything else.

When at last he nipped her gently, she thought she was flying to the moon.

Desperate now, she tugged at him. He didn't argue, broke away just long enough to get a condom and then he slid up and over her, filling her with himself in a way that answered a deep craving, filling a place that had never felt filled before.

He didn't move in her, though. Not immediately. He kissed her and teased her breasts some more, even as her hands clutched at him and stroked whatever she could reach.

Then a wicked impulse seized her, and she pinched his

nipples gently. Encouraged by the groan that drew out of him, she pinched a little harder.

"Witch," he muttered, and at last began to rock into her, meeting her rising hips with his own plunges. He slipped one of his hands beneath her rump, holding her steady for him, controlling the movements of her hips just enough to draw the minutes out.

It was as if he was determined to wring every last drop of pleasure from their union. Aflame with desire, nearly out of her mind, Nora forgot everything except Jake and the blaze he was building in her.

Nothing else mattered. Nothing. She could have died a happy woman right then.

But she didn't die. She exploded finally in a cascade of completion that ripped through her entire body. Lights sparked behind her eyelids. Her brain seemed to freeze in ecstasy.

A few moments later, he jerked and groaned, following her to heaven.

Later she lay on top of him, beneath the blankets, reveling in the close contact. He held her, running his hands gently over her back and buttocks. Their breathing had calmed, the perspiration had dried and now she began to inch downward over him, learning his body the way he had already learned hers. She listened to his sighs, to his quiet moans, felt the way his muscles tightened then relaxed at each touch.

She liked being able to make him respond the way he did to her. It made her feel good, but also gave her such a sense of power. Jake, trembling at *her* touches. An old dream revived, and so much better than the dream had every been.

Finally he laughed and rolled her over. "I'm going to need a warmer room if you want to keep exploring."

She smiled from the corner of her eye. "You don't mind?"

"I'm loving it." As if to prove it, he threw the blanket back and revealed his full glory to her hungry gaze.

But it was chilly. As if the wind had sucked the heat from the house despite the heater that pumped almost continuously.

She gazed on him, feeling her own insides clench with pleasure, even as goose bumps started rising on her own skin.

"Too cold," he said, and pulled the blanket back up, cocooning them. "Just you wait until the weather improves."

A promise? She hoped so as he drew against him again. He was a heater himself, rapidly filling their little cocoon with his warmth, easing the chill on her skin.

Tucked away in her memory now, though, was Jake's well-muscled, perfect body, offered to her until the cold intervened. She liked what she had seen and promised herself that one time soon she was going to explore every inch of that territory. Learn it. Memorize it.

It was only then that she realized the keening wind no longer made her edgy. It simply made her snuggle closer. Another demon had been defeated.

Smiling, she pressed her face into Jake's shoulder. She just wished that creep wasn't still out there.

The wind had eased. Langdon stood at the motel window, watching snow whip across the street out front, but it wasn't rising very high into the air any longer. He could see the businesses across the way, and the night sky was no longer gray and yellow with reflected light. It looked black and cold.

He turned on the small TV on the rickety stand and found some weather reporting. The worst conditions were over; tomorrow promised to be sunny and calm.

Smiling to himself, he decided he'd leave before dawn. He might make it all the way to Conard County tomorrow, and then all he'd have to do was locate Nora and get her at the right time.

Just the thought of getting his hands on her again was enough to make him harden and nearly salivate.

But first things first. He needed a meal since he'd slept a lot of the day, and a stroll in the cold to clear his head. Then, later, when the last of the locals were safely tucked in, he'd change his plate with a truck similar to the one he was driving. There was one that had spent the past few days in the motel parking lot. Best to get that plate before the owner decided to move on, too, with the improving weather.

Another day. Then maybe a day to find the woman and figure out his plan. Soon.

Then he'd be off on his grand adventure.

He had to struggle a bit with the compulsion to start out right now, but he won. He was still in control.

For some reason that made him feel very, very good.

Chapter 13

The light of morning was harsh, almost blinding, bouncing off the snow and shattering into a thousand colors. Grass still poked up, uncovered as yet, but the blades looked brown and lost amidst the sparkling white scattered everywhere.

Without the wind, the day felt warmer. The horses seemed delighted as Nora led them from their stalls and into the corral. They nosed around at the ground, but then made their way to the troughs full of hay. Even though they'd had food all along, being outside seemed to enhance their appetites.

She returned to the barn and made a stab at helping Jake and Al muck out their stalls. Rosa's breakfast was still warm in her belly, and the activity made her feel good.

Even though last night had been anything but inactive. She smiled inwardly, thinking of all the fresh memories she now possessed of Jake. She wished the whiteout had lasted longer, that she could claim just one more day alone with him.

But it was not to be. He had to work, and so did she. Real life had returned. She tried hard not to think about the parts of it that would upset her and focus instead on the fact that she liked the archival work Emma had given her. She'd have fun today, just a different kind of fun.

It struck her then that she was enjoying herself for the first time since the attack, and doing so without any hindrance. If that guy were just behind bars again, she was certain she'd be able to throw her arms wide and embrace all of life with joy.

She just hoped that wasn't only because of Jake, because he sure hadn't promised anything. Not really. A few references to the future, but casual ones that could be meaningless.

Tucked away inside her, the memory of his rejection all those years ago remained. She couldn't believe that it would be different now, even after what they had shared.

Maybe that was for the best, she thought. Could she really trust that she wasn't just feeling dependency? Enjoying the escape he offered? What if the blossoming, deep feelings she was experiencing turned out to be illusory?

At this point she couldn't tell.

What's more, she decided not to worry about it. She had enough to deal with now that the cover of the storm had passed. That creep could be moving closer again. And nothing, absolutely nothing, had changed her mind about whether he would pursue her. He was sick. Of that she was sure, and sick people who felt compulsions were rarely rational when it came to their compulsions.

Her view of him was shifting as she thought more about him and about what Jake had theorized, but none of it suggested that the creep was just going to head for the border and never be seen again.

Something about him going after his own wife was like a red flag in her head. She couldn't quite put her finger on why, but it seemed to bear out her feeling that he wouldn't give up on her. Maybe because the attack on his wife indicated that he no longer cared whether anyone knew what he did.

He had, after all, been found out. She had survived and had been able to help identify him. She had made it out of those woods when he was absolutely convinced it would be years before anyone came across her scattered bones.

So he had nothing to hide anymore. Only scores to settle. And she figured she still loomed large on his score sheet.

The weight of those feelings settled over her as she and Jake drove toward town on what should have been an absolutely gorgeous early winter day. The feeling of dread weighed on her even though he held her hand nearly the whole way.

It weighed on her even more when they reached the library.

"I have to go in to the office," he said. "I can take you with me or leave you here with Miss Emma. Your choice. But if I leave you here, I'm going to make sure one of my men is outside."

"I can't be following you everywhere like a lost lamb," she said, even though it was hard. At some point she had to face up to this. She couldn't remain a prisoner of her fears or be dependent on Jake every single moment of the day.

"You can," he said firmly. "These circumstances are unusual. I promised I'd staple myself to your side and I meant it."

It took every bit of her courage and determination to

shake her head. She didn't want to be away from Jake at all, for plenty of reasons that had nothing to do with safety. But she reminded herself, too, of her determination to take back at least some of her life. Letting the nightmare take charge wouldn't change a thing, but would leave her living only half a life.

"I'll be fine. I'm sure your officer can guard me as well as you."

"Hey," he said, sounding as if he were trying to joke. "I'm the best!" But the tension at the edges of his eyes gave lie to the humor.

"I know you are." She meant it.

He half smiled and leaned over to kiss her. "I'll watch while you get inside. Then I'm not budging until one of my men gets here, okay?"

"Okay."

Opening the car door was hard, but she did it, squaring her shoulders and marching up the recently shoveled path and salt-scattered steps. When the door closed behind her, the library's familiar silence and scents closed around her.

Safety was here. It had been here her entire life. She just hoped nothing wrecked it.

Jake made sure Ben Clews fully understood the importance of keeping an eye on Nora. Ben got it.

"I heard. We're all watching, remember, Chief?"

"I remember. I just don't want anyone to get careless or distracted. I'll be back as soon as I can to take over."

Then he headed for the office and hunted up Gage. "Anything?"

Gage shook his head. "It's like the guy vanished."

"Easy enough to do."

"Don't I know it. It's a big country. We don't usually

find them until they slip up or slow down for too long somewhere. Damn needles in haystacks."

"Anything more from Fred Loftis?"

"Should I be worried? The guy seems to have settled back for the time being. Of course, the weather hasn't encouraged any hijinks from any direction."

"I hope things don't start emerging from the woodwork today." He paused. "Or maybe I do. This waiting is killing Nora, and I'm ready to wrap my hands around any handy throat."

"I know that feeling," Gage said. "I know it well. Unfortunately…" He shook his head.

Jake got it. He just wished he knew how much more of this agonizing wait Nora was going to have to endure. What if the guy did head for the hills and never came? How long would this go on for her? Would she ever be able to move past it?

That concern settled in his chest like lead. She needed some kind of resolution, and while the thought that Langdon might get near her again chilled his very blood, especially after the scars he had seen on her, he knew that this had to be settled somehow so she could move on. Five years down the road, he didn't want her to still be looking over her shoulder, wondering.

But all they had to go on was Nora's conviction that Langdon couldn't let it go. He both feared and hoped she was right. Talk about the horns of a dilemma, he thought as he went to his office to scan messages and scheduling. Then he marked himself off for the next two days, hoping nothing would happen to change it, and went back to the library in his private vehicle.

He hated stakeouts, but that was basically what he was going to be doing until whenever.

It had been a month now. If Langdon was coming at

all, he must be getting closer by now. More and more convinced that everyone would believe he'd skipped the country. That they'd be growing more and more inattentive.

Well, Jake wasn't going to let down his guard. Not for a good, long time to come.

Nora had vanished into a diary written by one of the county's earliest pioneer women. Growing pain and approaching madness seemed to be oozing from the pages as the lonely woman wrote about the wind. The ceaseless wind. Nora's heart began to gallop.

It is almost all I hear, the woman wrote. *The children and the wind, and the wind has the worst voice of all. It sounds like a call from beyond the grave. It blows endlessly, dust settles over everything and I do not care anymore. When I step outside, it is even worse.*

The wind has a voice, and it cries in loneliness and pain. It calls to me until I put my hands over my ears. If only it would calm for a few days, if only it didn't pound me every time I step out, grabbing at my hair and clothing. It nearly whipped my skirt into the fire as I was making soap....

It is alive, this wind, and it is the voice of a demon.

"Nora?"

Startled, she jumped and looked up. Emma was standing in the doorway. The librarian evinced immediate concern.

"Is something wrong?"

"No...no. It's just this diary. This woman writes with such pain."

"Enough for today," Emma said. "Even if you don't need to quit, and I think you do, Jake has been sitting outside patiently all this time. I think he needs lunch, so why don't you go make sure he gets it? I'll see you tomorrow."

The argument about Jake needing lunch was all that could pull Nora away from this woman's story. She put the fragile diary aside, determined to continue with it the next day even though she suspected that might not be wise.

The demon wind. Nora could almost hear it. Had heard it that cold, terrifying night. It had tried to snatch the life from her as she had crawled weakly over twigs and rocks, cold, so cold. She felt that woman's suffering reaching out to her across the centuries.

The day had clouded over while she'd been buried in the past. The wind was gone, though, at least here in town, and after reading that diary, she was especially grateful. It had carried her to uncomfortable places, to a different kind of suffering, but suffering nonetheless. She wished she could reach back over time and offer that poor woman some solace.

"Lunch?" Jake asked as they pulled away from the library.

"Absolutely," she agreed, although she didn't feel very hungry right now. But Emma was right. Jake had been sitting out here patiently watching over her, and he certainly needed something to eat by now. A glance at her watch told her it was already past one.

"Is Maude's okay?"

"Is there another place?" She tried to sound light.

"Home," he said quietly.

"No, that's a long drive. You need some food. Maude's is fine." She'd even have agreed to the truck stop, although she wasn't sure she'd feel as comfortable there with so many strangers pulling in and out. At least at Maude's she'd recognize most of the faces, even if they weren't as familiar as they'd once been.

Maude's, however, was all but empty. A couple of older men had a table where they were drinking coffee and talking about football. Jake guided her to a corner booth, and then the fun began.

"Still too thin," Maude said, looking her over. "Gotta fatten you up some."

"I can't eat a whole lot at one time," Nora said.

"Well, I ain't getting you no salad. Eat what you can."

Nora mentally threw up her hands. If she'd wanted to choose for herself, she should have chosen the truck stop.

Jake picked up on her reaction. "We don't have to eat here," he said quietly as Maude stomped off to get coffee and God-knew-what to feed her.

"It's okay. Like she said, I'll eat what I can."

He waited quietly until they were both served, he with a steak sandwich and a heap of fries, she with a grilled chicken breast, a fresh roll and some broccoli. So Maude did make healthy food when pressed. She needed to remember that.

"So what's going on?" Jake asked quietly. "You came out of the library looking disturbed."

"I was reading a diary." Talking more about it left her feeling uneasy. She had enough hang-ups these days to qualify for some heavy-duty therapy. Did she want to convince Jake she was totally nuts?

"A diary? About what?"

"One of the first women to settle here. She was awfully lonely and the wind bothered her, too." Then she just said it straight out. "She said the wind was a demon."

"I can see why you were disturbed. Do you feel that way, too?"

She felt a flash of anger, maybe because he had come so close to the truth. "I'm not a lunatic!"

"I didn't say any such thing. I know the wind bothers you. I get why it bothers you. Reading that diary couldn't have been easy, and I couldn't blame you if the wind seemed demonic. You told me about crawling out of those woods."

At last she met his gaze and saw nothing critical there. No, not in the least. He looked concerned, but in a kind way.

She almost asked him if he were ever unkind, but caught herself in time. Given what lay in their past, that would be an ugly question, even if born of simple forgetfulness. "It's fanciful," she said finally. "I guess I identified with her too much."

"So you're okay? Honestly, Nora, that's the only thing I'm concerned about right now. You. If that diary is up-setting…"

She shook her head. "It is. It was. But that woman de-serves for someone to read her story even after all these years."

"I guess so. I won't argue with you."

"Wow," she said.

"Wow?"

"You have no idea how much of my life I've spent ar-guing."

"Until you left here, I presume?"

"Mostly, yes." The smile returned to her heart, however briefly, and she offered it to him. "Thank you for that."

"For what? You seem adult to me, capable of deciding things yourself."

Right then, that meant a lot to her, mostly because she wasn't exactly sure herself. Oh, she was old enough, but the events of the past few months had left her feeling like a child again in some ways—control of so much had been removed from her hands.

"I haven't been feeling very grown-up lately," she ad-mitted.

A spark heated his eyes. "Oh, trust me," he said in a low voice, "you're definitely grown-up."

And there it was again, the fire in her blood and in her loins, a fire he stoked so quickly and easily. All of a sudden she couldn't wait to get back to his ranch and forget everything in his arms again. Everything.

Rosa would be there, unfortunately, but eventually evening would come and she could once again reside in Jake's arms, once again feel his body moving inside hers.

Once again feel like a whole woman. Truly whole.

He must have seen something in her face because he suddenly lifted his hand. "Maude? We've got to go. Can I get some carryout boxes?"

Langdon was making great time. The compulsion sat in the driver's seat now, and while some part of him realized he was taking a risk in driving so fast, he couldn't prevent himself. He could almost smell his quarry in the open spaces ahead, in the mountains that began to loom over the surrounding plain.

He would get there tonight. Tonight. He could hardly wait now. But he wasn't a completely stupid man and he knew he had to deal with some things.

Small towns didn't talk to strangers without good reason. So he was going to have to explain why he needed to know the whereabouts of Nora Loftis.

He had a couple of knives. He preferred knives. Guns were too quick and offered little amusement. But a knife... that could amuse him for hours, inflicting pain the whole time.

He had bigger plans this time. Bigger hungers. He wanted the woman's pain as much as he wanted to hear her beg, as much as he wanted to see her die. He'd long since forgotten why he'd become obsessed with her. It didn't matter.

She had to be dealt with before he could move on to the next one.

And there were going to be a lot of them. Nora would be his true practice, his chance to learn the parameters of what he could do to make it all last as long as possible. His lesson in making sure he left no breathing evidence behind when he was done.

The past few weeks had been an advantage in one way: he'd had plenty of time to think about new ways to torture, to draw it out. He had developed some great ideas.

He made one stop at a big-box store in Casper. As he had hoped, they carried plenty of hunting and fishing supplies of the kind he wanted: mainly knives of a few kinds, but also some pretty big fishhooks that gave him some new ideas. And in the toy department, he even found a badge that looked real enough at a glance. He'd put in a cheap leather wallet to make it look more official, and wouldn't let anyone look hard at it.

But it would probably get him the information he wanted. His mind was already spinning the story, rehearsing it. All he needed was for one rube to fall for it. In a town full of hayseeds, that shouldn't be too hard as long as he was careful.

Knives tucked under the seat, he gripped the steering wheel until his knuckles whitened.

He'd get there tonight. At most, Nora Loftis had one more day, depending on how difficult it turned out to be to grab her.

Not too difficult, he assured himself. It had been easy the first time. She'd be more on guard now, but she was still a weakling. She wouldn't be able to fight him for long, and he would enjoy every bit of fight she put up.

Because that would make teaching her a lesson that much sweeter.

Grinning into the graying day, he pressed harder on the accelerator.

Al had things well in hand, although the weatherman was predicting some more light snow. Nora was glad to change into jeans and help however she could. It felt so good to be outdoors and the wind didn't feel at all threatening today. In fact, it was nearly silent, tossing her hair a bit but offering no other problems.

She spent a couple of hours in the corral working the horses, who seemed quite content to run in circles and work off energy. Her own spirits rose with the horses' and banished the last of the disturbing sorrow the diary had given her.

It wasn't the same now as back then, she thought. Maybe when there was a blizzard, but even so, people weren't cut off like that anymore. Maybe the diarist had more problems than the distance from her neighbors. Maybe she didn't have a supportive husband, a man who was also a companion. That could make life out here very hard indeed.

She wondered if she would find out as she read more tomorrow. She had never dreamed that an ordinary diary could grip her as much as a great novel.

But maybe it wasn't the diary, but the way she identified with the woman. Cut off, alone with the wind.

Maybe that's all it was.

"Hey, lady," she heard Jake call.

She turned from Daisy, who was nudging her for pets. "Yes?"

"You've been out here too long. I don't know about you but I think we could both use a hot drink. Come on inside."

She turned to pat Daisy's neck one last time and trot

ted toward the fence. She was running again. Very cool, she thought, and grinned. Only then did she realize how cold her cheeks had become.

She felt so good just then, in a way she hadn't felt in forever. Just happy to be alive. Yes, the lovemaking with Jake had helped start the cascade, but the beautiful day was adding to it, enhancing a wonderful sense of life. She needed more of this.

The grin remained, almost painful on her icy cheeks as she trotted through the door Jake held open for her. He smiled back at her, an expression that lit up his whole face. Apparently he, too, had shelved worry for the moment.

And why not? Living every moment on the edge of doom would serve no purpose. Whether she had many minutes left or only a few, no one could say. Regardless, it was a shame to keep wasting them.

She nearly danced as she pulled off her hat, gloves, jacket and scarf. The bootjack took care of her boots, and she giggled as she felt a sock pull halfway off. Bending, she tugged it back on, and felt Jake playfully swat her butt.

"Nice view," he said.

A laugh escaped her as she straightened. She could see Rosa through the glass panes on the interior door, standing at the stove, so she resisted the urge to turn and kiss Jake.

Amazing that she now felt as if she could do so anytime she wanted. Just amazing. How life could turn around!

Inside, Rosa's famous hot chocolate awaited them, along with a heap of peanut-butter cookies fresh from the oven. Nora ate with more gusto than she had felt in forever.

"Cold air," she announced, "is great for the appetite."

"That and working outside in it." Jake waved Rosa to join them.

She shook her head, smiling faintly. "Dinner is in the

slow cooker. If you don't mind, I'd like to go home. Some time with Al would be nice. Is he almost done?"

"We finished up. And more snow is on the way, so go, go, go. Thanks for everything."

When Rosa had disappeared out through the mudroom, Jake's eyes lit again on Nora. "I think she senses we might like some time alone."

"Now where would she get that impression?"

"I feel like I'm wearing a sign. Don't you?"

Nora flushed faintly. "Does it really show?"

Jake shrugged and grinned. "Who cares?"

Moments later they were racing up the stairs and giggling like schoolkids. What followed, though, was very grown-up.

It was late, snowing lightly and cold by the time Langdon reached the outer edges of Conard City. A mile outside of town he turned onto a quiet county road and found a place to pull over.

The pressure to get at Nora was almost overwhelming now, and he sat stiffly, drumming his fingers on the steering wheel, fighting it down. If he let the compulsion take charge before he found her, he might do something stupid.

On the other hand, he might get very smart. He'd been smart enough to get Nora the first time and smart enough to get his wife. All without being seen or detected.

The world changed as the compulsion took over. Colors brightened, and even the dark snowy world seemed almost to sparkle with the magic of the power that was growing in him. He'd know what to do, and he'd know instinctively. It had worked before.

The power thrummed through him, pulsing in every vein. There was nothing like the control over life and death. He'd failed so far to completely deal death, but he would correct that soon. Then the power would become complete, filling him with strength beyond compare.

He relished the thought, the anticipation, the knowledge that would soon be his. He no longer needed the excuses he'd manufactured to justify his first attack on Nora. Only the weak needed justification, and he was no longer weak.

In the next day or so, he would deal with Nora. Then, filled with refreshed energy, he'd be on his way to collect another life. Yes. He would become so strong that nothing could stop him.

He pulled out the map of Conard City he'd found online before leaving Minneapolis and his old, hampered existence behind. The Loftis address had been easy to locate because the idiot was in the phone book.

So he knew exactly where to start looking. Night would be best, he decided. No one would know if he took out the old man, too, but he wasn't interested in that unless the guy stood between him and Nora.

The important thing was to learn where Nora was right now. Then he could plan and choose his own time. And using that badge he'd bought would be easier with less light to give him away. It resided now in a leather wallet that would make it look all the more official, and he had no intention of letting anyone look closely.

The Loftis house. If she answered the door, he'd snatch her right now. If her father answered, he'd cover.

It would work. He had no doubt whatsoever. One way or the other. The power filled him.

Jake stood at the living room window looking out over a world that sparkled with lightly falling snow. Every so often enough thin moonlight would break through to create a magical world that seemed alive somehow.

He felt replete. Complete. Satisfied. Nora had given

him a sense of fulfillment beyond any he had ever known. It troubled him, because he was quite sure once they got that creep behind bars for good, she would want to return to the life she had made for herself, to all her friends. She sure as hell wouldn't want to spend her days in the middle of nowhere, not after living in a nice city with a great job.

So he had opened himself up to loss. Well, he could live with it. What mattered was that Nora had what she wanted and needed. He didn't want to make her unhappy. Quite the contrary.

Life dealt losses. They were inescapable.

He sighed and thought about making some coffee. At this hour that seemed crazy, but Nora had finally fallen into a deep sleep after hours of repeated lovemaking. He should have done the same, but instead he was wide-awake.

His gaze ceaselessly scanned what he could see of the world outside, and he realized he understood now what Nora had meant when she said she felt as if she were caught in a web and the spider was coming. He felt it, too, crazy as it sounded.

Not even lovemaking could relax him enough now to banish the feeling. Threat existed somewhere out there, threat to Nora, and he could feel it almost as if a tension whispered on the night air and crept inside him with nearly silent warnings.

Langdon was coming. Maybe even close. He could not sleep or rest now. His mind sorted through every possible way of protecting Nora, and he realized no protection could be perfect. How could it? One man. One woman.

Stapling himself to her side sounded good, but it was unrealistic. Sooner or later an opportunity would arise, and if that creep was around he would seize it. If he found Nora.

He had to remind himself that Loftis had been warned

not to give away her whereabouts, but anyone in the county could talk loosely, unintentionally. Langdon might already know where she was, and this ranch was a big place. Even three sets of eyes could lose track of Nora just long enough.

Maybe he should never have taken her from her father's house. Maybe she would be safer in town. But when he thought of how Fred had been treating her, his stomach churned with fury. No one should have to put up with that. No one should be subjected to the scene that man had caused right at Jake's front door. Accusations of sin in front of other people. What kind of father did that?

God, the woman had suffered enough, and he had the most ridiculous urge to shelter her from everything. Wrap her in bubble wrap or something. Which would only hurt her more, but his protective instincts weren't exactly rational. They just were.

His fists were clenching and unclenching, and for the first time in a long time he realized patience was about to kill him. He wanted this done with. He wanted Nora free of fear. He wanted that creep behind bars for the rest of his days. He wanted all that right this instant.

Instead, he had to stare out at a snowy night waiting and worrying.

And for the very first time in his life, he wanted to commit murder.

In the middle of the night, Fred Loftis answered the knocking at his door. It was quiet but persistent, and he figured Nora had finally seen the error of her ways and had come home to be a good girl. About damn time, too. He was envisioning his sermon on Sunday, when he would address how the fallen could be saved, indirectly using her as his example.

He didn't put on his glasses, which meant everything

closer than ten feet was pretty much a blur. Getting worse, too, thanks to cataracts he should have removed soon. Regardless, how much did he need to see at his own door?

It was all a fog, but he could see a man standing there, and despite cataracts and old eyes and dim light, he knew the flash of a badge when he saw one.

"Mr. Loftis, I'm Detective Fielding from the Minneapolis Police Department. I've come to speak to Nora Loftis."

"She ain't here no more," Fred grumbled and started to close the door. A hand stopped it.

"Where did she go? I need to let her know that her attacker is back in jail. I also need to remind her of a court appointment."

Loftis glared at him. "Boy, you go 'round knocking on doors at this hour, you'll get yourself shot, badge or no badge, especially out at the ranches. You talk to her in the morning, hear?"

"The morning? I have to get back. A ranch, you said?"

"Dang Jake Madison has her out at his place. Like I said, you'll get yourself shot, you go out there now."

"I can't stay. Will you just tell her for me?"

Fred started to close the door again. "I'll tell her in the morning. The guy's in jail. What court date?"

"I'm sure she remembers. Ask her to call if she doesn't."

Fred slammed the door. In an uncustomary action, he locked it.

He shuffled back to his bedroom, giving only a brief thought to calling out to the Madison place. He dismissed the notion. Idiot cops who banged on doors in the middle of the night sure as hell wouldn't hesitate to go out to a ranch.

Man, they did things different in Minneapolis. He couldn't imagine a local cop rousting him for such a thing.

Fool. He climbed back into bed and put it all from his mind. It wasn't important. Nora would learn soon enough.

* * *

Driving away, Langdon faced a new problem. How would he find the Madison ranch? Were they labeled? Who could he ask? He'd managed to get the information he needed from the old man, but pulling into a gas station at this hour asking for directions to a ranch might get someone's attention.

The old man, though, hadn't seemed at all suspicious, and had said he'd tell Nora in the morning that Langdon was back in jail. She might or might not have the cops check it out. If they did, then his time would shorten dramatically. He had to find this ranch and hide himself out there before the cops started looking for him. He doubted they'd believe a Minneapolis cop had come all this way so late at night. But the added pressure only enhanced to his excitement. A real cat-and-mouse game, eluding cops while getting Nora. He could do it. Look how long he'd managed so far.

He pulled into the empty supermarket lot and thought about it. The location of ranches couldn't possibly be a secret. All he had to do was figure out how to find the place without arousing immediate suspicion.

But the power was filling him, and when he considered how easily he had gotten the important information from the old man, he was sure he would find it easy to get the rest.

The badge, the reasoned approach. Or maybe a more casual one. He thought about it, then smiled to himself and headed out of town.

He knew exactly what to do.

Chapter 14

The afternoon had turned absolutely gorgeous: cold and sparkling with fresh snow. She and Jake had come back from town only an hour before to discover that Al was concerned about a couple of the cows in a far pasture. Warning Nora to stay indoors with Rosa, Jake set out with Al, promising to be back in a few hours.

"I've got to look, sweetheart," he told her with a light caress to her cheek. "Even bovines get sick, and if they are I need to deal with it quickly. We don't need something spreading through the herd, and we may need the vet."

She smiled, leaning into his touch, reveling in the joy he had brought to her over just the past couple of days. "Don't worry about me," she said. "Just hurry back."

She watched him leave with a smile on his face, feeling an internal warmth she had never known before. Knowing Jake was becoming something like living inside a big hug all the time. His lovemaking was spectacular, but it was far more than that. He made her feel truly special, truly cared for.

But then, he was special himself. A very special guy. She almost hugged herself with happiness.

Rosa insisted she wanted no help cleaning bathrooms upstairs. Nora stood looking out at the beautiful day and decided there was no reason not to go out in the yard. If she needed help, Rosa would hear her, and she wasn't likely to need any help.

Outside, bundled in her best Minnesota winter gear, she stood at the fence and fed carrots to Daisy, who was fast becoming the next best thing to a friend.

Before long, however, Daisy lost interest in the carrots and began to toss her head and trot around the corral as if she were disturbed.

Restless, Nora thought. Well, of course, she'd been cooped up over the past few days because of the weather, and while Al and Jake had ridden off on two of her friends, she was probably feeling neglected. Maybe even jealous.

Nora sighed. There wasn't much she could do. Well, she could. Jake had taught her how to saddle Daisy and she'd gotten pretty good at it. But going for a ride alone was forbidden.

Daisy pawed the ground and tossed her head repeatedly before cantering in another circle. Then she came back to Nora and nudged her so hard Nora stumbled back from the rail.

Well, that was a clear demand: *Get me out of here.*

She'd never seen Daisy act this way before, and when she thought about it, she wondered if the sickness Jake had gone to investigate in his herd might have infected her. Could horses and cows get the same disease?

But then Daisy cantered in another circle, tossed her

head some more and came to stand right in front of Nora. Definitely she wanted to get some real exercise.

Nora hesitated, and then decided it couldn't hurt. Out here in the middle of nowhere, she could ride around and even someone who knew where she was would have a hard time finding her.

She hesitated a little longer, but Daisy's agitation didn't diminish. Finally she decided to go get the tack and see if the sight of it calmed the horse. If so, they could ride just around the immediate vicinity.

She was pleased that she had enough strength now to heft the saddle, hard though it still was. With reins dangling over her shoulder, she panted her way out to the corral and slung the saddle over the top rail. Daisy's ears perked and she came over, assuming her usual stance for saddling. Yup, that was it.

Nora started to climb the rail when the back of her neck prickled with the unmistakable sense that she was being watched.

She froze and looked around, but except for the familiar buildings, there was nothing out there except a distant line of trees and the mountains. Not a soul or animal in sight.

Probably Rosa looking out the upstairs window. She'd better hurry or the woman would be out here in just a minute to scold her.

But Rosa never came, even as Daisy stood patiently, enduring Nora's inexperienced efforts to saddle her. Nora patted the mare's neck. "You're such a good girl, Daisy."

Ten minutes later, she and Daisy were trotting out over the snow, under the golden afternoon sun. Not far, Nora thought. They wouldn't go far.

When she felt the prickling of eyes on the back of her neck again, she was sure it was Rosa. There'd be a scolding when she got back, she was sure.

The notion brought a smile to her face.

* * *

It had been easy, Langdon thought. Amazingly easy. In the wee hours he'd stopped well outside of town at a gas station and told a half-awake kid he had a delivery for the Madison ranch but didn't know how to find it.

He'd gotten the directions, but he'd also gotten a serious shock of unease. Madison was also the chief of police in town.

Not that it really mattered. But it settled firmly in his mind that trying to get Nora in town might be a big mistake. This guy probably had his whole crew on alert.

That left the ranch for sure.

He had found the place midmorning and had driven up and down the surrounding roads casing the place. Finally he parked out of the way and went into the woods. He had no idea what Madison looked like, but there was a guy there working around the barn. No sign of Nora.

Then shortly after noon another car had driven in and he had finally seen Nora. Sweet, sweet Nora, who was going to enhance his powers with her suffering. He was pleased to see she looked healthy again, which meant he could torment her longer.

But even in his Minnesota winter gear he was starting to feel the chill as he hid in the woods, growing increasingly aware that the house was awfully far away, and that there were two men around Nora. Two men. Finding the right time was going to be difficult. He hated thinking he might have to wait a day or two, especially under these circumstances.

But he counseled himself to patience, battering down the now nearly overwhelming compulsion to act. If he didn't get her today, he'd sleep in his truck tonight somewhere out of the way. There'd be tomorrow. It would give him time to really plan now that he knew the lay of the land. Clearly, he needed a decent plan.

But then he saw the two men ride away to the north. He was debating whether to wait or chance striking out for the house when Nora came out and began paying attention to one of the horses. This could be it. He just had to bide his time for an opportunity.

Daisy seemed glad to be out of the corral, even though she was still being ridden in circles. But they were wider circles and Daisy could get up her speed a bit more than when she was within the confines of the fence. Nora was loving it, too, even as her cheeks burned from the cold, and slowly widened the circles so Daisy could move even faster.

With every swing around the outer arc, Nora looked in the direction from which Jake and Al should come. They were taking longer than Jake had predicted, and she hoped they hadn't discovered something awful.

Her circles were bringing her closer to the woods, and she decided to ride along the tree line, letting Daisy open up to a gallop on the long straightaway and level ground. Then they could head back in.

She still wasn't used to a full gallop and felt unsteady in her seat. Worse, her boots still had snow frozen on them, and her feet slipped the stirrups from time to time. She was just about to rein in Daisy and take a slow walk back to the barn when a figure jumped out right in front of them.

Daisy reared. Nora slipped backward off the saddle. Her head hit hard and she saw stars just before everything went black.

A foul mood had settled over Jake as he stood over the dead cattle. "Damn!" he swore to Al.

Al didn't answer, but his expression was grim enough for both of them. Two cows put down because someone had baited a trap with poison, probably to catch wolves or coyotes, and somehow the cows had ingested some of it. Maybe from the meltwater. Regardless, they'd spent all that time searching to find the problem, and once they'd realized what had probably happened, there was no alternative.

They'd wrapped the bait for now in a poncho, but were going to have to go right back out and clean it up, along with the dead cattle, which were now probably almost as toxic as the bait. If he was right, he knew that poison. It was supposed to be illegal except in authorized livestock collars, but some still used it anyway, and it could get into the water. Once there, his whole herd would be at risk. They'd moved the remainder to a different pasture, but now he had his whole ranch to protect. Hell, he had hundreds of square miles to protect.

"I gotta call the sheriff," Jake said. "Then we get a drum to put that poison in and we're going to have to get those cows removed fast, before something moves in to eat them."

"Okay."

"Today."

"Yes, boss."

He was still moving in a black cloud of rage, wondering if his dogs had eaten any of that crap. They'd driven the rest of the herd away from the sick animals and were standing guard, but that didn't mean they hadn't eaten some of that bait. Hell, how could it not have tempted them?

"Dammit!" he swore. "I'm gonna have someone's hide over this." But even as he railed, he figured it was going to be next to impossible to find out who had done it. Bait was a lot harder to follow than traps. It could have come from anywhere. Hell, it might not even have been bait, but some animal that had died after eating the poison two days away. He swore again, wishing the USDA had never allowed the return of the poisoned-filled collars for livestock. Killing coyotes wasn't worth this price.

It was a hellacious death. Just thinking about it made him grind his teeth. Hours of convulsions, vomiting, confusion… Oh, he wanted someone to pay.

Leaving Al to keep watch over the carcasses so that no scavenger ate the poisoned flesh and carried it even farther, he mounted up to head back and make the call. He took the dogs with him to confine them to the barn until he could get the vet to check them.

But every single thought of his ranch, his cattle and his dogs flew from his head as they rounded the barn and saw Daisy, saddled and riderless, standing outside the corral, reins on the ground.

Those reins gave him a cold chill. All his horses were trained to stay put when the reins were dropped, but Daisy still showed a faint lather. She'd been ridden hard. Maybe had fled. And where was Nora?

He slid out of his own saddle, shooed the dogs into the barn, where they started yapping about being confined, and went running into the house, shouting Nora's name.

Rosa answered from upstairs. "She was at the corral."

"How long ago?"

Rosa shook her head. "Twenty minutes. Half hour?"

"Did you see her saddle Daisy and ride out?"

The way Rosa clapped her hand to her mouth told him all he needed to know.

"Dammit, I told her not to go out!"

Rosa dropped her hand, still looking pale. "Just to the corral, Jake. The girl isn't a prisoner."

"No. But she's missing and Daisy is outside. Call the sheriff. Now."

Rosa nodded and went to use the bedroom phone.

"Emergency," Jake shouted after her.

He grabbed his belt and holster out of his office, and his shotgun out of the locked cabinet. Then he grabbed a flare gun and a couple of flares.

Rosa had come back downstairs. "Jake?"

He turned to her. "I'm going to hunt for Nora. Al is out keeping a watch on the cows. Somebody poisoned them."

Rosa gasped. *"¡Madre de Dios!"* She didn't lapse often into Spanish, but she was upset now. "Yeah, boss."

"First Nora," he said. "You watch and tell the sheriff which way I go, okay? Al can handle the poison problem until we find Nora."

Rosa nodded. "Nora first. Find her, Jake. Please." He hated to leave Daisy saddled and lathered, but had no choice. He put her in the corral so she could keep moving without getting chilled.

He set out, following the clear path of hoof prints in the snow.

He prayed harder than he'd ever prayed in his life that he'd find her unhurt, that she had just taken a spill.

Except Daisy wasn't the kind of horse to run off when that happened. Something had scared her.

Dread settled in his heart like icy lead.

"I've been waiting for you to wake up."

Nora knew that voice. Terror filled her until she thought her heart would burst from the panic. She didn't want to open her eyes, didn't want to see that face again.

She could feel that she was tied to something, her arms behind her, sitting on the cold ground. A tree trunk. God, all those self-defense lessons were useless now. She had to find away to get loose.

"Your breathing changed," her nemesis said. "I know

you're awake. How nice to see you again, Nora. How nice that you're healthy again. It will make my job even more pleasant."

At that her eyes snapped open. "Your *job?*"

"My avocation, really." He was holding a large knife, and he ran the edge of it against his leather-covered thumb. "This takes skill, you know. I apparently wasn't skilled enough the first time. And let me tell you right now, if you try to scream or raise your voice, I'm going to shove a rag so far down your throat you'll have trouble breathing."

She gasped, feeling her head swim, trying to think of something, anything she could do. Thoughts raced frantically but settled nowhere. Panic ruled. Calm, she told herself. Find some calm. Panic wouldn't help. But panic refused to listen.

"It would be such a shame not to be able to hear your cries, but I guess it would be best to gag you anyway. I'd hate for someone to hear your screams."

She didn't answer, but forced herself to stare into the face from her nightmares. He was oddly handsome for a man with so much evil and cruelty in his heart. He should have looked like a troll.

She found her voice with difficulty. "You don't need to do this. Let me go and I'll tell the police it wasn't you."

"Then they'll just believe you're trying to protect me again." He shook his head. "I thought you were smarter than that."

He was enjoying the anticipation, she realized. Her stomach rolled sickeningly even as she tried to figure out how to keep him enjoying these moments before he started cutting her again. There had to be some way.

Ego? She wasn't sure she knew exactly what made him preen. He didn't like defiance, so she squashed any thought of arguing. No, she had to find a better way.

Her heart fluttered like a bird that desperately wanted to escape, and her thoughts still remained fractured, only fragments of sense making their way through the din of terror. *Think!*

Finally she hesitantly spoke the only thing she could think of, hoping to sound out what would get to him.

"You're very strong."

That was it. She saw it on his face. Somehow that was the key. Now she had to figure out how to use it.

The circles Nora had made riding Daisy around were clear enough still that Jake barely had to follow them. Then she had ridden along the tree line. He followed her path, listening with every ounce of hearing he possessed. Right now there was nothing but the sound of the horse's deep breath and snorts, the jingle of the harness. Not another sound.

Then he found it, the spot where Nora had been thrown. Daisy's footprints all of sudden became deeper, as if she had reared, and there was no mistaking the imprint of Nora's body on the thin layer of snow, nor the broadening of Daisy's stride as she suddenly turned back toward the corral.

It had happened here. He looked into the woods and felt his heart sink. No snow to speak of under those trees, and frozen ground didn't yield to feet. Tracking would be difficult, if not impossible.

But he had to try.

He dismounted and dropped the reins, knowing his mount would stay put unless frightened, and if frightened he wanted the gelding to get away.

He pulled the shotgun from his holster and the flare gun from one saddlebag, stuffing it into one of his pockets. Into another he shoved a couple of handfuls of shells.

In the distance Jake saw the first patrol vehicle arriving, lights flashing, no siren.

Help was coming. The only question was whether they'd find Nora in time.

"Yes," the beast said, "I'm very strong. And you're going to make me even more powerful."

Nora felt a moment of confusion. What did he mean? It made no sense. "How do I do that?"

"You give me strength with each of your cries. With your pain. With your death. If you had just died the first time, I would have had power beyond imagining."

Oh, God, she had fallen in with someone who was not only cruel and evil, but crazy, as well. She forced herself to drag in a couple of deep breaths. What had one of her professors said? The crazy aren't illogical at all. Their logic is just based on a different reality.

Well, this was one reality she couldn't imagine, and fear wasn't helping her clarity of thought. Or maybe the blow to her head had dazed her. Fighting against every desire to just give in to a primal scream of terror, she ransacked her memory, trying to find a clue. Gain strength from her suffering and death?

She had heard or read that somewhere. Some kind of magical belief. Maybe even a ritual one in some cultures. But how exactly was it supposed to work?

How did *this* guy think it worked?

Not knowing, she finally just asked, her voice cracking. "How does that work?"

He settled back a bit, still fingering the knife, as if deciding how much he wanted to say. How much he wanted to brag. She hoped he wanted to brag a whole lot.

Behind the tree, she was working her wrists, seeking

to free them from what felt like nylon rope. Her hands were growing numb from the cold. Soon they'd be useless.

Time. She had to buy time.

"Your essence," he said, "combines with mine."

"My essence?"

"Energy." He said the word as if speaking to a child who couldn't understand. "But mostly, the power of life and death I have over you enhances my strength. Soon no one will be able to stop me."

Her head had begun to pound, not helping her think at all. So somehow the power he held to kill her empowered him? The thinking was so foreign to her that she had trouble understanding how he could believe that. Then another thought popped out.

"It makes you godlike."

He smiled. She didn't like that smile at all. "Exactly."

Elaborate, she thought desperately. "Tell me more. I'd like to understand why this is happening to me."

"You don't need to understand."

Panic speared her once again. Any moment... She had to delay him again. It felt as if the binding on one of her wrists was stretching. Time had become everything. Seconds, minutes, whatever she had left, she had to draw them out.

"But..." She hesitated. "Maybe if I understand how this...strengthens you, you'll get even stronger."

He almost froze, struck by the thought. "Stronger because you understand? I don't..." He trailed off, then began fingering the knife again. "Perhaps," he said finally.

She pulled hard with one arm. Was the rope slipping farther down her hand? "Think of it as a ritual," she said desperately. "Rituals make more energy because they have meaning. There's meaning in my death only if I understand it."

He lowered his head a moment, studying the knife.

She waited, holding her breath, tugging at her bonds. Let him bite. Please, God, let him believe me.

Jake was as close to losing his mind as he'd ever gotten. Terror for Nora filled him, and he struggled to keep it in check so he wouldn't miss any important clues as he ventured into the woods. He prayed they were still here, that she hadn't been carried away in a vehicle. He prayed he'd find her, because it suddenly seemed that without her life would be meaningless. Pointless. He didn't even care about his herd anymore. All he cared about was Nora.

The forest was quiet and it muffled sound, making it harder to hear if someone was around, but also covering his own movement. Blessing or curse, he didn't know at that point.

He could see where Nora had been dragged across the ground for a short distance by the disturbed needles and occasional leaves, but then the guy must have picked her up. The drag marks disappeared.

So he looked higher, for bent and broken branches, for trampled undergrowth. The trail grew fainter, it seemed, but he kept looking, moving slowly when he wanted to run, because running would do absolutely no good. None.

This creep, he thought, holding the shotgun, wasn't going to get another chance to hurt anyone. Ever. Today was going to be his last day, if Jake had anything to say about it. The blackness filling his heart would have frightened him under other circumstances.

But right now all he could feel in his heart were terror and rage. And murder.

Then he heard it: a voice.

* * *

"A ritual would be good," the beast said. He apparently liked the idea. "I should plan one."

"Yes," Nora agreed. "From everything I've read, there has to be an order, a meaning. And to work it has to be done just right." God, it was hard to squeeze out words when she was breathless with a galloping heart. She managed anyway and tugged harder at the bonds.

If she could just get her hands free, get to her feet fast enough… The thought of being able to move faster than he could, fast enough to evade that knife, caused a wave of despair to wash over her. This was it. She could do nothing to prevent a rerun of the nightmare.

But then she forced her spine to stiffen. No matter what, she would not go meekly. Meekness was, for now, keeping him in check, but when the time came he was going to get the fight of his life.

Then she realized her hand was nearly free.

Making as little noise as possible, Jake moved toward the voice. A man, but he thought he could hear a woman, too. Nora.

His step quickened, and he lifted the shotgun, already cocked, to the ready. God, he hoped she wouldn't be in the way.

He hoped she was still okay. He couldn't bear the thought of another scar on her, another wound, or the pain it would cause her.

Not now. Focus on getting the guy, whatever it took. Nothing else. Just get him.

An eternity seemed to pass before he caught sight of them through the trees. She was seated at the base of a lodgepole pine, appeared to be tied up. The guy was sitting cross-legged on the ground, facing her, holding a wicked-looking hunting knife.

Too close. He might catch Nora with the spray from his load. He edged around, trying to get a better angle, allowing himself a moment of relief when he saw that Nora had not yet been attacked. In fact, she was talking to the guy.

God, she was brave.

Then, in an instant, the entire picture changed.

Nora leaped to her feet with amazing speed and jumped toward the man. The guy sitting on the ground tried to scramble up. Jake stepped out, yelling, "Nora, run!"

Thank God, she reacted fast and switched directions on a dime.

Langdon got to his feet just before Nora escaped the line of fire. Instinctively he turned toward Jake, and just as instinctively, Jake shot him, getting him in the chest.

But that was not the end. It seldom was, despite the movies. The guy grinned and stepped toward him. "You can't kill me." He started coming toward Jake, knife ready. Jake shot again. The guy didn't fall.

Being a rancher and not on duty, he wasn't carrying a riot gun, but a double barrel that needed reloading. His mind raced as he tried to decide whether to move in on the guy, or if he had time to reload.

Then, astonishingly, Nora leaped into the fray, jumping at the guy from behind. She mounted his back, wrapping her arms tightly around his throat.

He swung around wildly with the knife but couldn't reach her. And now it didn't matter if Jake could reload or not. He'd shoot Nora. No choice but to move in.

And move in he did. He ran forward, keeping the knife in his peripheral vision, watching the guy's eyes.

Langdon might have thought he was invincible, but he was beginning to look panicked. Nora was not only strangling him, but she was also kicking the backs of his legs with her pointed-toe cowboy boots.

Moving in on the side away from the knife, Jake managed to take a swing at the guy's head. He was bleeding badly and couldn't keep this up much longer. Or so Jake hoped.

A shout of rage escaped Langdon, but it was followed by a gurgle. Jake pounded him again, this time right on the chest wound.

The knife fell. A second later it was followed by Langdon as he collapsed to his knees.

"Get off him," Jake shouted, and shoved two more shells into his shotgun as fast as he could. Nora pushed away, but as she did so, Langdon fell face-first.

"Stay away, Nora," Jake ordered.

She backed up.

Walking over, Jake prodded the guy with the barrel of his gun, rolling him over. He could see the man's gaze dimming at last.

Then Nora did the most surprising thing. She leaned over the guy and said loudly, *"Now* who has the power?"

That was probably the last thing Langdon ever heard.

There were cops everywhere. EMTs treated the rope burns on Nora's wrists, declared that her concussion should be checked out if she developed any symptoms, but judged her to be okay for now.

At last Jake squatted in front of her, taking her hands gently. "I have to go out for a while. Two of my cattle were poisoned with something really bad. The sheriff and I have to take care of it before it spreads."

"Spreading poison?"

"If it's what I suspect it is, yeah. If an animal eats the flesh of a poisoned animal, it gets poisoned, too. The decaying flesh can let poison seep into the groundwater. We have to deal with it now. I'm sorry."

"Could that creep have done it?"

He shook his head. "Why would he? Anyone with half a brain would realize that the instant I found the animal I'd call the cops. How would that help him? Besides, the stuff was banned back in 1989. These days it has to be sold in sealed collars by USDA-approved vendors. Even if Langdon had known about the collars, he likely would have killed *himself* by puncturing one. It's that toxic. No, most likely some coyote moved in for a kill and got a mouthful of collar instead of ewe or cow."

She freed one hand and touched his cheek. "I haven't thanked you. But go. I understand. I'll thank you later."

"Keep a close eye on her," he told Rosa, then he and most of the deputies departed, leaving only one who wanted to ask her questions about what had happened.

Unlike last time, this time she *wanted* to tell the whole story.

But it seemed like forever until Jake returned.

Gage and Jake stood over the wrapped bait and the two dead cows.

"This is bad," Gage said. "Nobody's supposed to be using that stuff anymore."

"Well, it's allowed in a few states in livestock collars. I locked my dogs in the barn. They seem fine right now, but I have no idea if they ate any of that carcass."

Gage swore. "The cows wouldn't eat that bait, so it must be in the water now."

"At least the meltwater from the snow."

"This could kill the whole county and beyond, and no way to tell where that dead animal came from."

"None."

Gage swore again. The vet was on his way, and a flat-bed was coming to take the carcasses. They touched everything with thick rubber gloves now. If it was the poison they were both thinking of, it could kill them, too. "The vet needs to take the dogs, too. To check them out."

"Dr. Windwalker will find out what it is," Gage said finally.

"I hope I'm wrong."

"Me, too. More than I can say." Then he turned to give Jake a half smile. "Get back to your woman, Jake. We'll handle this. There's going to be a hell of an investigation, but right now, the important thing is that Nora is all right."

"Amen," was all that Jake said. Even now, getting back to Nora seemed more important than the poisoning. That would change, but right now he was more concerned with the woman who had brought so much joy into his life.

Chapter 15

When he got back to the house, not all was what he'd hoped to find. Fred Loftis had called and Nora was livid.

"He told that creep where I was! My own father! Said he thought it was a cop from Minneapolis. How stupid can you get? Claimed the guy had come all this way to tell me they'd caught Langdon."

Jake wrapped her in his arms and held her close. "He called?"

"Yeah. He wanted to know if I felt better now. *Better?*"

Jake continued to hold her. The deputies were gone now, at least from his house. He heard Rosa say dinner was in the oven, then heard her go out the back door and head home.

And still he continued to hold Nora. Through her anger, through the reaction that left her shaking like a leaf, holding her until she at last became quiet against him.

"I'm proud of you," he said finally. "The way you took

that creep on... God, Nora, my heart is bursting with pride. You're so damn brave."

"I was terrified out of my mind," she admitted in a small voice.

"So was I," he answered truthfully. "All I wanted was to get to you and kill him."

At last she hugged him back. He felt her sag a little, so he settled in the armchair, swinging her onto his lap.

For a long, long time, as the events of the day rolled through them both, they didn't say much. But at last the emotional storm began to recede as night settled over the world outside.

"I'm free," Nora said finally. "Free of him forever."

"I can testify to that."

She lifted her head and gave him the first smile since that morning. "I'm just starting to believe it. I don't have to be afraid anymore."

"I think you did a damn good job of getting past it these past few weeks. It didn't just happen in an instant."

"Maybe not." She kissed his cheek. "Thank you."

"For what?"

"Everything."

"I didn't do that much."

"You gave me a haven, a place to get my strength back and reason to believe in myself again. Confidence."

"I think you always had that. You just had to rediscover it."

Then he gave her the kiss he'd been wanting to give her for hours: deep, hungry and possessive. Even though he didn't have the right to claim her, the claim already existed in his heart.

"What will you do now?" he asked her.

"That depends."

"On what?"

She lifted her head and looked straight at him. "On you, Jake. On you."

His heart leaped. His head whirled. God, she had come so far from the woman who had arrived here. "On me? You really want to know what I want?"

"Yes." She faced him unflinchingly.

"I want you. Forever. As my wife. Mother to my kids. In my bed and at my side. But Beth couldn't stand it here."

"I love it here. I love you. I love everything about this place."

"But your career…"

"I'll find one here. I know I can. If not, well, I do love taking care of the horses."

"You won't get bored?"

"I think I'd like to get bored once in a while, but around you, I never do."

He squeezed her so tight, she squeaked. "I love you, Nora Loftis. I love you beyond words. But don't say yes unless you're sure. It hurt when Beth left, but if I lost you… Well, I figured out today that losing you would leave my life empty forever. There'd be nothing left worth living for."

She cupped his cheek. "I feel the same way about you. Part of me always has."

He frowned, but she touched his lips. "It's in the past, Jake. I needed it, and you did what you had to do, given your promise to Beth."

"There's no excusing my cruelty."

"Youth," she said finally. "What I did was pretty stupid, too. I was embarrassed for years that I'd try to pay you with my body to take me to the prom."

"Oh, no. No, don't feel that way."

"Then stop feeling the way you do. We're older and wiser now, I hope. And I've found heaven with you."

He kissed her hard and long, never wanting to let go. "I've found heaven with you, too. You're in nearly every thought I have. I can't want to set eyes on you again when you're away. I even hate your damn job at the library."

She gave a little laugh. "It hasn't been as much fun lately because I'm away from you."

"Marry me, Nora," he said, catching her face and turning it toward him. "A big fancy church wedding. All the trimmings."

"Not at my dad's church."

He laughed, feeling his heart grow lighter than it had in years. "Not at your dad's church," he agreed. "So, will you?"

"Of course I will." She sighed, lifting her arms, wrapping them around his neck and burrowing into the only place that she had ever felt was home: his arms. "I love you, Jake Madison."

"And I love you. Wedding tomorrow?"

She tipped her head, laughing joyously for the first time in forever. "What about the trimmings?"

"Okay, I'll wait a few months," he agreed.

Then, without another word, he rose with her still in his arms and carried her up the stairs. They were going to begin their new life in the best way possible: wrapped in each other.

* * * * *

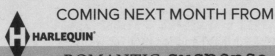

REQUEST YOUR FREE BOOKS!
2 FREE NOVELS PLUS 2 FREE GIFTS!

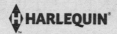

ROMANTIC suspense

Sparked by danger, fueled by passion

YES! Please send me 2 FREE Harlequin® Romantic Suspense novels and my 2 FREE gifts (gifts are worth about $10). After receiving them, if I don't wish to receive any more books, I can return the shipping statement marked "cancel." If I don't cancel, I will receive 4 brand-new novels every month and be billed just $4.74 per book in the U.S. or $5.24 per book in Canada. That's a savings of at least 14% off the cover price! It's quite a bargain! Shipping and handling is just 50¢ per book in the U.S. and 75¢ per book in Canada.* I understand that accepting the 2 free books and gifts places me under no obligation to buy anything. I can always return a shipment and cancel at any time. Even if I never buy another book, the two free books and gifts are mine to keep forever.

240/340 HDN F45N

Name _____
(PLEASE PRINT)

Address _____ Apt. # _____

City _____ State/Prov. _____ Zip/Postal Code _____

Signature (if under 18, a parent or guardian must sign) _____

Mail to the Harlequin® Reader Service:
IN U.S.A.: P.O. Box 1867, Buffalo, NY 14240-1867
IN CANADA: P.O. Box 609, Fort Erie, Ontario L2A 5X3

**Want to try two free books from another line?
Call 1-800-873-8635 or visit www.ReaderService.com.**

* Terms and prices subject to change without notice. Prices do not include applicable taxes. Sales tax applicable in N.Y. Canadian residents will be charged applicable taxes. Offer not valid in Quebec. This offer is limited to one order per household. Not valid for current subscribers to Harlequin Romantic Suspense books. All orders subject to credit approval. Credit or debit balances in a customer's account(s) may be offset by any other outstanding balance owed by or to the customer. Please allow 4 to 6 weeks for delivery. Offer available while quantities last.

Your Privacy—The Harlequin® Reader Service is committed to protecting your privacy. Our Privacy Policy is available online at www.ReaderService.com or upon request from the Harlequin Reader Service.

We make a portion of our mailing list available to reputable third parties that offer products we believe may interest you. If you prefer that we not exchange your name with third parties, or if you wish to clarify or modify your communication preferences, please visit us at www.ReaderService.com/consumerschoice or write to us at Harlequin Reader Service Preference Service, P.O. Box 9062, Buffalo, NY 14269. Include your complete name and address.

"What are you doing?" Laila asked, taking his arm.

Harris stared at her. "Why didn't you go with your family?"

"And leave you here alone?" Laila asked.

He didn't want Laila in the thick of this. An attempt had
been made on her life in America and he didn't know if she
had been one of the targets of the bombing here. "You need
to be somewhere safe."

She gripped his arm harder. "I am safest with you."

Another explosion boomed through the air. Harris grabbed
Laila and shielded her with his body, pulling them to the
ground. Was the sound a building collapsing from the damage
or another bomb? Harris guessed another bomb. Laila was
shaking in his arms. Harris waited for the noise around him to
quiet and concentrated on listening for the rat-tat-tat of gun
shots or another bomb.

His protective instincts roared louder. He wouldn't let anything happen to Laila. "I'm going to help where I can."

Her eyes widened with fear. "What if there is another bomb—"

He had some basic first-aid training and he'd been a marine. Dealing with difficult situations had been part of his training. "There might be another one. There's no time to wait for help."

"I can help, too," Laila said, lifting her chin.

"You aren't trained for this," he said.

"No, but I'm capable and smart. I will be useful. Don't treat me like a crystal vase."

Laila wouldn't back down. She wouldn't leave the scene, not when her countrymen needed help. Arguing wouldn't get him anywhere. He'd seen her strength many times before. She might act like a shrinking violet in front of her brother or other males, but she had an iron core. "You're stubborn when you want something."

"So are you," Laila said, giving him a small smile.

**Don't miss
PROTECTING HIS PRINCESS
by C.J. Miller,
available November 2013 from
Harlequin® Romantic Suspense.**

HRSEXP1013

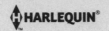

ROMANTIC suspense

THE COLTON HEIR

Ranch hand Dylan Frick threatens to turn
in a gorgeous intruder, but Hope begs him
to keep her deadly secret. She isn't the only
one whose identity is under wraps.
Will the truth set them free?

Look for the next installment of the
Coltons of Wyoming miniseries
next month from Colleen Thompson.

Only from Harlequin® Romantic Suspense!

Wherever books and ebooks are sold.

Heart-racing romance, high-stakes suspense!

HRS2784

HARLEQUIN®

ROMANTIC suspense

Two *USA TODAY* bestselling authors in one book!

Two deadly missions have these men in uniform
putting their lives and their hearts on the line for
service, duty and love.

Look for *COURSE OF ACTION* next month,
featuring *Out of Harm's Way*
by Lindsay McKenna
and *Any Time, Any Place*
by Merline Lovelace.

Only from Harlequin® Romantic Suspense!

Wherever books and ebooks are sold.

Heart-racing romance, high-stakes suspense!

www.Harlequin.com

HRS27845